THE HAUNTING OF KENMORE ASYLUM

JJ CARPENTER

THE HAUNTING OF KENMORE ASYLUM © 2025 JJ Carpenter

Published by Graveside Press 2025
graveside-press.com

Editing: Lauren Woods, Kelley York
Cover illustration: Design by Definition
Interior Formatting: Sleepy Fox Studio

Digital 978-1-967547-43-2
Paperback (KDP) 978-1-967547-40-1
Paperback (Trade) 978-1-967547-41-8
Hardcover 978-1-967547-42-5

CONTENT NOTES

Please note: it should be assumed that basic horror tropes will apply. These include death, gore, and violence.

For a list of other potentially triggering subjects,

please refer to page 260.

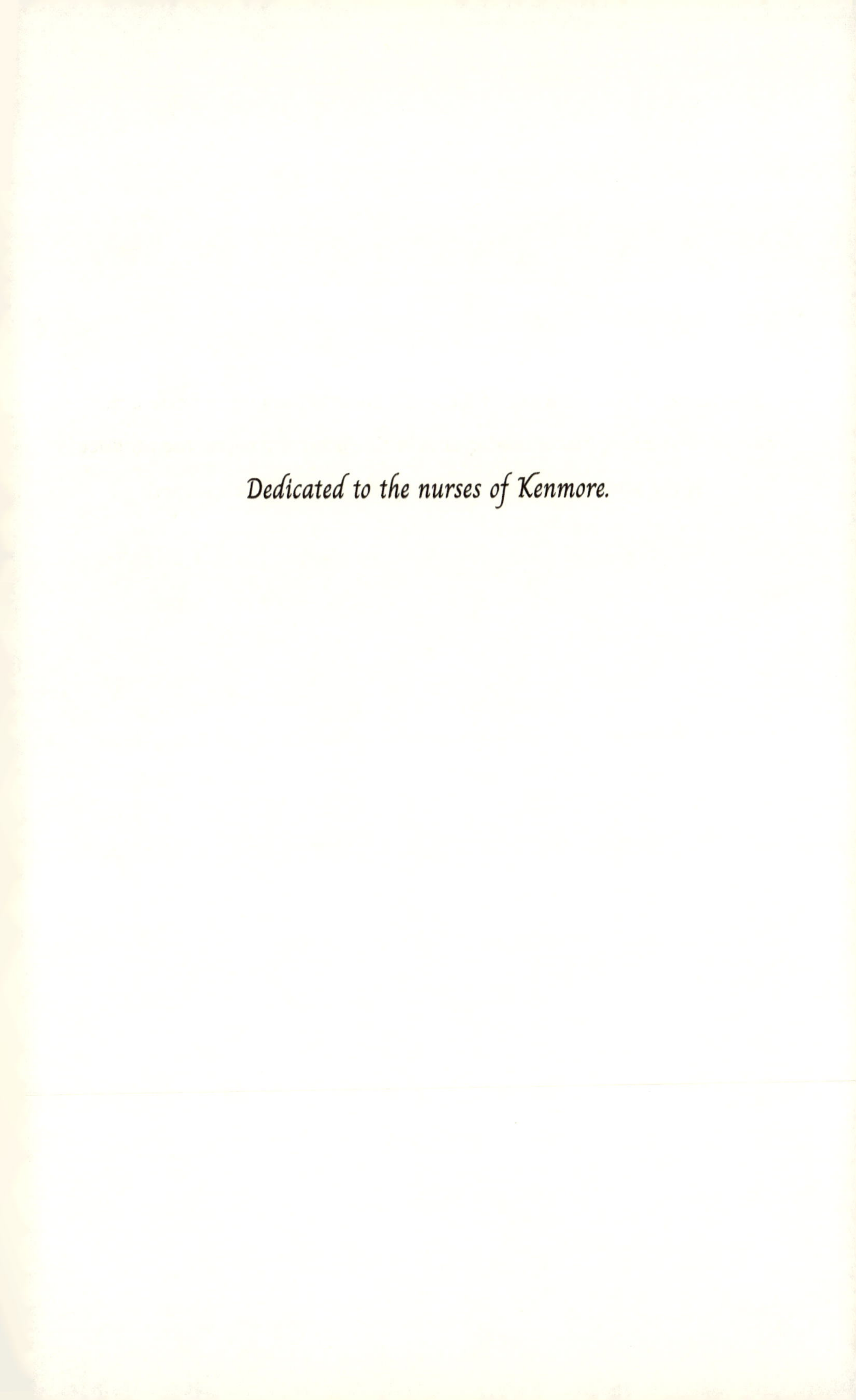

Dedicated to the nurses of Kenmore.

Disclaimer: This is a work of fiction. Unless otherwise indicated, the names, characters, places, and events in this book are either the product of the author's imagination or used in a fictitious manner.

The wild winds weep,
      And the night is a-cold;
Come hither, Sleep,
      And my griefs infold:
But lo! the morning peeps
      Over the eastern steeps,
And the rustling birds of dawn
The earth do sorn …
      —William Blake, 18th Century

CHAPTER ONE

I WATCH THEM *come and go. The men. The women. Even the occasional children. The only constant is their passing. Forever moving through, never staying. One by one, they always leave. One way or another.*

I observe their loneliness. I see their imperfections. I feel their insanity. Once they come here, the world forgets them. They are abandoned. But not by me. Never by me.

I keep them all. I haunt them all. From the moment they step foot through those gates, to the moment their breath no longer mingles in the air of the grounds. They are mine.

I am always here. Perhaps I always have been? It begins to feel like it, anyway. Perhaps, I will always be here now… Perhaps there is no end for me…

⁓◆⁓

1953
SUMMER

BONNIE COULD ALMOST feel a change in the air as she passed the open gates of Kenmore Asylum. It wasn't a tangible thing, per se, but a feeling. A tingle deep inside her skin that ran gentle shocks through her sternum to the pit of her stomach. The rumbling of the bus didn't help the sensation. *Temporary paraesthesia,* Bonnie thought to herself. *Most likely caused by a narrowing of the blood vessels, reducing blood flow to the nerves, due to a momentary spike in anxiety. Perfectly normal.*

At eighteen years old, Bonnie had flown through her preliminary nursing school to the sparkling praise of her teachers. She'd always known she wanted to be a nurse. Her mother had been one, before Bonnie and her brother came along, and she always spoke of it as the best years of her life. However, Bonnie hadn't counted on completing her training at a psychiatric facility. Working in an asylum had never occurred to her before, but the pay was good. *Very* good. The demand for psychiatric nurses was high and growing. One thing society could always count on in today's world was insanity.

The bus navigated around a beautifully kept circle of garden, coming to a stop before a building that —to Bonnie—was more a work of art than simple bricks-and-mortar. Beautiful red bricks and sandstone blocks had been patterned together beneath a solid Welsh slate roof, with plenty of bright white shuttered windows and carefully carved details. Archways encompassed the lower level, drawing the eye towards a large front doorway. The paraesthesia returned momentarily, this time as flutters in her stomach.

"Last stop: Kenmore Looney Bin. All disembark; final destination," the old bus driver yelled over his shoulder in a gruff, self-amused voice. No doubt a regular joke, one he snickered to himself every time. Only half a dozen girls rode on the bus with Bonnie. Most appeared as bug-eyed and bewildered as she must have looked. She knocked into one, a tiny thing with long blonde hair, as she reached above her for her mother's old leather suitcase.

"Excuse me!" the girl squeaked, flinching with both of her hands up before her face. Bonnie was pretty certain the bump hadn't been the girl's fault. "I'm such a klutz, really I am!"

Bonnie chuckled softly as she sized the woman up. Petite was the perfect summation of this trainee, from her frame right down to her manner. The largest thing about her was her well-pointed nose. She looked even younger than Bonnie herself; perhaps a mere seventeen years.

"Not at all, it was my fault. I'm Bonnie. Bonnie Thatcher." She thrust her hand out in introduction. The young woman looked at it carefully, as though assessing the safety of a regular handshake, before tentatively pinching Bonnie's palm and jiggling it.

"L-L-Lucy. Lucy Mills. That's me. That's my name."

"Nice to meet you, Lucy." Bonnie grasped her suitcase firmly and began extricating herself from the bus, joining the gaggle of girls on the road before the administration building. Lucy followed quickly behind, standing so close to Bonnie that she felt the need to squeeze her shoulders together.

A woman waited for them, hidden within the shadows of the archways. She stepped forward, her white nurse's uniform bright and creaseless. White cuffs were buttoned to the sleeves of her dress, and not a hair was out of place beneath her smart white cap. More crinkles appeared on her pinched face than on her clothes. Her white heeled shoes clacked on the paving stones as she strode forward. While her face was well-etched, it was clear that none of them were smile lines.

"Don't dawdle, you ninnies! Quick step, that's right. I don't have time to be wasting on you lot." The final girls lined up before the woman, suitcases clutched almost protectively in their hands. Bonnie swore she could hear the bus driver still snickering as he drove away.

"I am Matron Dunn. I make it a point to personally welcome all my new charges, but I *do not* expect to see *any* of you again anytime soon. Am I clear? You will pay attention. You will learn quickly. You will do as you are told. Otherwise, you and I will meet again, and I can promise you, it will not be pleasant *for you*." Matron Dunn strode forward purposefully now—despite her professed lack of time—looking each girl up and down unhurriedly as she passed. "Sloppy…fat…dull…" The matron mumbled under her breath as she passed each one. She stopped at Lucy, who cowered and shrivelled under her scrutiny. Venom dripped from her words as she clearly enunciated, "Barn mouse."

When the matron stepped in front of her, Bonnie squared her shoulders, her upper arm pushing Lucy back a little. She concentrated on smoothing any signs of nervousness from her face, looking straight ahead to a slightly cracked brick in one wall. She focused on that little crevice—its dark edges and veins—as Matron Dunn looked her over. What did she see? Tall. Slightly plump. Shiny, well-kept dark hair, cut short after her mother's suggestion. Sharp, dominant features—courtesy of her father's Italian ancestry.

"Try-hard," Matron Dunn muttered as she moved past her. Bonnie felt herself deflate like a sad balloon. The matron turned towards the row of arches as another woman strode forward. "Sister Hatchet, you have your work cut out for you."

The second woman looked even older than the matron, though she wore a pale blue nurse's uniform in contrast to the matron's white. Every hair on her was white, from the tight bun on her head, to her washed-out eyebrows, to the fine hairs on the backs of her swollen knuckles. She stood proudly, even though a slight hunch had formed at the base of her neck. In stark juxtaposition, her skin hung loosely like a plucked, uncooked chicken. She pursed her lips and made a disappointed noise in the back of her throat as she observed the trainees.

"Nurse Hatchet is your Charge Nurse, ladies," the matron continued. "She will oversee your training, your shifts roster, and your placements within the hospital. She'll also see you to Buna House, where *all* trainees reside until the end of their training."

"The matron is far too busy to waste any more time with you lot," Nurse Hatchet said in a stiff, monotone voice, sniffing as though the very sight and smell of the trainees repulsed her. "So hurry along, come with me. First rule of the Hospital: always be prompt."

BONNIE LAY BACK in her metal-framed bed, which creaked noisily as she did so. The mattress was too firm by her standards, and she thought she could feel a spring starting to push through the fabric. She wriggled until she was off the spot, committing to herself that, very soon, she would flip the mattress. But not today. Today was exhausting. Her mind still reeled from everything that was thrown at them during orientation.

The tour of Kenmore took the better part of the day. This place was not so much a hospital as it was a small town. It seemed to have everything: from its own crops, dam, livestock, and orchard; to its dozens of wards, administration buildings, residences, laundry, kitchen, boiler house, library, and even a dentist and hairdresser. She hadn't stepped foot inside any of the wards yet, and she'd only seen a handful of the patients—those who were trusted enough to assist with the gardening and laundry.

Lucy had stuck like an unwelcome fly to Bonnie's side all day. To make matters worse, Lucy had been assigned to sleep in the same room as Bonnie. All the other trainees and nurses in Buna House had their own rooms. Small as cupboards, maybe, but at least private. Lucky for Bonnie to be squashed into the only room large enough for two beds and wardrobes. At the news of the arrangement, Lucy tried, and failed, to hide her grin of excitement. Bonnie—never one to conceal her emotions—had both inwardly and outwardly winced. She was surprised Lucy didn't lie next to her in the same bed at this very moment.

As Bonnie liked to do when her mind refused to settle, she focused on a single point in front of her. The ceiling was weatherboard, just like the rest of Buna House, and a tight knot in one of the planks proved to be the perfect focal point. She felt herself become calm as her eyes traced its concentric circles.

"Right, enough of that, Miss Bonnie," she whispered through gritted teeth. "Time to meet everyone…"

She'd pleaded apologies to the nice Aboriginal woman who'd shown her to her room, begging for just a moment to freshen up before joining the rest of the trainees downstairs. She could have kissed the woman full on the mouth when she'd taken Lucy away with her, back down the steps. It gave her at least a moment's reprieve from her new shadow.

Buna House was two-storeys high. The second floor contained separate rooms, like the one she shared with Lucy. Even more rooms filled the first floor—according to the slim Aboriginal woman who'd introduced herself as 'illian (which Bonnie took to mean "Lillian")—and a communal area and kitchenette.

Bonnie pushed her suitcase under her bed and walked quietly to the door. Buna House creaked and groaned, as if protesting her every step. It was probably just the stress of the day, but the whole building felt eerie to her. Like she'd stepped out of the sun of Kenmore's gardens and straight into the shadow of something cold and slightly damp. The cedar stairs creaked just as loudly as she made her way down, then passed through the foyer to the communal space, where Lucy sat—engulfed, really—in an old, worn armchair. A gaggle of women of all shapes and sizes surrounded her.

God help me if I need to remember all their names, Bonnie groaned in her head. Lillian sat right next to Lucy, and Bonnie made a beeline for them. "Hi Lillian, Lucy, everyone!" Her voice sounded far too chipper, even to her own ears. She toned it down. "I'm Bonnie Thatcher, from Gundagai. Pleased to meet you all." Lillian grinned at her broadly, showing a mouth missing half its teeth. Parts of her gums had started to blacken.

"Evenin'," Lillian beamed, her voice raspy, as though a cough waited behind each breath. Lucy grimaced as bits of Lillian's spittle flicked the side of her cheeks; she sunk down even further into the chair–and into herself. Bonnie decided to stay standing. "That 'er is Bertha," Lillian continued, nodding her head to the only other Aboriginal woman in the room. A huge woman, by any measure, perhaps not in height but certainly in girth. Her limbs looked like the shiny links of a sausage. Bertha grunted but smiled, her mouth almost entirely sucked in behind her great round cheeks. "Thissum's Cora." The next woman Lillian motioned towards was a tall, slim, older woman. Her skirt and blouse were neatly ironed and tucked, her hair smooth and non-fuss, and her nails perfectly trimmed. The rest of her, however, seemed as wasted and shrivelled as a month-old orange.

"Are you a nurse, too?" Bonnie couldn't help herself before the question was out of her mouth. The women burst into uproarious laughter—poor Lucy flayed with more spittle—and Bonnie felt her cheeks flush with burning shame. *Damn my sympathetic nervous system…*

"I'm a patient, dear," Cora said calmly, brushing imaginary lint from her shoulders. "They let me stay downstairs with these fine ladies, and we help with the laundry. Don't worry, they've put bars on our windows and they lock us up good and tight at night."

"I doos the polishin'," Bertha mumbled in a voice as deep as Bonnie expected. "Yessim, that's right. I doos all the polishin' of them floors over in Ward Five." She emphasised her repeated statement with a firm nod of her head.

Still processing the fact that she shared her accommodation with patients and, presumably, housekeeping staff—*because who else could those Aboriginal women be?*—Bonnie grasped at the only thing that sounded familiar. "Oh, Female Five? That's where I've been stationed. I start there the day after tomorrow." The ladies exchanged glances with each other, some smirking slightly, others just staring knowingly.

"Ah, Ward Five, eh?" Lillian rubbed her knees and stretched dramatically. "Watch yerself there, aye?"

"Oh, are the patients a bit unruly?"

"Hm," Lillian shrugged noncommittally. "You best watch the patients everywhere you goes, me love. Mind the patients. Mind the nurses. Mind Sister Hatchet. But most of all, you mind them ghosts in Ward Five."

2021
15 OCTOBER, 16:42

Aiden swore as one of the tangled branches stuck in his backpack, flicking him across the face when he broke free.

"Fucking shut it," a second boy hissed at him, pushing him hard in the offending shoulder. Devin, the second boy, was a year older than Aiden—a whole thirteen months, actually, if you were counting. And Devin always did. Devin was shorter than Aiden and had barely a scruff of fuzzy orange facial hair on his chin. Aiden always assumed that's what gave Devin such a foul temperament. His insecurities about his short, podgy size, his pale freckled cheeks, and his youthful appearance. That was Devin: constantly out to prove himself.

Aiden, on the other hand, was tall and lanky with a tan so thick and rough he wouldn't be surprised if he bled brown. He'd had dark facial hair for three years now. He always shaved every morning, partly to keep Devin on his side, and partly to ensure his monobrow didn't make a reappearance. It didn't matter, though. The term twelve o'clock shadow was all too apt where he was concerned. By the afternoon, he'd be as stubbled as Devin after a week.

"You fuckin' shut it," he jibed back, pushing the older boy. They both started laughing nervously, filled with excitement and—if they were honest, which they never would be—a little fear as well. "That groundskeeper caught a bunch of shitheads the other day, did ya hear?"

"Pathetic losers." Devin kicked a stone for emphasis, which bounced off the trunk of a nearby tree. The clack as it hit resounded painfully loud in the silence of the grounds. The boys made their way into the abandoned Kenmore Asylum through the botanical gardens, which had overgrown into a tangled wilderness. Perfect cover, and if Devin was right about those maps he'd found online, it should get them pretty close to the main buildings. "You brought the spare batteries, yeah?" Devin asked for the hundredth time.

"Yeah, loser, I got 'em. Sheesh, how many times do I have to tell ya?"

"Yeah, well, we're not getting back out here anytime soon." They'd driven up from Canberra that morning, keen to shoot footage for their new YouTube channel. Urban exploring had started to boom again ever since the COVID pandemic restrictions had eased up. They wanted their share of whatever advertising royalties were going well.

"Do you wanna shoot any of the intro shit here, or what?" Aiden asked, hiking his pack up higher on his shoulder. Devin would be the star of the show; this point hadn't even been a question. The older boy looked around him at the knotted garden, daylight barely seeping through the canopy of leaves and branches. Eerie green light cast twisting shadows at their feet, where nature took over the broken pathways.

"Fuck it. Let's do it, aye?" Devin pulled up the bandana he'd been wearing around his neck to cover his nose and mouth. A cheaply painted skull revealed itself as the fabric stretched over his face, hiding most of his freckles. Next, he tucked his loose red hair into his black beanie. Aiden fumbled with their equipment. "Hurry up, bumfucker."

"Okay, ready when you are."

Devin took a moment to compose himself and then began his pre-scripted speech, his voice lowered in a B-Grade Horror Movie rasp. "I'm here at Kenmore Asylum, the largest lunatic institution in New South Wales. Opened in 1895, this once grand hospital now lies rotting and abandoned. Plagued by rumours of malpractice, mysterious deaths, and unexplainable accidents—this place is one of Australia's most haunted locations. We're the Ghost Heads, and *this* is Kenmore Lunatic Asylum. Enter with us if you dare."

CHAPTER TWO

1953
SUMMER

BONNIE COLLAPSED INTO a vacant chair in the staff dining hall, barely aware of who sat on either side of her. Her stiff cotton dress irritated her skin; she wondered again what starch they used to get the fabric to bend like cardboard. She flexed her arms, the rigour-mortis cuffs on her sleeves slightly inhibiting her movement. The stiff seams of her dress scratched at her underarms. Bonnie drew a breath through her nose so deep it pained her lungs, then exhaled forcefully through her mouth. Her head spun from the morning's orientation with the Charge Nurse, Hatchet.

Watch out for Sister Hatchet, Lillian's raspy voice sang in her head. Bonnie had already been rapped over the knuckles four times and across the back of the head once. For showing too much hair. For "daydreaming," when she was actually trying to memorise all the rules. For stuttering before answering one of the several barrages of questions. For making a face at the smell within one of the isolation rooms. And finally, for gawping at the elderly patient in the corner of the recreation hall of Ward Five who took a dump against the wall in broad daylight. She *dreaded* her first round the following morning. None of her neat-and-tidy desktop lessons or the quiet conversations over tea with her mother had prepared her for this.

"You must be one of the fresh bloods."

The voice was firm, yet with the hint of lilted laughter. Bonnie looked over her right shoulder and met the sparkling eyes of an old nurse. By old, the eighteen-year-old Bonnie meant middle-aged. Early forties at most, but a veritable lifetime away for her. The nurse had dirty blonde hair curled tightly beneath her cap. Her thin lips were pursed, though the pulled-up corners betrayed a waiting smile, as did the glint of mischief in her eyes. "I'm Gerald. This here is Patsy." She nodded to the towering, square-shouldered woman on her right, whose dark hair was as stiff as her blue nurse's uniform. "You're one of the trainees who just moved into Buna House, right?"

"G-Gerald?" With her head whirring, it was the first word to fall from Bonnie's lips.

"Nurse Geral*dine* Doyle," Patsy chimed in. "And I'm Patricia Martin. We shack up in Buna House, too." Patsy's voice was mellow, though with a quaver which gripped notes of determination. She held her chin high, too, not quite looking down her nose. Her precise accent spoke of fine English heritage.

Bonnie found her voice. "Yes, that's right. I moved in last night with another trainee called Lucy. I'm Bonnie Thatcher. Ward Five. As of tomorrow, that is."

"Ah, you're the girl who was staring at Ethel." Gerald nodded her head sharply, referring to the patient who'd used the rec hall as her personal latrine. "Patsy and I are Ward Five too. Best ward in the whole damn place." Bonnie flinched at Gerald's use of the word "damn" before she could catch herself. She'd heard the word maybe once before in her lifetime, when her Father had cut himself on his letter opener and hadn't realised she'd been behind the study door. Her face had bloomed crimson then, as it did again now. "Well, fuck my hairy arsehole, child. You'll have to get used to much worse than that."

Bonnie's mouth dropped, and she felt her eyelids peel back into her face. Patsy tsked and rolled her eyes, tapping the tips of her fingers on the long dining table. If Bonnie thought her face had flushed before, the roar of blood which now swam in her head was loud enough to drown out the raucous bellows of the male nurses across the dining hall. The men and women shared a dining hall, even with segregation still in full effect. "W-w-what…?"

Gerald laughed in clipped, rich murmurs, and even Patsy had to smile.

"You've just had Nurse Hatchet's orientation, right?"

Bonnie nodded in answer to Gerald's question, pushing at her green-ringed crockery plate with her fork.

"No wonder you're sitting there like a stunned mullet. That woman is a piece of work. You mind Nurse Hatchet, see."

There it was again, Bonnie thought. *Mind Nurse Hatchet.* "Why does everyone call her Hatchet? What's her actual name?"

"Nobody knows her real name." Patsy leant forward across her dish of cold, dry meat and stodgy vegetables. "Even the matron calls her Hatchet. You know why I think she got that name? The woman may be small, but she's tough, hard, and sharp enough to do real damage. You mind her, and you'll be right."

Mind Nurse Hatchet.

"She's just got one or two more years left until she can get her pension. Then she'll be off."

"Now, *our* orientation," Gerald said and smiled broadly, putting an arm around Bonnie's shoulder. Bonnie stiffened as the skinny, muscled woman pulled her closer, their starched uniforms scratching together like the legs of a cricket. "That's the one you need to pay attention to."

Gerald and Patsy spent the next thirty minutes of their lunch break forcing Bonnie down a vortex of even more viciously swirling tips and lessons. Lessons which, to Bonnie, felt more like gossip. Which nurses were secretly running off to "tousle between the sheets." Which of the staff were engaged or married, "so mind what you say to one about the other. It's incestuous here!" Which patients to avoid and at what times of day. What to *never* do in Ward Five; whistling was a sure way to start a riot.

At first, Bonnie stuttered one-worded questions or affirmations, but as lunch drew to a close and the two older nurses stood to return to Ward Five, she was utterly dumb-founded.

"We'll see you back at Buna House." Patsy smiled devilishly. Gerald just gave Bonnie a wink and a thump on the shoulder before she trundled out of the staff dining room.

SHORTLY AFTER 6:00 p.m., Bonnie fell onto one of the couches of the Buna House common room. Apparently, the trainees were given an "early mark" to get a good night's rest ahead of their first shifts in the morning. Her stomach groaned loudly in hunger, but Bonnie just squeezed her eyes shut and sank further into the old, musty sofa. She felt a depression in the cushions when Lucy flopped in place beside her. They sat in companionable silence, their minds so full of words that their mouths were lost for them.

"Mind Ward Five..."

Bonnie's eyes shot open at the whispered warning, adrenaline momentarily zapping her limbs and brain awake. Lillian had silently joined them, and sat across from them in the large, fraying armchair from the night before. She cackled at the look on her and Lucy's face.

"Good orientation then, ladies?" Her smile pared back her thin lips to reveal her missing teeth.

"I'm not sure. I can barely remember what happened today," Lucy breathed in her usual mild manner. "I didn't know there were *so many* patients here. Papa told me Kenmore was overcrowded when he tried to convince me not to come. But still…"

"Yessum." Lillian's mouth closed as she leant back with her hands over her tiny stomach, still smiling. "We's headin' into Autumn now, gals. Me and the other 'nebriates done make our homes here for the cold times."

"Nebriates?" Lucy asked gently. Lillian just smirked, the edges of her smile pushing into her lower eyelids.

"Inebriates," a clipped near-British accent said from behind them. Patsy pulled at the cuffs on her sleeves as she entered the common room. Gerald trailed behind her with her cap and cuffs already in her hands. Bonnie could now see just how tightly Gerald's dirty curls clung to her head. "Drunkards." Patsy said the word tightly, but with no malice, smiling over at the slim Aboriginal woman. It was after 6:30 p.m. now; perhaps the two girls had managed a little nap in their chairs.

"Yessum. Bertha, too. And about a dozen of them white trash in the dorms. Least me and Bertha got reason, see. Done owed after what you's all done ta us. What you's all took."

Bonnie exchanged inquiring looks with Gerald and Patsy.

"Lillian had her kids taken away from her back in the late 1800s," Patsy clarified. "And Bertha was taken from her parents and placed with a Caucasian family. If you've got white skin, you're guilty as sin. Isn't that right, Lillian?"

The woman tsked in reply, throwing up her hands and looking over her shoulder at nothing. "Not me nurses from Kenmore," she grumbled. "But we done owed a warm bed and supper sometimes, ain't we?"

"What about Cora and the other patients?" Bonnie piped up, diverting the conversation as tactfully as she could manage. "Why are they in Buna House? What're their stories?"

Gerald undid the top button of her dress, flopping into the armchair beside Lillian, her legs spread apart so you could almost see all the way up her stockinged legs. "Room's tight at the moment. Any well behaving, useful patient can end up here at Buna if they're good enough and lucky enough. Cora's been here…" she trailed off. "Hmgh, how long has Cora been at Kenmore?"

"At least twenty years." Patsy perched on the edge of Gerald's armchair. "As long as I've been here, anyway. Apparently, her husband put her in here when he got tired of her. Told their kids she was dead."

"That's *awful*," Lucy gasped, holding a hand to her mouth as though she might burst into tears.

"Ha!" Gerald laughed. "Where do you think you are, love? Luna Park?"

"And the others?"

"Who knows," Gerald yawned, closing her eyes as she stretched out her legs. "Half the time they get moved here from other institutions and we never know the full story. And often, it's just better not to ask."

Bonnie felt all the words and instructions of the day settle down in her stomach acridly, like fluttering pieces of burnt paper. Had she made the right choice? Was she really cut out to be a nurse like her mother? Or, more precisely, a nurse like Gerald or Patsy?

"Well, I don't know about the lot of you, but I'm ready to wash off the piss and shit from the day." Patsy stood up from her perch. "And I'm starving. Anyone else want to try to grab a feed?"

BONNIE PAUSED IN the entranceway to Buna House. She'd barely eaten, leaving the dining hall early to return to her room. The grounds at night felt empty, ghostly, and despite her fatigue, she'd spurred herself on quickly. Perhaps it was just the insecurities and doubts following her orientation, but as she'd stepped hastily through the well-mown grass, the breeze attempting in vain to ruffle her stiff uniform, she'd been unsettled. Out of place. Like she trespassed somewhere off limits.

The feeling didn't improve as she crossed the threshold to Buna House, the wooden step groaning in protest beneath her minimal weight. The entryway light had been turned off for some unfathomable reason, and a woman stood in the hall, her slim frame merely a black shadow against the wall. The shadow faced the hall mirror, silvery moonlight and bright external lights reflecting a pale, familiar face.

"You're so beautiful," Cora whispered to her reflection, stretching out the words. It sounded like she was crooning to a young girl rather than paying a compliment to the elderly woman she was. *"So…beautiful…"*

Bonnie lowered her head and coughed slightly, hoping that— combined with her creaking footfalls —it might be enough sound to break the woman from her trance.

"She was beautiful too…" Cora's eyes appeared silver when they flicked up to stare at Bonnie in the mirror, her back remaining unturned. *"You can still hear her…pacing…whispering… You can still feel her…so cold…but* burning. *Beware the ghosts of Ward Five."*

"Are you okay, Cora?" Bonnie said more loudly now, taking a step towards her. She looked around for another person, perhaps a nurse. Why was the patient out of bed, and most importantly, how had she got through her locked door? Cora started, as if waking from a dream. Perhaps she had been sleepwalking, talking to herself in her fitful slumber. Somewhere in the building, a door slammed and Bonnie jumped, making a startled choking sound.

"Oh, sorry dear," Cora said, back to her normal self. She smiled at Bonnie, and through the wrinkles, Bonnie could almost imagine how beautiful the woman would have been in her youth. *So beautiful.* "The doors here do that, you see. We're not allowed to lock the bottom-floor external doors. Too much kerosine polish on the wooden floors and walls. Too high a risk that the place will go up in flames and we'll be bolted up in here to burn. Even if you wanted them to, these doors never stay secured. They're always opening and closing on their own. Doesn't matter if you latch them. Doesn't matter if you lock them. But what can we expect? This House was constructed by hospital staff and patients forty years ago, before the Great War. It only got the name Buna after World War II, though, when the army took over. They named it after that battle in Papua, I think… We need a good locksmith, that's what I say."

"Oh-oh—" Bonnie found herself smoothing her dress as Cora rambled. She could feel her heart pounding in the centre of her chest, sending shockwaves up to the lump in her throat. Had Cora's door opened on its own? "Are you okay Cora?"

"Hmm, yes, just fine." Cora walked off then, practically gliding down the hallway. Bonnie considered going after her, ensuring she'd make it to her room okay, but hesitated. As a trainee, and a brand-spanking new one at that, perhaps she had got the rules wrong. Perhaps she had missed something. The entryway light snapped on again. Bonnie screamed, a strangled gasp that pushed its way through the lump between her vocal cords.

"For heaven's sake!" she chastised herself, ascending the rickety stairs. "Get a hold of yourself, Bonnie Thatcher. Otherwise, what good will you be?" She peered over her shoulders, feeling even more uneasy now she knew Buna House could not be secured. *Why* had Cora had to tell her this now, just before she tried to sleep? "Tomorrow can't be any worse," she muttered, steeling her resolve and pushing fanciful thoughts out of her head.

CHAPTER THREE

2021
15 OCTOBER, 17:07

AIDEN COULD JUST make out the back of Devin's curly, red-haired head through the gloom. While the sun still shone outside— somewhere beyond the dirty windows —inside the asylum, the walls were cast in muddy shadows. Leaves, soil, plaster, and shards of glass crunched beneath the boys' feet as they entered the asylum buildings. This first place had been easy to get inside. The door handle had been removed long ago, and they'd pushed against the peeling white wooden door with no resistance. It had barely creaked in protest to their entry. Standing in this hallway, peach-coloured paint peeling from the walls, Aiden could see that most of the doors didn't have handles anymore. The floor, too, had been stripped of carpet, leaving behind bare concrete to grate against the debris and heels of their boots.

It felt colder inside than out. The logical boy inside Aiden tried to convince himself this was due to all the concrete, insulation, and shade. The fear- and adrenaline-driven junkie beat those reasonable thoughts away. *Cold spots. Ghosts.* This irrational part of the boy latched onto the chilly air, drawing it in to settle in the pit of his chest like an icy stone.

If this place isn't fucking haunted, nowhere is…

The door behind Aiden made a soft noise as it gently closed. He watched it swing with a fluid motion, settling in its natural resting place within the doorframe. It was only inertia and gravity that drew the door closed, yet he still felt that stone of ice solidify behind his sternum.

"This is sick," Devin whispered ahead of him, disappearing through one of the open interior doors. Devin's footsteps echoed off the walls, yet Aiden still felt alone. Very alone.

"Yeah, fucking epic," he called out after his friend, willing his trepidation away. *It is cool. It's* fucking *cool.* He followed behind as Devin entered another open, empty room. Empty aside from the strips of peeling paint littering the floor, and an old pillow, blackened with age and mould. Aiden continued filming from the hallway, slowly panning to get a good shot of the interior. A galah screeched beyond the broken window, the beating of its large wings audible as it passed by. Everything sounded louder in here. Aiden looked over his shoulder as, once again, the door closed behind Devin. It had become warped so it didn't close properly, instead knocking against the wood in a rhythmic "tap, tap-tap, tap". The glacier in his belly sent out foggy tendrils to curl under the skin of his upper arms and at the base of his neck. *It's just the wind from his movement, pulling the door closed behind him.*

"Come on…" Devin shoved Aiden's shoulder as he moved back into the hallway and out of the room. "There's three storeys to explore in this one. I wanna see as much as I can before the sun goes down."

Aiden followed as closely as he could, suddenly afraid one of the doors would close behind Devin before he could get through, separating them.

And then what would happen?

As the boys put their feet on the base of the first wooden step, a loud bang sounded beyond them somewhere on the lower floor. "Fuck," Aiden breathed, trying to disguise his jump by peering down the hallway.

"It's just a door slamming, fuckwit. Are you recording, though? Did you get that?"

He simply nodded, pulling back to focus on the stairs again, determined to stick as close to Devin as he could without getting called a fucking chicken. It looked like a carpet runner had once hugged the stairs. The wood was pale and smooth in the centre. Anything not securely bolted down had been ripped out of the building. "*No going back*", a large black swirl of graffiti on the wall above the cedar staircase taunted. He punched the wall with his fist as he passed it, hearing the sound echo below him. Another door opened and closed on the ground floor.

"You really think this place is haunted?" Aiden called up the stairs, taking them two at a time to reach the landing.

"Shit, yeah," Devin answered excitedly. "Some fucking nutter killed a nurse here after World War One. He was a soldier with PTSD or somethin', convinced the doctors were out to get him. He shot her by mistake while he was chasing the doctor through the grounds." Aiden peeked into the various rooms as he followed Devin down the hall, hoping to catch something with his camera. "That gutless skulker of a doctor survived, but the nurse wasn't so lucky. Then, like, a bunch of patients died here. Some hanged themselves, others died in, like, that fuckin' flu pandemic. Apparently, one guy murdered his wife when she was a patient here. Heaps of shit. Whoa—"

Devin cut off as he pushed his way out onto a white, flaking balcony. The trees had grown so high that they partly obscured the view of the never-ending grounds. So much muck and filth coated the ground that Aiden could no longer tell what colour the floor had been. His footsteps grated.

"My pops said they used to come out here in the 80s when there were still patients," Aiden said in a slightly louder voice as they moved back inside. He was getting used to the chill in the air, and feeding his own ego emboldened him. "Said they drove through the gates one time, dropped my uncle out the front, then drove off yelling out the window 'new patient!' He fucking cried." Aiden flinched as Devin's barked laughter echoed back at them, and the whole place creaked as if in protest to its silence being broken. Yet more doors in the second-storey hallway creaked shut, seemingly pushed by unseen people, objecting to the disturbance of their peace.

"Let's get the fuck out of here, man." Devin lowered his bandanna and ran his arm across his nose, sniffing as he did so. He left a barely visible stream of glistening mucus on his sleeve. The chilly air and falling dust within the abandoned hospital made Aiden's nose run, too. "It's just all the same shit. I think I saw some BBQs out back. Let's go check 'em out instead."

1953
SUMMER

THE SUN HADN'T risen yet when Bonnie made her way to one of the tables on the ground floor of Buna House. The green padding of the chair she'd chosen was slightly ripped, and the metal legs grated across the floor. She was pleased to see that someone had made a pot of black coffee and left some jam and rolls in the middle of the table. They'd even laid out a red-chequered tablecloth. Buna House might be old, poorly made, and groaning in protest against being left standing—but the nurses, trainees and other residents did their part to make it homely.

She breathed the steam of the coffee in deeply, letting it wake up her stomach, before taking a tentative sip. Her eyes fluttered in appreciation.

"Good to see you've remembered one of the most important lessons," Gerald said as she walked up behind her, grabbing a roll from the middle of the table. "Coffee is fucking life!"

Bonnie didn't outwardly flinch at the curse word this time, though it literally made her feel like her ears burned, the fine hairs along her ear canal sizzling and shrivelling.

Lucy joined them next, her cuffs and cap already secured, a huge yawn barely concealed behind a delicate hand. "I didn't sleep well *at all*," she mumbled in her fiercest voice yet. "All that banging and creaking. I don't know how you stand it."

Gerald chuckled, reaching for a mug and the pot of coffee this time. "Tell me after a week if you're still hearing noises. I doubt it. You'll be out cold like the rest of us as soon as you hit the pillow."

"Cora told me how old this place was and how it was built," Bonnie began conversationally, tearing small strips from her bread. "Why don't they fix it up?"

"Ha! They'll let it burn down before they do anything to it," Gerald spoke around a thick mouthful of food. "It was always supposed to be temporary accommodation, but nothing is ever really temporary here. There's always chatter about building a permanent nurses' quarters. Proper brick walls. Enough beds. Can you imagine?"

"Oh, that'll be lovely," Lucy breathed, straightening an edge of the tablecloth, which was already neatly in place. "When is that happening?"

"It's been happening for the past twenty years," Gerald grumbled. She slammed her empty mug down on the table and Bonnie's eyes bugged out of her head. Gerald made an art form of drinking hot coffee quickly. "See you two over at Ward Five. Don't be late or you'll get another rapping across your knuckles." She smiled coyly, wagging a finger at them, and then was gone.

The two sat in silence for a while, the only sounds their tentative slurps of hot coffee and soft chews. "This place is a little eerie," Lucy finally piped up, needing to fill the silence.

"They're not allowed to secure the lower floors, and the doors don't shut properly." Bonnie felt good to have some kind of information Lucy didn't. She wasn't used to being the new girl, or feeling out of control, or having none of the answers. She was a quick study and a bit of a know-it-all, if she was honest. This conversation brightened her little corner of the world slightly. "They don't even lock."

"Did you hear the whispering…?"

"What?"

"The whispering…" Lucy looked over her shoulder and bent low to the table as if imbibing some great secret. "Beneath our window early this morning. Sounded like a man."

"What did he say?"

"I don't know! It was all low and scratchy and blended together. Like gibberish."

"You must have a secret admirer," Bonnie jested, not in the mood for any spooky conversation. Lucy tittered in exasperation. "Come on. I'd rather be early than late."

BONNIE SHUFFLED HER feet into the thick gumboots, thanking Lucy for helping her to don the rubber apron. These items of clothing were even more irksome than the cuffs and collars. Those felt positively pliable compared to the rubber, which chafed and squeaked with every movement. Nurse Hatchet had unlocked the shower room before shepherding half a dozen of the trainees inside. Every door, cabinet, and cupboard always remained locked. Before staff could leave one room or progress to the next, the door had to be locked again behind them. There was always at least one, though more likely two or three, locked doors between them and the outside world.

"You and Lucy will do the washing," Hatchet intoned forcefully to Bonnie before moving on to the next pair of girls. "You two will clip the nails. You two will do the drying. And the rest of you will help the patients re-dress." They'd already carted out the bundles of labelled clothing that morning, each one strangely wrapped and tied together. Hatchet turned to Bonnie and Lucy again. "The water temperature is to be *no higher* than 36.5 degrees Celsius, and no colder than 32. *Always* turn on the cold water first. But *never* bathe a patient in cold water, unless under the strict direction of the Medical Superintendent or myself, on his orders. You are to move promptly, thoroughly soaping each patient from top to bottom. Make note of *any* marks, bruises, sores or anything abnormal on the patient's body. You are to report any such findings to me, *immediately*."

Hatchet turned to the next girls and began drilling them on the rapid speed with which they must dry the patients, how short to trim their nails, and whom to assist with getting dressed. Bonnie let out a deep breath. It had burned in her chest, but she'd dared not expel it in Nurse Hatchet's presence.

"*Now*," Hatchet turned to address them all fiercely. "The Senior and Junior Nurses are rousing the patients for their bathing. They will come through those doors unclothed and ready to move promptly through. If I catch anyone slacking off or dawdling, I'll dump a cold bucket of water over your head and see how *you* like being left out in the cold. Understand me?" The trainees all nodded their heads solemnly. Despite the summer season, the air always seemed cold inside the walls of the wards. "Right then. They'll be coming through now."

Bonnie and Lucy rushed to turn the water on as Hatchet's heeled shoes clicked on the tiles. Bonnie's fingers tingled numbly as the two of them fidgeted with the taps. *Damn that paraesthesia.* She sighed in relief as steam finally began to fill the room, then checked with her thermometer to find the water rested at a comfortable 33.9 degrees. The victory was short-lived as the room filled with other sounds beyond their squeaking shoes and aprons, and the running water. Bonnie turned and nearly staggered back into the running faucets.

Dozens of naked women of all different shapes and sizes shuffled into the room. Some were large, their corpse-white bellies sagging over their privates. Others were so thin and stretched that each bone protruded like an underfed dog's. Many had breasts that dangled like pendulums, knocking into each other and the women next to them. Nipples of all colours, sizes, and even shapes stared at Bonnie like sad, unblinking eyes. She never knew wrinkles could extend so far…downwards… Of course, she'd seen wrinkled faces, chests, arms, and legs. Somewhere deep inside her, she'd known wrinkles would cover the whole body. But it was one thing to know something subconsciously and quite another to be confronted by an endless procession of reminders.

Most of the women moved like zombies from black-and-white horror films: their legs and arms stiff while their skin and bellies jiggled, and their eyes—their actual eyes, not their nipples—stared vacantly. Others were almost manic in their movements. Never able to stand still, practically vibrating on the tips of their toes, pulling at their skin or the edges of their mouths. One woman in particular stood out to Bonnie. Unlike the others, she stood erect and still, her eyes bigger than any she'd ever seen, the whites as round and large as boiled eggs. She had a stiff grin on her face that showed each one of her yellowed teeth, and her wiry, grey hair stood out from her scalp as though electrocuted.

The stillness unsettled Bonnie most. Or perhaps it was the noise? Not just the shuffling of feet, and the slapping of breasts and thick thighs, but the grunts, the moans, the giggles. Each noise on its own was barely noticeable, but together, they made a sea of sound that crashed over her like a wave meant to drown her.

"Nurse Bonnie!" she heard Hatchet yell from *somewhere* beyond the oncoming hoard. Its own wave of flesh, rising above and down to crash into her. *"Nurse Bonnie!"*

"Here," Lucy passed her a cake of thick yellow soap. It wasn't the bars she was used to. She could practically see the white fat leaching out. The gesture was enough to snap her out of it; if not to her senses, then at least to action. She encouraged the patients to come forward one at a time and stand beneath her faucet. Two other nurses soon joined them—the Senior and Junior nurses, she guessed—and the four of them gently scrubbed each woman with soap all over before sending her further down the line.

Bonnie wasn't sure what she would have done if the patients themselves hadn't been so indoctrinated to this routine. She barely had to encourage the first two at all, who lifted their arms and chins, turned, and parted their legs. The second patient had thick globs of dark black tar running up her back and down her legs. Appalled, Bonnie was about to call for Nurse Hatchet before the smell hit her. The pungent, flesh-curdling stench crawled its way past her taste buds and into the pit of her stomach. She gagged before she could help herself. The woman was covered in her own faeces.

What have *I got myself into?!*

1913
ALICE: DAY 257 IN THE ASYLUM

ALICE SAT IN complete darkness. Her bottom, back, and legs had long ago turned numb. Her only movements were the twitches of muscle spasms that protested her confinement, as though trying to remind her she was still alive. That blood still pumped through her limbs, however sluggishly.

They put something in there, Alice thought viciously to herself, trying to steel her muscles against the spasms. *They're poisoning me…*

She wasn't sure if her eyes were open or closed. She tested them, gently fluttering her eyelids, feeling tingling spasms in her cheeks as she willed her body to obey. If not for the cold stinging against her dry eyeballs, she couldn't have said if her eyes were actually open. Perhaps she had finally become blind? *They want me blind. They want me mute. They want me quiet…* Nothing but blackness waited for her here.

Blackness and flies. She thanked whatever God or demon still watched over her that her legs, at least, were numb to their constant buzzing and tickling. Alice realised that as her train of thought progressed, she increasingly enjoyed the flies' company. She occasionally felt them on her face, her neck, the tips of her fingers. She focused on them whenever she felt them. Focused on each of their six little legs. The sucker that spat and sucked filth from her skin. In this utter stillness and silence, she could almost identify each of their tiny limbs as they tracked across her. Imagine the veins in their beating wings. She welcomed the buzzing. If it ever ceased, as it sometimes did—at night, she supposed—then the ringing would begin again. The whining and droning in her ears that made her feel dizzy, like the whole world spun.

They're making me insane, the thought panted in her mind. *They're all in on it.* I hate *them.*

She hadn't felt the flies on her skin for a while now, though she could still hear them. Perhaps it was night? Or perhaps she was on her period, and they were all busy down below? Perhaps that's why her stomach knotted so tightly, like tiny fists pummelling her from the inside. *Or perhaps it is the venom. They are moulding me into a lunatic.*

Alice closed her eyes again, letting her head rest back on the hard wooden top of her chair. *How long will they leave me here this time? How long until they come back to finish me off?*

CHAPTER FOUR

1953
SUMMER

Bonnie flinched and threw her hands up before her face. She tried to remember her training in this moment: what to do, but most importantly, what *not* to. *Don't hurt the patient.* The patient's fist made contact with the protruding edges of Bonnie's wrist instead, rattling off pain that vibrated through her forearm. It felt like the patient had tolled a church bell inside her bones. Bonnie pulled her hands down, instinctively grabbing her throbbing wrist, and instantly regretted her mistake. The patient's fist barrelled towards her. She barely blinked in preparation as it made contact with her left cheekbone. All she saw were twinkling spots, then blackness.

"It's alright now, Maggie." The words were the first thing to break through the ringing in Bonnie's left ear. Then came Maggie's— the patient's—grunted screams and panting. She sounded like a cornered animal. Perhaps that's what she was at this moment. Other patients filled the rec hall with their soft moans, nervous laughter, or bristling silence. Gerald's voice—because Bonnie now realised it was Gerald speaking—was a soft, yet forceful, beacon in the midst of it all. "You hungry, love? Thirsty? Come on, let's make you a cuppa."

"I needs me ciggies!" Maggie screeched, launching herself at Gerald, this time with hands clawed for scratching. Gerald gently grabbed Maggie's wrists, but the patient—seemingly fuelled by some unnatural, demonic strength—pulled herself free and swiped her across the face. Every nurse in the room had some kind of mark on her: a swollen red lump, a shallow bleeding scratch, even an angry bite. One nurse's hair and cap had been pulled free and hung down one side of her face.

"Why don't we just give her a cigarette?!" Lucy moaned, suddenly beside Bonnie, her expression betraying her hopelessness. Bonnie inwardly chastised the girl for her frantic tone.

Stay calm. Don't shout. Don't fight back. Listen, but don't give orders. Offer food, water and quiet. Don't overstimulate. Ascertain the cause of any pain, discomfort or distress.

Bonnie observed Maggie from her momentary safe distance. The woman was likely in her sixties, at least. She was heavy-set, short in stature, with arms as broad as Lucy's thighs. Her thick, wiry hair was more grey than black, and her skin was as pale as winter frost. She spoke with a slight accent that could have been from any number of eastern European countries.

Why don't we give her a cigarette? Bonnie thought fervently, in agreement with Lucy. *It's obviously why she's distressed.* Bonnie could feel her own craving for a quick fag growing hot in the top of her stomach. As she breathed, she could almost feel the warm, soothing smoke easing down her throat.

"Oh, dear Lord…" At Lucy's distressed call, Bonnie's attention was diverted from Maggie. She looked up to see Nurse Hatchet making her way into the common area. Lucy and Bonnie weren't the only ones to notice, and Maggie turned as if in slow motion to fixate her attention on the steadily approaching woman. Bonnie's stomach fell—warmth and all—to the top of her groin, at the thought of watching a confrontation between the demon-powered Maggie and the sharp, immovable force that was Nurse Hatchet.

Moreover, she worried about any fallout that might blow back on the rest of the trainees. Maggie raised her hands, fists forming, and that made the decision for her.

"How about I get you that durrie, Maggie?" Bonnie kept her voice even, calm, as she slipped her hands into the side pocket of her dress. She always kept a packet of Craven A 20s there, on hand for any break she could catch. The soft tone worked; Maggie turned back to her, lowering her fists, her eyes brimming with hopeful tears.

"I needs me fags…" she practically begged as she took a couple of steps towards Bonnie. Her hands and lips trembled as she locked eyes on the small red box.

Fully distracted, Maggie didn't see Nurse Hatchet until she stood right behind her. With strength belying her advanced years, Hatchet swept her arms down past Maggie's shoulders, pinning the woman's limbs to her side. Maggie instantly bellowed, writhing and wriggling beneath Hatchet's grip like a snake on fire. Bonnie could do nothing but gape as she watched the fierce struggle between the two women. The Charge Nurse was almost half Maggie's size, her petite arms barely reaching around the woman. Perhaps Hatchet had her own demon inside her, fuelling her unbelievable strength, and the two devils were now battling it out.

"Get the camisole, Nurse Gerald." Hatchet's words remained flat, if said through gritted teeth. "And for God's sake, you lot, stop gawking and come help me."

Bonnie snapped forward, lending her strength to Hatchet's, along with two other nurses. Gerald was soon back with a straightjacket, and the room became a flurry of whipping arms, legs, spittle, and white cloth and buckles. At one point, someone grabbed Bonnie's own arm, wrenching it painfully into a sleeve of the camisole. "Wait!" Her lessons to use soft and even tones were momentarily forgotten as her shoulder joint was wrenched, shooting zaps of pain down through her elbow to her still pulsing wrist. "You've got my arm, you've got my arm!"

"Get out of the way, you absolute ninnyhammer!" Hatchet wrenched Bonnie's arm out of the straightjacket sleeve and sent her careening backwards. When Bonnie took two steps backwards, she realised it had been the Charge Nurse herself who had grabbed onto her arm in the flurry. She felt not only her cheeks flush with exertion and frustration but also the tips of her ears. The task was nearly done, both of Maggie's arms secured and the buckles of the camisole meticulously fastened. Saliva and screams were the only things flaying the nurses now. "Take her to a solitary room, if you please." Hatchet wiped at her apron, breathing heavily from the exertion. "And *you*." Hatchet turned to face Bonnie.

"Yes, ma'am."

As Maggie was led away, other sounds in the room seemed to amplify. The moaning, rocking patients. The women who let out short, sharp shouts to alert the others to their distress. The ones who giggled or cried. The ones who remained silent. One short patient wandered back to her chair, muttering under her breath, "Maggie's fingers are screaming…"

"What in heaven's name were you thinking?" Nurse Hatchet rounded on Bonnie.

"I-I…ah… That is, it was *you*, ma'am, who put my arm into th—" She cut off as Hatchet's lips practically disappeared beneath her scowl, and her own flushed cheeks grew progressively more burgundy. *How many more mistakes could I possibly make today…?*

"What were you thinking, offering Maggie a cigarette?"

Maggie's cries were now distant echoes, and the rest of the staff settled the other patients to return to their routines. Bonnie still felt their eyes on her. She didn't think it was possible for her face to turn any brighter. Surely it would burst into flames at any moment.

She lowered her eyes to avoid looking at any of the other ladies in the room who were watching the spectacle unfold. At least, Bonnie could still *feel* them watching her.

"I-I-I thought it might calm her down, Nurse Hatchet. I was trying to think of ways to make her comfortable."

"Foolish girl. Do you even know what a cigarette is, hm?"

"Oh, ah…" Bonnie was lost for words, unsure if this was some sort of trick question. Who didn't know what a fag was?

"It's a *stimulant*. The very last thing a patient like Maggie needs."

"I saw other patients smoking, ma'am. I thought…"

"And you think we treat every patient the same, do you? Shall we give morphine to suicidal patients or shock therapy to the ladies with menopause? Let's have less of that apparent 'thinking' out of you." Hatchet scoffed and turned to leave. Bonnie raised her eyes ever so slightly to watch the blank expressions of all the faces staring at her; now anger made the blood in her cheeks and ears boil.

"She was going to hit you, Nurse Hatchet." *I've made plenty of mistakes today, why not one more?* She squared her shoulders and drew her spine erect. More than anything else, she resented being made to feel stupid or uneducated. That was one thing she was not.

Hatchet turned slowly, her lips still folded inward. "*That* I am used to, young girl. *That* would have been much easier to handle."

2021
15 OCTOBER, 17:41

"That was a fucking car," Aiden whispered, crouching back behind the window from which they'd filmed the bell tower. They could still hear the sounds of its tyres ricocheting from the gravel in the distance, beneath the sounds of galahs and cockatoos.

"I wanna get footage of that church," Devin hissed back through his teeth. In his efforts to move away from the window, Aiden had unintentionally stood right over the top of Devin's head. Something he knew the short ranga hated. He moved backwards to allow Devin to lead the way down the stairs and outside of yet another red-bricked building. The light turned yellow as the sun dipped closer and closer to the horizon. They were losing daylight. "Let's just hope that car was that bitch caretaker getting the hell out of here for the night."

Aiden nodded in agreement as they hit the black road. On the tarmac, there were no tall trees or walls to hide behind. The sudden openness made him feel like eyes stared down at them from every window. He could still faintly hear the car far away from them; or at least he thought he could. It didn't stop him or Devin from jogging around the clock tower building and towards the large church to get out of the open. The stained-glass windows were a beacon showing them the way. The boys flew through the open doors, checking over their shoulders with every second step. They didn't loiter in the broken, messy vestibule—where their feet echoed loudly on the hollow wooden floor—but ran straight through the next set of solid, polished wooden doors to find themselves in a rotund room with the stained-glass windows.

The half-green walls weren't peeling so bad in here, but were still covered in graffiti. Even greater quantities of broken chairs, plaster, and glass crunched underfoot, and it looked like someone had burnt something on an old wooden table. Ash had settled in its centre in a wet, congealed mass.

"Come on." Devin's whispers echoed off the wooden floors, just as their footsteps did, as they made their way through to the main hall.

"Did you see the latest YouTube video of that confrontation with the caretaker?" Aiden needed to fill the silence with more than just their panting and echoed footsteps. They couldn't even hear the galahs in here anymore. The place was eerie in its silence.

Devin answered with his trademark chuckle, a high-pitched *hugh-hugh-hugh.* "Yup, I thought she was fuckin' gonna cry. And then she took a swipe at that skinny cunt."

"Nah, they were all pussies," Aiden laughed back, pushing Devin's shoulder. The bravado helped force back some of the niggling fear that had crept in unseen along with the cold, to settle on his bones. "Fuckin' calling out for all the ghosts and demons but too chickenshit to come back at night. We're gonna be fuckin' famous, brah." He bit his words off at a rattling noise behind him, the sound of something rolling across the floor in the previous room. There was one thing Aiden could agree on with those other YouTubers: Kenmore Asylum was one of the freakiest places they'd ever explored. Strange sounds gathered in every building, like the very walls were breathing.

"Whoa," Devin said as they stepped into the main hall of the chapel. None of the videos they'd watched had prepared them for the immensity of the space. The windows were largely untouched, and the ceiling soared above them. The nave was completely empty, aside from a small pile of broken doors under a central window against the longest wall. On one end was what looked like a small stage, and on the other, a typical altar padded with thick green carpeting. "Fuckin' aye, look at this. The pipe organ's still here." Devin's voice echoed, reverberating back louder each time. Aiden's palms began to sweat. Devin noticed his friend's discomfort and smirked, giving his high-pitched guffaw again. "*Coo-ee!*" The loud call practically shook the walls and windows as it echoed back at him. If the caretaker was still close by, there's no way she wouldn't have heard it. Aiden couldn't help but flinch, knowing Devin filmed him to make him look like a skulker.

"Nah, man." Aiden threw an open hand at him in frustration. "Not cool. Don't have to be such a fuckin' wanker." He strode off to the other side of the hall towards the stage, filming as he went. The walls creaked, then a loud bang came from one of the back rooms. His muscles tensed even tighter, and his nerve endings practically sparked with electricity.

"Hey, come check this out." His mate slowly ambled up behind him. "Check it. There's a trapdoor up at the top of the stage."

As they peered up at the dark hole, a rumbling grew in the distance. "You fuckin' hear that?" Devin didn't yell or make a fool this time. It was almost like the sound of a truck or street-sweeper coming closer. Maybe more like a tractor, or… "It's a ride-on mower." They'd seen videos of the caretaker chasing other YouTubers through the grounds on it. The growling sound continued to build as the presumed mower came closer.

"Just had to be a fuckin' smart arse, didn't you, Devin!" Aiden exclaimed. "You've brought that bitch right down on top of us."

The two boys looked around the hall, just as exposed as when they had sprinted between buildings. They dodged into a side door which led behind the stage. The small room was in complete disarray, packed with broken chairs, church pews, and rotting, discarded clothes that stunk like an old public restroom. It would be impossible to move through without making a sound. They'd gone from feeling like rabbits in an open field to being claustrophobic amidst the tangle of junk and debris. The room was also a dead-end; the only way out took the boys back into the hall or up onto the stage. Neither seemed like a tempting option.

The walls practically vibrated with the deep engine-like sound, which filled the room with more intensity than any previous echo had. The energy was palpable, sounding as if an aeroplane prepared to take off from *inside* the building. They were trapped. Aiden suddenly felt a strong urge to piss.

"Up that fucking trap door, mate." Devin gave Aiden a gentle push and they both hurried onto the stage, each creak of the floorboards practically screaming *we're over here* as they hurried to the old wooden ladder. Aiden tried to step softly, but his adrenaline-pumped ears amplified every sound. Luckily, the square wooden hatch was already open. He pushed his way inside, crouching in the corner on shaking calves as Devin followed behind him.

They were too scared to even close the trapdoor as the engine cut out and they were thrown into absolute, groaning silence.

CHAPTER FIVE

1913
ALICE: DAY 1 IN THE ASYLUM

HARRIET HURRIED ALONG the gravel path, her head bowed low to keep the light of the rising sun out of her eyes. The tiny woman strode with a purpose straight into its glare, her light blonde curls shining and her heels clipping on the tiny stones beneath her, as she made her way to the other side of Kenmore's grounds. Harriet had been working at Kenmore for only one week, but the route was already firmly ingrained in her. She let her mind wander as she marched toward the reception houses where she had been temporarily stationed.

The reception houses were a place for people suspected of insanity to be "received" into the care of the asylum. A place to wait for a few days and see what prognosis might befall the patient, and—should they stay—to which ward they would be assigned. At times, Harriet found the process to be a gentle way to ease herself into psychiatric nursing. The female reception house, like its male counterpart, was small, contained. In essence, it was her job— along with the other staff—to observe, not to treat. There was no attachment made to any patient, as they soon moved on. At other times, Harriet imagined it to be one of the most distressing jobs at the hospital. To see individuals unwillingly discarded by their loved ones was heartbreaking. And, of course, she witnessed all kinds of diseases of the mind. The violent, depraved, depressive, manic, deformed, or retarded. The falling sickness had been most shocking to witness. Harriet had seen a lot in her five years of nursing at the Mooroopna District Hospital. She'd seen as much within a single week at Kenmore.

She reminded herself, as she passed the sporting field to her left, that this was to be a *temporary* assignment. She had always been meant for the wards. With voluntary admissions on the rise—growing at a rate faster than staffing could hope to match—Harriet had been provisionally subpoenaed to the reception houses. She had a great distaste for the Medical Superintendent assigned there and couldn't wait to move on. Since he did not officially treat the patients, he seemed to take his allowances by doing whatever he pleased to them. It turned her stomach how sickly sweet he spoke to anxious family members, then how quickly his mood and ire shifted when they were out of sight and hearing. Especially towards the women who obviously would not be released back into the world.

This brought Harriet's mind back to Alice, a patient who had arrived at the reception house the day before. Remarkably, Harriet not only remembered Alice's name but also almost every detail of her arrival. The other patients passed like shadows through limbo, but *her*... Perhaps it was the way Alice glared as she was led into the asylum. The fierceness and intelligence of it, like she could see into your very soul to weigh and measure each of your sins, starting with your first childhood fib. Perhaps it was how slack the rest of her seemed compared to those hard eyes; like a porcelain doll, face forever frozen in pensive nonchalance. Most likely, it had been how she'd arrived. Her husband—for obviously that's who it must have been—had entered with his arm securely fastened through hers. Not as a gesture of love, but as one of forceful intent. If

Harriet had to guess, she would have said the furtive look in his eye contained both guilt and fear.

Alice had stunk of brandy, and a small amount of sick had made its way down one side of her mouth and onto the collar of her shirt. She was so intoxicated that Harriet had been surprised the woman managed to stand at all. She remembered each word of the husband's answer when asked the nature of his wife's ailment. "*I fear she may have a hereditary disposition,*" he'd said grimly. "*If I'm honest, perhaps a hint of the dropsy, a wandering uterus, and…*novel reading, *if you catch my drift.*" The husband's true intent was as plain as the daylight that blinded Harriet: the man had simply become weary of his wife, and the asylum was as good a dumping ground as any other. Perhaps he'd even picked out his next wife already. No doubt a fledgling, passive thing who could help him feel like a young man again, while she cared for his ageing body like his nurse. "*She can be a bit of a handful, I warn you. Downright assertive at times.*"

Harriet had taken Alice's arm, talking softly, encouraging her towards the bathing rooms. The first order of business in any asylum: wash the patient, dress her, and above all, ensure there were no dangerous belongings on her person. Alice had looked up at Harriet with those piercing grey eyes, so dark they seemed almost black. Her plump, pale lips had parted, trembling. Despite her inebriation, she still appeared quite aware of what was happening to her. Or perhaps she was awake within her mind, but simply lacked the control over her body to make any protest. Alice had breathed shallowly, and Harriet remembered positioning her fingers on the woman's wrist to take her pulse. Her heart had beaten so slowly. The woman's pupils hadn't been all that small, but that didn't negate Harriet's strong suspicions.

Chinese Molasses, she'd thought to herself. *The poor woman has been doped with enough opium and brandy to suppress a bullock.*

"SISTER, HAVE YOU seen a patient by the name of Alice? She's got long brown hair streaked with grey. Fierce dark eyes. Quite pretty. About a head taller than me. She came in yesterday." Harriet had caught a moment between the flurry of rounds and admissions to think of the poor woman again, to wonder what had befallen her. Alice was not in any of the beds, and it was certainly too early to have sent her on to the wards or back home. She doubted the husband would have come to retrieve her, even if they tried to call him back.

The nurse Harriet had addressed hissed slightly as she sucked breath in through clenched teeth. "Oh aye, Sister. I most certainly 'ave. She's in the box."

"*The box?!*"

"Yes, solitary."

"I know what the box is," Harriet replied curtly. Her colleague, who towered over her by head-and-shoulders, sniffed. The box was worse than solitary confinement. It was a wooden prison with no light. A cage, essentially, where the most violent, deranged and uncontrollable patients were shut away from everyone else until someone could figure out what to do with them. "What happened? She seemed quite calm yesterday. Though she was quite full, if you catch my meaning."

"She came 'round last night," the nurse continued in her strong Irish accent. "Almost suddenly she awoke. She must have realised what happened to her. She was screaming, kickin', scratchin', biting—anything she could to inflict harm. Attacking not just nurses, but the other patients, too. 'Twas a sorry scene, I heard, Sister. They managed to get her wrangled into a camisole, doused with water, and into the box. And then they calmed the other patients down before the mornin'. Thank the Lord."

"And she's just been in there ever since?"

"Yes. The Medical Superintendent will get around to her when he can. For now, he's happy enough to leave her there. She's got her two pots. So long as she don't confuse them, she'll at least have fresh water."

Harriet nodded in thanks, breathing sharply through pinched nostrils. *Happy enough… Sweet Fanny Adams…* Harriet hurried to the wooden boxes, noting on arrival that only one was secured. How fortuitous, she supposed, that she wouldn't have to check each one. She pulled aside the round wooden peep-hole, which she begrudged was just her height. Anyone else would have to stoop, but not little Harriet. "Ms. Alice?" She realised as she stood there that she'd forgotten the woman's last name. Perhaps that no longer mattered. Who would want to be continually called by the family name of the man who had abandoned you? There was a scrabbling beyond the door, and Harriet pushed her face slightly closer to the small hole.

The smell of faeces instantly assailed her. She pinched her nose, while breathing out quickly through her mouth, trying to expel the sickly stench. It was so thick that she could almost taste it, and she tried not to gag. The woman had evidently *not* utilised her second rubber pot for its intended purpose. "Ms. Alice, this is Nurse Harriet speaking. I welcomed you in yesterday. I've come by to check how you are." The scrabbling behind the door intensified, scratching as though the claws of dozens of rats were pulling themselves up into the shape of a human. That mental image came unbidden, and she flinched. She breathed out low and long through her mouth. A loud thud came from the other side of the box, rattling the wooden panels, and Harriet jumped, startled. She dropped the round door to the peephole in her shock, which fell back into place.

"Please, you have to help me," Alice whispered in a hoarse voice. Hoarse, no doubt, from the amount of screaming she'd managed the night before. "I need to get out of here, *please…* I don't belong in here! I need to get back to him."

"My dear," Harriet whispered back through the wooden panels that separated them. "I do not think your husband has any intention of taking you back." Harriet was never one to mince words or give out false hope like lollies to rot your teeth. She found a fresh dose of reality and honesty the best way to push onwards. There was no use looking back. "You are safe here, I promise you."

Silence answered her, though she imagined she could hear Alice breathing from behind the door. Much more laboured than it had been the day before. She took a step forward again, reaching for the peephole. She pulled it back to find one of Alice's deep, dark eyes staring back at her. In the dark, with her pupils widened, it wasn't as if her eyes were *almost* black. They *were* as black as pitch. Like the eyes of a demon. Her grey-streaked hair, wrapping around a pale and drawn face, didn't help with the image. Harriet wasn't sure which was worse: a person made from rats or a black-eyed demon.

Alice screamed. Not a whimper of hopelessness, or a polite cry of grief, but a banshee-from-hell shriek loud enough to shatter glass and peel paint from the walls. Harriet stepped back again, the peephole covering Alice's intense glare, and put her hands over her ears. The wailing continued, drawing attention from all within that side of the reception house. In between the shrill shrieks, Harriet heard a familiar pair of heeled oxford shoes clicking on the floor behind her. The Medical Superintendent approached. Harriet rounded her shoulders, prepared to show him just what a little "assertiveness" from a woman really could look like.

1953
AUTUMN

BONNIE SHIVERED AS she made her way back towards Buna House after her shift. She needed to remember to wear her cardigan tomorrow. The sun was already setting beneath the horizon, casting the grounds in black and orange shadows. Lucy, Bonnie's ever-present tail, stumbled behind her. As they approached the wooden two-storey building, now a black monolith in the approaching night, they caught sight of smoke. Even in the fading day, it was thick and grey. Bonnie's cold chest immediately constricted and she quickened her pace, fearing the old wooden house might have caught alight. Her thoughts in these moments weren't fear of the fire or even for the lives of the people inside, but fear of a good night's rest being stolen from her. She didn't have the brainpower or stamina to face the prospect of her bed going up in flames after the day she'd had.

Closer to the house, the sound of laughter drifted to her along with the smoke. "What is it?" Lucy puffed. Bonnie had almost forgotten she'd been behind her. Like failing to overtly register your own appendages. Rather than answer, Bonnie continued around the back of Buna House towards the origin of the laughter and smoke. Not just smoke from a small, well-contained fire, but also from a circle of women chain-smoking cigarettes. Though her back was turned, Bonnie recognised the unmissable girth of Bertha sitting in a chair that had evidently been moved from inside the house. A group of other inebriates she'd seen with Bertha and Lillian kept her company, either in their own borrowed chairs, or on old blankets spread on the filthy ground.

Lillian was one of those sitting atop some kind of material, unidentifiable in the dim light, but unmistakably filthy. "Me baby nurses!" she cried upon seeing Bonnie and Lucy, motioning for them to join the others around the fire. Bonnie hesitated a moment, thinking of her bed calling to her—and the stern frown of Nurse Hatchet if she were to catch them—but the warmth of the small fire and the smell of cigarettes were even more welcoming than Lillian had been. She suddenly felt the weight of her own packet of cigarettes deep in her pocket.

"Well, just for one quick durrie…"

The ladies let out a loud cheer, and the cloud of smoke thickened momentarily as they took their drags in near unison. Bonnie again briefly thought of the chastising Nurse Hatchet would give her if she caught her fraternising, but instantly dismissed the worry. It would just be one more failure to add to the long list of mistakes she'd made that day.

"You want wanna mine, darlin'?" A woman whose name Bonnie hadn't learnt yet proffered her a soggy, white stick that just barely resembled a cigarette. Bonnie repressed her shiver as she looked at the sores around the woman's mouth, then at the swollen lumps beneath her ears where her lymph nodes bulged beneath her skin. Who knew what kind of diseases these women had. Syphilis, probably.

"N-no, thank you." She pulled a cigarette from the packet within her pocket and smiled as she lit a match and breathed in the rich, hearty smoke. The warmth in her chest seemed to reach out caressing fingers that eased the aches of the muscles in her shoulders. She sighed audibly, letting the sense of calm fall over her like the smog around them.

"Doncha worry, love," Lillian croaked, breaking Bonnie's temporary reverie. "Any time ya want to go handin' out ciggies, just swing 'em this way, 'ey?" Her yellow teeth—what were left of them—glistened in the flickering fire as she smiled at her, her eyes narrowing in mirth.

"Oh God, has everyone heard what happened in Female Five today?!" The women burst into uproarious laughter again, and Bonnie felt Lucy huddle so close that her skin prickled with annoyance beneath her stiff uniform. With that reminder, she pulled at her collar and cuffs, loosening them. "It was *a day*, that it was."

"Ah, not any different to most days in Female Five, then." Bonnie didn't recognise this inebriate's voice or face either, but shrugged politely anyway.

"You were right, Lillian," she breathed deeply through her cigarette. "You were right about minding the patients, about minding Nurse Hatchet. Let's just hope your ghosts don't give me more trouble than they already did." She'd said this in jest, but silence fell over the group until only Lucy's whiny breathing could be heard. Bonnie wriggled her shoulder blades to encourage Lucy to take a step back from her.

"Well, I'm surprised you haven't met them yet yerself. But I s'pose you haven't been there at night yet."

"How do you know it's haunted?" Lucy piped up.

"Noises ya can't account for," Bertha grunted, lighting up another cigarette. "Scratchin' in the walls. Cold spots. I hears it and feels it when I's doin' the floors, see. They like it when yous alone."

"Sounds typical of a big building to me." Bonnie shrugged, coming towards the end of her cigarette. Her thoughts strayed back to her bed.

"Footsteps from the attic," Bertha added. "And folks 'ave seen 'er. A woman in white. Or a woman in grey. Depends who ya ask." Excited murmurs spread through the women, and Bonnie chuckled, sucking the last of her cigarette and lamenting how quickly it had burnt down in the brisk night air.

"Not to mention the screaming," Lillian nodded along. "And the knockin'. Comin' from *her* room."

"Her?" Lucy whispered from behind Bonnie. Bonnie turned to see the pale nurse clutching at her skirt with twitching fingers, eyes wide. Evidently, not all of them were so entertained. Lillian smiled, those yellow teeth once again glinting. Now that the sun was fully hidden, and the shadows of the flames danced across her squinting eyes, she looked almost ethereal—eerie—as she leaned forward.

"*Alice.* She was a patient here, long before any of us. One of the maddest these walls have ever seen, or ever will see, again. So crazed that they left her tied to a chair for weeks, for months, at a time. I heard that once they even left her tied to that chair for a whole year. Locked alone in that small room in the attic of Female Five. Screaming and knocking about, but no-one ever let her free."

Lucy shuddered, and Bonnie put a hand around her shoulders and gave her a quick reassuring squeeze. "Thank you for inspiring tonight's nightmares, ladies." She nodded jovially, flicking her cigarette butt towards the fire. "But it's bedtime for us. And you ladies should be getting inside, too. No doubt they'll want to be 'settling you in' for the night soon."

"Yes, ma'am." Lillian nodded her head deferentially. But as soon as the two trainees headed back around to the front of Buna House, the cackling picked up again behind them.

"I *knew* it," Lucy whispered as they pushed through the door and into the relevant warmth. "I *told* you I heard whispering. This place really is haunted…"

Bonnie laughed as she reached up to unpin her cap from her hair. "I'd be careful whose stories you believe. Hallucinations are a common symptom of psychosis. And those ladies seem to like a good story."

Lucy looked fervently over her shoulder as she closed the front door behind her. The darkened grounds of Kenmore were swallowed in its woody maw as it clicked shut. The creaking of the house began almost instantly, a door past the common room banging open and shut. "But it sure is easy to believe sometimes," she muttered under her breath as she turned for the stairs.

CHAPTER SIX

2021
15 OCTOBER, 18:14

AIDEN THOUGHT HE was going to pass out. He could feel his heart thumping in the centre of his chest and hear the sound it made between his ears. It seemed to rock him with each thundering beat. The edges of his vision had gone white, and his head felt like a helium balloon. Light and gassy, like it could float away at any moment. His eyes grew wetter as he stared across the wooden hatch at Devin. If Devin hadn't looked so pale and terrified, Aiden might have been ashamed of his unspilled tears. There was no room for that emotion now, though. All he could feel was terror; at any moment, the caretaker would climb that rickety ladder and they'd be caught. Their night—and their YouTube dreams—shattered. She'd probably call the cops. Worse than that, the cops would call his Mum.

The chaotic noises of the old building continued. With adrenaline rushing through him thicker than blood, Aiden heard every door and window creaking and banging. Every strip of paint or chip of plaster clattering to the floor. Every piece of debris or rubbish shuffled around with every step the caretaker took. Her footsteps echoed in the hall of the church. Aiden pictured her exploring each room, and he prayed she wouldn't think to check the trapdoor. When she finally came towards the messy, cluttered room behind the stage, he almost choked on his own breaths. His chest literally burnt from trying to suck oxygen in through his clenched teeth.

She was so close. They heard her slightly laboured breaths and her grunts as she pushed some of the chairs aside to make her way further into the room. Flecks of black swirled within the white edges of Aiden's vision, and he squeezed his eyes shut, lowering his head slightly between his bent knees. Fainting at that moment would be just the sound to bring her racing up that ladder. After what felt like hours, the woman finally left the room, then the church. They heard her steps growing distant as she exited the building, and then the ride-on mower started up again. Dust shook free from the ceiling and rained down on them like sparks in the fading light of day as the engine rumbled to life. Aiden sighed in relief and let a groan slip before he could help it. He fell back onto his bottom, the muscles of his calves and thighs finally relaxing.

"That was clo—" Aiden cut off when Devin shook his head, a finger pressed to his lips. Immediately, the anxiety returned, like a fist clenching tight around his stomach. Devin couldn't possibly think she was still there? They'd heard the mower leaving. But even the slightest chance that someone still waited for them in the hall below was enough for him to nod his head in agreement. They stayed there for at least another ten minutes, not daring to let out any sound but their own breaths. The church continued to creak around them. Once again, Aiden pictured the walls breathing, like the asylum was a living thing.

Fifteen minutes later, the sound of the mower a distant memory, the two boys finally crawled back to the ladder. It was dark enough now that all they could see of the stage was its black outlines. They'd done it. They were *inside* Kenmore Asylum at night. And it had happened almost against their will. Aiden switched his camera to night mode, filming down the ladder and onto the stage, watching the green of the view-screen to make sure no-one waited in a corner to jump out and grab them. Finally reassured, he made his way back down, limbs trembling.

1953
AUTUMN

BONNIE FOUND HERSELF subconsciously staring at a crack in the dining table of Buna House, her trick to quiet her mind. It was still dark outside; each day the sun seemed to rise later and later. She lifted her mug of coffee to her lips and sipped slowly, willing the caffeine to wake up her sluggish brain. Lillian sure did make a good pot of coffee. Gerald and Patsy joined her silently, each filling their own mugs and sliding into mismatched chairs beside her. Lucy broke the silence, and the reverie, as she practically collided with the doorframe when she ran into the room. The three of them looked up at her. Strands of Lucy's long straight hair hung loose under her poorly secured cap, she had sleep crumbs in the corners of her eyes, and she panted. It was unlike her to be so dishevelled.

"I heard it again!" she exclaimed as she staggered forward to join them, rubbing her upper arm where it had hit the door. "The *whispers* beneath our window."

Each woman around the table reacted differently. Bonnie rolled her eyes and sighed, returning her attention to the coffee. She needed to drink it fast to have the stamina for this conversation. Gerald barked out a harsh laugh, her voice still rough from sleep. Patsy was the only one to respond with any kind of curiosity or empathy.

"Whispers?" Patsy queried, scraping her chair to the side to make room for Lucy to join them.

"Lucy reckons there's someone whispering beneath her window at night," Bonnie groaned, reaching to refill her coffee mug. "A *man*."

"There *is*," Lucy said petulantly, stomping her heel beneath the table. "He's not speaking real words either. I looked out the window this time, and there *definitely wa*sn't anyone there."

"What?" Bonnie snickered. She wasn't normally this cruel, but days of constant dressing-downs from Nurse Hatchet and endless restless nights had sharpened her edges. "You think it's a *ghost*, then?"

Gerald laughed again, this time at least into her coffee cup. Lucy's eyes widened with hurt and a little embarrassment; only then did Bonnie feel a twinge of shame in her own chest. She sighed loudly, wishing she'd been allowed to wallow in her own silent self-pity a while longer.

"Well…" Patsy started, breaking the awkward silence only to pause to sip her own drink. "Some of the nurses and patients *do* think this place is haunted. I haven't heard any stories of male ghosts whispering beneath windows yet, but I sure have heard plenty of others."

"Oh?" Lucy asked, almost desperately.

"You know, the standard things. Unexplainable noises, footsteps in the middle of the night, feeling cold or nauseous. Some folks even think they've seen dark shadows or floating orbs, those types of things."

"Absolute nonsense," Gerald said firmly. Her cup was, as always, the first to empty. "Big buildings make noises. *Patients* make noises. And breezes and draughts account for all the cold spots and ruffling papers you can imagine. Not to mention all the rats and possums. Have you ever heard a possum? They sound like the devil himself."

Patsy smiled conspiratorially. "Oh, come on Gerald. I *know* you've had weird stuff happen to you…" The square-set woman's grin deepened as her dark eyes sparkled. It was infectious and Gerald smiled back at her, letting out a little chuckle.

"There's a rational explanation for that too, I'm sure."

"What?" Lucy piped up, eager to talk with someone who might actually believe her tall tales.

"Gerald was on night duty one month," Patsy explained. "She was doing the rounds of Ward Five, and she found the door to the top floor—the attic—wide open. She'd locked it behind her earlier that night. And all the adjoining doors. *And* she had the only keys. But somehow, there it was, standing open." Despite the warmth of her coffee, Bonnie felt a chill tremble its way through her. How did you explain that one away? "You might think maybe she just didn't remember?" Gerald rolled her eyes as Patsy continued her story dramatically. "But Gerald locked that door good and tight *again*, only to find it exactly the same, wide open, the next time she did her rounds."

"*See*," Lucy whispered. "This place is haunted."

Bonnie didn't answer, instead focusing her eyes on that split in the dining table again. Tracing its dark edges. Calming her mind as she prepared for another day of real-world problems.

"There'll be a rational explanation," Gerald said stubbornly, standing and stretching her limbs. "There always is. Don't let your mind get carried away with you, I say. Unlike insanity, these stories are catching. It's the power of suggestion. All it takes is one person believing and then suddenly you've got yourself a haunted asylum."

Do I believe in ghosts? Bonnie thought to herself. She'd never considered it before. She'd never had cause to. Her life before coming to Kenmore had been completely ordinary. *What even* is *a ghost?*

THE MORNING IN Ward Five had been blissfully quiet. The patients' showering had gone off without a hitch. It surprised Bonnie just how quickly she'd got used to the knots of naked flesh. Just how quickly her nose had inured itself to the stench of excrement and other bodily fluids. There was a lot to be said for routine.

The patients each had their breakfast without fuss or complaint. A *miracle*. Bonnie even had time to sit with Ethel—the patient who had defecated in the corner that first day—and had an almost normal conversation about bees and honey and how different flowers made the honey taste different. It was obviously something that fascinated the woman to the point of fixation, and she'd found herself impressed at Ethel's depth of knowledge on the subject.

"Did you know bees shiver to keep themselves warm?" the older woman said, staring out the window at the gardens. The day was bright and warm, the sky blue. Bonnie was surprised to find she was enjoying herself. "Did you know bees have five eyes? And that they can see the colour blue better than they can red? They're so smart." The old patient's voice quivered with excitement.

"I didn't know that, no," Bonnie smiled politely. It was in this moment—Ethel so calm and happy, the patients all clean and well-fed, and the sun shining through the window—that Bonnie realised she *was* enjoying herself. *I'm making a difference.* She smiled at the thought, reaching out to hold Ethel's hand. She found herself caring deeply for this woman, and for all the women she was getting to know here, in a way she'd never cared for anyone else. In a way, perhaps, she never could care for anyone else. These women needed her unlike anyone ever had. And her feelings towards them felt more real than any she'd ever felt before. Not just for the Ward Five patients like Ethel and Maggie—who was also having a good day, finally over her nicotine withdrawal. But also for the inebriates like Lillian and Bertha, and the Buna House patients like Cora.

Ethel stood up slowly, her chair grating across the floor. At first Bonnie thought she might be going to the window to get a better look outside. But instead, she walked towards the fireplace at the opposite end of the room. Despite the slight chill in the Autumn air, it hadn't been lit yet. A large protective cover enclosed it—mitigating the risk of open flames in an asylum. Bonnie followed behind her slowly, more out of curiosity than anything else. It was actually quite normal for conversations to finish abruptly here. Ethel stopped in front of the fireplace and frowned, bending low to look at the empty grate through the gaps in its protective cover. Soon enough, the days would be cool enough to warrant a fire.

"Are you okay, Ethel?" Bonnie smiled, standing a couple of paces away. "Do you need anything?"

"It's cold…" Ethel murmured, turning to look at Bonnie with frightened eyes. Her entire demeanour had suddenly changed. From being bright-eyed and happily talking about bees, to a sudden paleness and frailty that made Ethel look her years. Though she still had dark hair, she was stooped and wrinkled top-to-bottom. Bonnie knew this from the morning showerings. Ethel suddenly looked ancient.

"Do you want your cardigan?" Bonnie took a step forward, and felt the chill, almost like she'd stepped out of the sun and into the shade. Almost, but deeper. The air felt positively icy. It clung to her exposed skin and pushed its way inside her until she couldn't help but shiver. Involuntary trembles ran up her limbs. Perhaps there was a gap, allowing cold air to blow in from outside. Another thought struck her, Patsy's words repeating in her head: *cold spots*. And then Lillian's words, *mind the ghosts of Ward Five.*

She reached a hand out to Ethel, about to encourage her away from the spot, when the woman suddenly spoke. Her words were soft but hollow, holding none of the emotion from moments before. "Did you know that bees never sleep?" The thought was as chilling as the air around them, though Bonnie couldn't put her finger on why. "They're not the only things that never sleep here…"

With that, Ethel pinched her face, frowning in concentration and squatting slightly. Bonnie heard the sound of wet, thick flatulence as the smell of fresh faeces hit her. Ethel hadn't even bothered to remove her underwear this time.

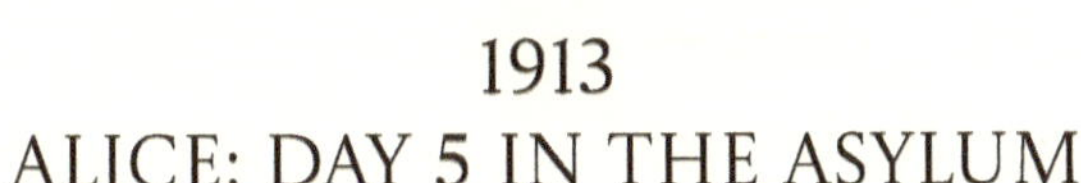

1913
ALICE: DAY 5 IN THE ASYLUM

IT TOOK TWO strong, tall male wardsmen, accompanied by both medical superintendents—from the female wards *and* the female reception house—to get Alice into Female Ward Five. Harriet trailed behind them, out of range of the thrashing woman, but not out of range of her screams. She wasn't sure anyone on the grounds of Kenmore were beyond the range of Alice's screams at this point. The woman's once shiny hair wrapped around her face in long whipping tendrils. It had only been one week, but already the colour seemed darker, more dull. The grey and brown tones had shifted to shades of black. Of course, Alice was well-secured in her camisole, but that didn't stop her from flailing like a mighty, muscled fish out of water.

The nurses in Ward Five had obviously heard them coming and had shepherded most of the other patients into their rooms before bringing Alice inside. She had thrashed so spectacularly as they'd approached the stairs that they'd let her fall to the ground, and then heaved her up like a heavy sack of writhing rats. Harriet winced as the woman repeatedly hit her head against the back of the stairs.

"We'll need to shave her head," the Ward Five Superintendent grumbled as he made his way up the steps behind them. He turned over his shoulder and noticed Harriet there, directing his mumbled observation to her as a command.

"Yes sir," Harriet said firmly but obediently. She'd heard good things about this man. At least in comparison to the man she'd just been working for. Firm and stiff—perhaps even uncaring—but at least not deliberately cruel.

"You're Nurse Harriet, am I correct?" The two of them paused on the stairs as the others continued to wrangle Alice to the upper level. He spoke as if this were a run-of-the-mill day. Perhaps it was.

"Yes, sir. I spent five years at the hospital before coming to Kenmore. They temporarily reassigned me to the Reception House, but I'm looking forward to starting in Ward Five as soon as possible."

"Hm," the man grunted, turning to climb the stairs again. "They didn't tell me you'd been temporarily reassigned. You'll start here tomorrow, Nurse Harriet. We're short-staffed all over. I don't know *why* they thought I could handle a gap any better than the reception houses. And with *her*, we'll need all the staff on board we can get."

"Yes, sir," Harriet said, elatedly. If she'd known it would be this easy to take up her desired post, she would have found a reason to come to the wards far sooner.

Her elation dipped as they reached the top floor. The attic. The roof beams were visible here, sloping at a gentle angle. There were beds crammed up here as well, showing just how overcrowded Kenmore was since the attics and verandas—and she assumed basements or any other empty space—had been converted. Alice wasn't in any of these beds, though. They'd dragged her off to a small room off the main hall. Harriet could hear her crying and cussing. It didn't sound like words at all. It didn't even sound human. She remembered the day she'd seen Alice's black eyes staring out of the Box, and had imagined her pulling her body together from rats. Perhaps she really was more demon than woman.

Harriet and the Medical Superintendent got to the door in time to see Alice, now free of her camisole, being strapped to a hard wooden chair. Its legs were bolted to the floor, and Alice was secured with buckles at her ankles, thighs, wrists, and waist. She pulled violently. One leg of the chair wasn't as secured as the rest, and it tapped brutally against the hard wooden floor. Harriet felt physically and violently ill as she watched the life drain from the woman's face. As the realisation of her full captivity, worse than a dog chained in a yard, fell on her. It was like the acid from Harriet's stomach had found its way inside her veins.

"This is abnormal, you understand," the Ward Five Medical Superintendent said beside her. "You'll find the other patients here quite reasonable by comparison." Harriet could only nod, feeling it difficult to rip her eyes away from the sight of the panting wardsmen, chests heaving as they exited the room. "Now, unless you're needed back at the Reception Houses immediately," he continued, looking at his colleague as he did so. "I'll ask you to fetch a bucket of warm water, some soap, scissors, and a razor, and shave the patient's head before I lock the door."

CHAPTER SEVEN

2021
15 OCTOBER, 18:26

Aiden had to manoeuvre carefully over the chairs and other rubbish the caretaker had moved around the room in her search for them. He cursed as he grazed a shin against broken wood. "Fuck this shit, man…"

A red glow suddenly lit up the room, and with that new illumination, he saw the broken church pew he'd run into. He looked over his shoulder to see Devin had switched on his headlamp. Devin had gone on some ghost hunting tour where the tour guide had told them the red light was: a.) less likely to scare ghosts away, b.) not as harsh on the eyes, and c.) not as bright. He must have figured it was a good way to light up the room without attracting much attention.

"It's alright, numb nuts. The cunt is long gone."

The two of them carefully climbed out of the side room and back into the large main hall. With the sun now set, it felt even larger than before. The ceiling wasn't just high, it was a wide gaping maw that stretched further than Aiden could see. It was literally cavernous. And colder, too. Colder than he'd thought possible for the temperature to drop in such a short space of time. The building still groaned and settled. Tapping noises and rattling echoed all around them. Aiden could almost imagine the hallways surrounding them, hundreds of unseen spirits flooding towards them.

"Let's get the fuck out of this church, man," Aiden groaned as he subconsciously scratched an itch that tingled at the base of his throat.

"I want us to film one more commentary first. It's, like, perfect. I've never seen anyone else film this place at night. It's, like, a totally different vibe, you know? Like we've Silent-Hilled this motherfucker and gone into some totally new and creepy dimension."

Aiden knew exactly what Devin meant. It did feel like they hadn't come out of a manhole, but through a portal to some creepy underworld. With his camera already in hand, Aiden raised it and simply nodded, willing Devin to keep talking.

"I'm standing in the abandoned church hall. The sun has set, and the vibe here is next-level. The place is totally empty, except for church pews and even the old pipe organ. But it doesn't feel like we're alone." A bang sounded at that moment, like a piece of falling wood had crashed to the floor somewhere further in. The two of them jumped, and Aiden knew he'd ruined the shot with his jerky motion. "Did you catch that?" Devin asked excitedly and Aiden merely nodded. "As you can hear, this place has been making crazy noises ever since we got here. And now it's time for us to make camp. Can we survive the night?"

Devin dropped his hands and raised his eyebrows in a query. "I got it," Aiden said before his mate could ask. "Now let's get the fuck out of here!"

"I want to set up for the night in one of the wards," Devin grinned. In the green light of the night vision camera and the red light of the torches, his white teeth lit up like a terrifying Christmas tree. Aiden marvelled at how little fear the boy showed. He also wondered how much of it was bravado and how much of it was stupidity. Aiden suddenly felt less certain of the plan.

"It's so fuckin' cold, man." He slipped his backpack off his shoulder and rummaged inside for the lightweight hoodie he'd brought with him. It wasn't supposed to be this chilly during this time of year. He pulled it over his head, the tip of his icy nose protesting slightly. "Which ward? We're pretty much in the middle here. We could head anywhere."

"I hear the most stories about the female wards," Devin answered, making his way back through the hall to the entryway. "Ward Sixteen is supposedly the noisiest ward, where they kept some of the worst patients. I hear there's even fingernail scratches on the back of the doors. That would make for some awesome video. Then Ward Fifteen is said to be the most haunted."

Ward Sixteen was slightly closer, and that decided it for them. They'd make their way there first and see if they could set up for the night. "What else did you hear about Ward Sixteen?" Aiden whispered as they exited the church. With the sun now set, the birds had stopped chirping, and the bugs started up their nocturnal chorus instead. The place had felt eerie during the day. At night, eerie took on a whole new meaning. He wished Devin hadn't compared the asylum to an alternate Hellish dimension.

"Not much. The solitary cells are where the scratches on the doors are meant to be. Apparently, they locked them in those cells for days. And if they got too noisy, they'd spray them with a hose! That's, like, full-on torture."

"Where'd you hear all this shit?" Aiden kept his voice low. He didn't just whisper because they trespassed; it was also pitch dark. The more superstitious members of his family had always whispered in the dark to avoid attracting unwanted attention from things they couldn't see. Perhaps his eastern European upbringing was what made him so skittish.

"There was a news story about ten years ago. Not to mention all the local talk on the Reddit chats. It's also how I found out you could be sent here for frequent masturbation. You'd be fucked, mate."

Aiden snickered and bit back. "You and me both, wanker."

They arrived at the edge of the large central courtyard. It was an open expanse, but also the most direct route to the wards. Moonlight broke through the clouds to cast the whole area in a silvery glow. Just as Aiden was about to suggest going around, Devin took a step out of the shadows and into the open. He lifted his camera again and began filming.

"I've never seen this place like this…" he trailed off as he panned the area. "It's kinda magical. We're gonna get so many subscribers."

Aiden followed Devin out into the courtyard, also panning his camera. The clock tower was iconic, and with the moonlight and parting clouds, it looked ethereal. The boys took their time crossing the courtyard. Aiden made sure to get Devin in some of his shots. He felt almost artistic. Yet despite the beauty, being so exposed redoubled the feeling they were being watched. By the time they reached the other end of the courtyard, Aiden's chest was so tight he could barely breathe.

They paused, listening. The nocturnal sounds had changed. The crickets became overshadowed by another noise. A familiar noise: the distant rumbling of that ride-on mower.

"Shit!"

"Fuck!" Devin yanked Aiden by the collar of his sweater, pulling him down to his level as they dashed back into the shadows. The rumbling got steadily louder. The ride-on mower was approaching fast, and by the sounds of it, making a bee-line straight for them. "How the Hell does she always know where we are?!"

1953
AUTUMN

Bonnie woke up early, like she did every day. It was her first weekend off since she'd arrived at Kenmore, but her internal body clock wouldn't permit her to enjoy a sleep in. Still, she revelled in the fact that she didn't have to get out of bed straight away and snuggled further under the covers, stretching languorously as she did so. The broken spring in her mattress attempted to poke her back as she wriggled. *I still need to flip the mattress,* she thought to herself distractedly, before rolling over. *I'll do it this weekend…but not today…*

Today, Bonnie planned on joining Gerald, Patsy, Cora, Ethel and some of the other patients for a swim in the dam before it got too cold. Best of all—though Bonnie felt slightly ashamed to admit it—Lucy had declined to join them, fearing it was already too chilly. This just made Bonnie want to go even more. If Lucy couldn't do it, then she *had* to. *Cold be damned,* she smiled to herself beneath her blankets.

A few hours later, Bonnie had one arm through Ethel's, and the other through Cora's, and practically skipped through the grass for the final few metres to the "swimming pool", as Gerald and the other older nurses called it. The dam had been constructed forty or so years earlier, fed by the nearby river, for the farm. During World War II, when the military had temporarily taken over the asylum, the soldiers had used it as a "swimming pool". It was now surrounded on one side by a wooden fence in need of mending, with a small wooden shed at one end. The "pool" itself was roughly thirty metres long and less than ten metres wide. Its concrete edges had turned black with age, and the water looked slightly dark. To Bonnie, whose hometown had nothing of the sort, it looked wonderful. It reminded her of the days her family would travel to the town of Wagga Wagga to swim at the "beach" at the Murrumbidgee River.

The day started with a chill in the air, but the sun quickly came out, not a cloud to be seen in the bright blue sky. Not a single breeze shook the trees surrounding the dam. A perfect day for a swim, and perhaps their last, before the cold truly settled in. Ethel hummed excitedly as they drew close, and Bonnie turned to smile at the woman. Ethel's wide eyes stayed fixed on the water and an eager smile pulled at her thin lips. "Hmmmm," she hummed again, pulling on Bonnie's arm now, which caused her and Cora to laugh companionably.

"Best get in your togs, ladies!" Gerald called from just behind them. Bonnie turned to see she'd already offed her cardigan and unbuttoned her white cotton dress to reveal a flower-patterned bikini underneath. The top was well structured with wire, and the shorts tailored perfectly to her muscular hips. Prompt as always, Patsy had already folded her clothes and stood proudly in an equally well-tailored one-piece suit with navy and white stripes. She was already tucking her ringleted hair into a black nylon cap. One of the other patients behind her had stripped down to a singlet and bloomers.

"Hmmmm!"

Bonnie laughed again as Ethel recaptured her attention.

"Did you know," Ethel practically whispered, "that bees use water in their hives to help regulate the temperature? Like air conditioning."

"You know, I didn't," Cora said, winking as she removed her own dress to reveal a bra and bloomers. Falling behind, Bonnie extricated her arm from Ethel's and excitedly stripped down to her bikini. A beautiful red and black one, not quite so well-tailored as Gerald or Patsy's—her mother had made it for her—but still the most thrilling piece of clothing she owned. Her black nylon cap tied the whole outfit together. Gerald wolf-whistled behind her, making her flush, but smile, which she bent her head to hide.

"You'll be beating off the male nurses with a stick," Gerald teased, walking to the edge of the pool and stretching, each of her ribs standing out. Gerald wouldn't have done too badly with the male nurses herself, if she'd been remotely interested. The older nurse dived into the water with a delicious splash, which encouraged a flurry of excitement and a rush from the other nurses and patients to the water's edge.

"Hmmm!"

Bonnie turned in time to see Ethel remove her singlet, bloomers, *and* underwear, to embrace the sun like the day she was born. Starkers.

"Oh… Ethel, dear—"

"In we go!" Patsy cut Bonnie off, jogging past her with another naked patient padding excitedly along behind her.

When in Rome…

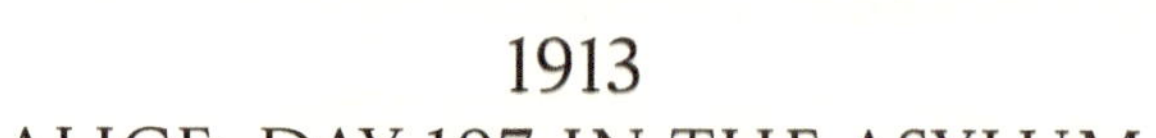

1913
ALICE: DAY 107 IN THE ASYLUM

HARRIET PEEKED OVER her shoulder at the closed solitary cell door while she folded down the patients' beds in the attic of Ward Five. Alice had been out of the chair only one day this time before finding herself back behind that door. Harriet could hear her in there, that one chair leg still not quite as well secured as the others, tapping the wooden floor rhythmically.

Alice's time in the ward with the other patients was getting fewer and farther between. After her first week in Ward Five—and her first week in the chair—Alice had seemed determined to at least try to behave. Although she'd barely spoken to the doctor or the other nurses, merely nodding or shaking her head in answer to their questions, she'd at least followed directions. Doing so with such meekness, eyes downcast, tongue muted, probably helped her cause. Harriet had truly hoped this pattern would continue. That perhaps Alice had accepted her fate. It had, however, been merely a ploy.

After only a few days of contriteness, Alice had been caught trying to escape the ward via the catwalk that connected Ward Five to Ward Six. *How* she'd got through the door, no-one could figure out, but regardless, she hadn't got very far. Caught at the door to Ward Six by one of the nurses. How she had *howled* and scratched when the wardsmen had pulled her back to the chair. After that, Alice's escape attempts had continued for days and weeks. From attempting to steal the keys from the nurses, to wrapping herself in bundles of dirty linen, and even running at any open door as fast and as hard as she could. After several of these failed escape attempts, Alice had given up the pretence of compliance. Refusing to eat with the others, refusing to bathe.

Harriet observed that the more Alice resisted, the more she was punished. Now, simply refusing to look a nurse in the eye, or moving slowly in defiance, resulted in a fist to the stomach or a slap to the face. Harriet never raised a hand to the patients, where she could help it, but some of the other staff… The older nurses, especially, held no such compunction. Now, if Alice refused to bathe with the others, there was no attempt to force her. She simply got thrown into her cell and viciously sprayed down with a hose. If she spoke back, she ended up in the camisole. And, increasingly, the staff resorted to the chair for any other misbehaviour.

Several months after Alice had first arrived at Kenmore, she began whispering to herself. Hissing, cursing and muttering constantly. Whether she roamed the wards or was tied to the chair, a near-constant stream of sound escaped her lips. If she wasn't speaking, she'd be tapping. A foot against the floor, her nails against her skin, her fingers against her teeth. Harriet would sometimes press her ear to Alice's door and hear her in there. The scratching of Alice's voice reminded her of that first time she'd found her in solitary. Reminded her of the sounds of rats. Harriet could never bear to eavesdrop for long, always fleeing to the floor below, icy pins and needles running down her spine.

Harriet didn't know whose circumstance was worse. Alice, seemingly entrenched further and further into her own insanity and darkness. Or herself, increasingly relieved to turn a blind eye to the woman in the chair. To put her from her mind so she could simply make it through the day.

CHAPTER EIGHT

1953
AUTUMN

Bonnie flinched as Charge Nurse Hatchet's spittle flayed her chin. It felt like her stomach was a led balloon filling up with helium. It wanted to both weigh her down and expand to escape through her throat, away from this embarrassment. Bonnie hunched her shoulders protectively towards her chest, scrunching her eyes shut as her bottom lip pushed up into its sister. Nurse Hatchet only came up to her shoulder, but standing this close and staring up at her, Hatchet was the most intimidating thing she'd ever seen. Bonnie was the one who felt self-conscious about the height difference. Like she was a bumbling buffoon of a woman and wanted nothing more than to shrink down beyond Nurse Hatchet's sight.

"How *dare* you!" Nurse Hatchet viciously spoke again. She hadn't laid a hand on Bonnie, but her fists trembled by her sides as if she desperately longed to. The vibrations were almost physical things, shaking the air around Bonnie. She could feel the tension almost as much as she would have felt those old, gnarled fingers, had Hatchet given into her urge.

"I—I—I—"

"This is your first warning, girl, and you won't get another. If I *ever* see you stealing from a patient again, you'll feel my boot in your arse on your way out the gates. I don't care how short-staffed we are. I won't tolerate it. Not in my ward."

Flames burnt to life at the tops of Bonnie's cheeks. She was many things—a novice who made mistakes among them—but she was *not* a thief. She drew a sharp breath through her nose, feeling the cool air burning her nostrils. Her lips pinched tighter, and she let her chest expand as she retorted in whispered defiance, "I did *not* steal anything from Ethel."

Nurse Hatchet's eyebrows raised and her own lips pinched. This was a woman who was not used to being talked back to. The vibrating air turned colder, and Nurse Hatchet's face darkened. Bonnie could almost see the thunderclouds gathering in her eyes.

"Ms. Ethel told me her Brussel sprouts were rotten." Bonnie tried to fill her voice with as much air and gusto as she had her chest, but her words merely breathed out like a soft spring breeze. Nothing like the gale force winds she feared were about to come out of Nurse Hatchet. "I wasn't stealing her food, ma'am. I was *tasting* it to make sure the sprouts hadn't gone bad. They had a particular smell tha—"

The thunderstorm broke. The spittle had been a mere taste of the lashing rains to come. "They're *spouts*! Fart grenades from Belgium. Of *course* they don't smell right. Of *course* they taste like three-day-old cabbage."

"In North America…" Ethel calmly piped up around a mouthful of instant mashed potatoes, sitting to their left and still eating her lunch. "…Honeybees have to collect pollen from skunk cabbages. They're the first plants that bloom through all that snow. Skunk cabbages smell like dead, rotting bodies. And honeybees *eat* them…"

"Hm," Nurse Hatchet grunted shortly. "Very good, Ethel. Now eat your skunk cabbages." The nurse hooked her cold fingers around the base of Bonnie's upper arms. Despite her age, her grip was fierce, her fingers as cold as ice. It felt like the hand of the dead had reached out from the grave to snare her. Nurse Hatchet used the vice-like grip to steer Bonnie through the patients' dining hall and out through the first locked door into the corridor. The keys still jangling on the ring on her belt, Nurse Hatchet swung to face Bonnie yet again.

"I don't care *what* these patients say to you." She didn't yell any more, and her tone held more exhaustion than anger. The half whispered icy words still made Bonnie want to flee. "The other day, good old Vera claimed she was the Virgin Mary. And Rose thought the Government was listening to her through the cutlery. If Ethel told you God was a wart-covered toad at the bottom of the dam, would you dive in and go looking for Him?" Hatchet paused, hands on her hips, looking up at Bonnie with fiery intensity. This was not a rhetorical question.

"No, ma'am."

"*No*. So you are not to eat a patient's food again, am I clear?" This *was* a rhetorical question, as Nurse Hatchet quickly had her keys in hand again and made her way back into the dining room.

2021
15 OCTOBER, 19:44

"Can you feel that?" Devin said. Night had well-and-truly set in. Despite Devin being just three or so steps in front of Aiden, he was barely a grey shadow in the dark. Aiden watched his mate through the green screen of his digital camera, night-vision mode capturing his friend's form far better than his own eyes could. Devin's eyes glowed white through the camera when he turned back, holding his hand out in demonstration. "I've never felt cold shivers like this before. I don't just feel them in my arms, I feel them in my *chest*. I've never felt that before. It's like popping candy."

Aiden could feel it. Not just in his chest, but in his whole body. He worried he'd never be warm again. It had been a balmy enough day, but now that the sunlight was gone, it no longer felt like spring. Somehow, they'd again evaded the caretaker, turning their torches off, and ended up in a ward with solitary cells. Almost as though the asylum had led them here. Through the static-y green of the camera screen, he could see each of the heavy, thick wooden cell doors. Some were closed, still locked, but most hung half open. Each had a small metal grate in its centre; a small door within a door that could be opened, he supposed, to pass food through or to check on the patients without going inside.

One of the metal grates squeaked loudly as Devin pulled it back-and-forth, testing it. "You're still filming, yeah?" he whispered. Aiden nodded back. "I'm going in. You close me in, then film me through this grate, yeah?"

"Is that a good idea…?" Aiden trailed off. "What if the door locks and I can't get you out? There aren't any keys."

Devin pushed the heavy door closed, and it clicked shut with a dull boom that echoed down the long hallway. Aiden couldn't help but look over one skinny shoulder, into the complete darkness behind him, hearing the building sigh as the sound settled. Another creak came from somewhere far beyond his sight; that popping-candy shiver burrowed deeper into his chest. Aiden looked back just in time to see, through the green screen, Devin twist the handle and pull the door back open.

"See? It's fine." Devin's smile filled up the screen with a black yawning grin that made Aiden physically shiver this time, shaking his limbs as though trying to shake away the ice from his fingers.

"Okay, stop fucking wasting time, then. Get in."

As Devin pulled the door wide to enter, he paused at the last moment. "No funny business, got it?" He took a deep shuddering breath, as though reconsidering, then steeled himself and stepped into the cell as if pushing through an invisible barrier. He may have been the shorter of the two. He may have looked the youngest. But in that moment, Aiden's respect for his short, freckled friend doubled. He reached out a hand to nudge the door closed. In that moment, the stillness to the air seemed to solidify, pushing with Aiden's hand against the door with vigour. He could feel the door swinging forcefully, as though it were not just being pushed but *sucked* closed. An unseen wind bellowing against it.

Just before it slammed with a deafening rumble, Aiden caught a glimpse of his friend's face. So pale he looked like a ghost. Terror etched into every fine line. His mouth hung slightly agape. *"Devin?!"* Aiden hissed, pulling open the small grate with fumbling, numb fingers. "Devin, are you okay? Why'd you slam the door like that?!" He must have pulled it closed as well. It was the only explanation.

Aiden gasped and jumped back as two white eyes suddenly filled the gap in the grate, wide and flickering. Aiden felt like his skin vibrated off his bones; everything tingled.

"Why'd *I* slam it?" Devin hissed. "Why'd *you* slam it?!"

"I didn't... I—I—"

"Just start filming, would ya?" Devin's eyes disappeared from behind the grate. Aiden reached forward to secure it again. "Fucking little bitch. I'm the one in the fucking cell."

"Okay, man, but you're the jumpy one!" The momentary embarrassment and anger helped to bring a touch of warmth back, at least to Aiden's face. As did the bluster. After all, they were both being jumpy. "You ready? I'm filming now. Just start talking when I open the grate again, okay?" Aiden filmed a shot that dramatically panned the full length of the cells. A door behind him creaked at just the right moment, and he steeled his spine so he wouldn't flinch and ruin the shot. The sooner he got this done, the sooner they could get out of solitary. The creaking noise stopped just as the camera finished panning and focussed on the cell door behind which Devin waited. He could almost feel unseen eyes watching behind him, where that creaking sound had come from. Aiden didn't dare turn to check, and instead moderated his heavy breathing so it wouldn't ruin the shot. His long, tan arm came into view as he reached forward, pulling the grate down.

This time, Aiden didn't jump when Devin's eyes came into view, opened even wider than they had been before. In the night-vision of the camera, they shone like a demon's. Like he'd actually become possessed by a malevolent spirit. It was YouTube gold.

"I'm standing in one of the solitary cells, locked within these walls like so many lunatics before me." Devin made his voice deep and dramatic again, but whispered his words so he sounded like the narrator of a cold case murder show. "Patients unfortunate enough to end up in here were tortured daily. Hosed down with jets of water. Left in the dark to drift further and further into insanity. It's said that some of these doors still bear the scratch marks left by terrified patients' desperate fingernails. Standing here, in the dark, in solitary, I can understand. I myself want to scratch my way free." He paused, and then the grate snapped back into place with a bang.

This time Aiden shook the camera, jumping back and gasping. He hadn't touched the grate. There'd been no breeze. It was as though unseen hands had whipped it shut. "Devin, Devin?!" Pounding shook the door as though Devin threw his whole weight against it.

"Come on, man!" Devin's voice came through even more muffled than before. "Not cool! Let me out! Stop holding onto the door!"

"I—I—" Aiden stammered.

"Let me out, dickhead!"

Aiden dropped the camera to the ground, not bothering to turn it off. Without the camera to see through, the darkness appeared even more oppressive. He couldn't see anything but the door in front of him, the rest of the hallway swallowed up by such blackness that it had winked out of existence. He used his rising panic to fuel him and rushed forward, grabbing onto the door and pulling with all his might. The handle twisted, but the door didn't budge. Like it was swollen. Like the cold had made the door warp and bulge into the frame. His shoulder pinched and groaned in protest as he yanked.

"Aiden!" Devin's voice came out shrill. *"This isn't funny, man! Th—th—there's something else in here..."* Behind Devin's rising terror and the groaning of the door, Aiden could almost hear it himself: a scraping sound. The kind that seemed to jangle across your nerve endings. Like chalk on a blackboard. Like metal forks across ceramic plates. *Like nails across wood.*

"Argh!"

The fear in Devin's scream was like a living thing. A black, translucent worm that spewed from one boy into the other. Aiden yanked at the door again and finally it burst free. Devin sprawled on top of him, knocking him to the dusty ground and almost on top of their camera.

With one hand still free, Aiden fumbled for the button on his headlamp, flicking the red light on. He felt his pupils dilate almost painfully with the sudden change. The light illuminated a small, dark cell. Little more than two metres by two metres. The light barely touched the corners, but still, it was obviously empty. Not even a rat to explain the scratching sounds. Void of anything but darkness and dust. Devin panted and shivered at the same time. He pushed Aiden roughly as he got to his feet.

"What the fuck, man?" His voice quavered. "Not cool. Not fucking cool." He shook out his hands, but still they trembled.

"I didn't…" Aiden trailed off, his eyes still locked in rotation on each corner of the cell. Another door slammed somewhere in the gloom behind them, causing both boys to jump. Devin let out a gurgled groan. "Th—the wood," Aiden whispered, grasping for reason. "It must've warped…must've stuck…"

"There was something in there with me, man." Devin ran one hand through his tangled mop of red hair. "I heard its footsteps, stumbling out of *that* corner." Aiden followed the length of Devin's finger to the far right corner. "And it fucking *touched* my shoulder. It was cold, and wet, and…" He shuddered again, going silent.

"Bro," Aiden whispered. The light of his lamp now fell on something else. Something they hadn't noticed before. In fact, he was *sure* it hadn't been there before. He lifted his own trembling finger, pointing at the back of the door. There were scratches. Dozens of them, peeling through the top layers of wood and varnish. But they weren't old scratches. They looked new. As if they'd only just been gauged into the wood. And then that sound, that scraping, echoed again.

CHAPTER NINE

1953
AUTUMN

BONNIE TWISTED IN her bed, trying to get comfortable. That blasted, broken spring in the mattress seemed to poke her no matter which way she moved. *I have* got *to flip this mattress*, Bonnie thought to herself, not for the last time. She pulled her blanket tighter over her shoulders, tucking her chin into her chest. The swim in the dam with the patients, mere weeks before, had heralded the end of balmy days. The chill of winter was well-and-truly descending. With no heating in Buna House, her bed was the only haven from the steadily declining temperature. Her toes had just started to warm, but the tip of her nose still felt like a small, dripping icicle.

Bonnie rolled again, now looking up at the ceiling, the scratchy blanket pulled up to her eyes. Through the blueish gloom, with moonlight streaming through the window, she could see that same knot in the weatherboards she'd focused on her first day in Buna House. She concentrated on it again now, tracing its circular patterns, counting its rings, trying to quiet her mind enough for sleep to take her. Somewhere below her, a wall in the house creaked and moaned. In the stillness of the night, it was as audible as thunder in an otherwise empty sky. A moment later she heard a gust of wind batter the windows, and the groans echoed as the breeze wound its way through the corridors of the house.

"Bonnie?"

She rolled over at Lucy's whisper, watching as the slim girl propped herself up on her elbow.

"Did you hear that?"

"It's just the wind, Lucy. Buna House is always making noises."

Bonnie and Lucy lay facing each other a few moments more as the house continued to settle. Lucy's jitters made Bonnie think again of the alleged whispers beneath the window. The ones only Lucy could hear. She strained her own ears, hearing nothing more than the light tap of leaves and twigs on the glass as the wind continued beating the weatherboards.

"There…" Lucy whispered again, sitting fully upright this time. "Did you hear that?"

Surprisingly, beyond the creaks and wind, another muffled noise *could* be heard under the din. Bonnie sat up as well, pulling her top blanket around her shoulders. It wasn't whispering. At first Bonnie thought it was just more groans of a settling house. But these creaks had a pattern to them. "Footsteps?" she thought aloud, to Lucy's avid nodding. It did sound like someone shuffled around on the ground floor beneath them. Bonnie thought again about how it was impossible to lock up Buna House at night and wondered if it was another nurse, or maybe someone had wandered in from outside. She stood, walking to the chair at the end of her bed to pick up a thick dressing gown. She shivered in the moments between offing the blanket and donning the robe. The icy tentacles of winter instantly wrapped around her toes and fingers again, stealing their momentary warmth.

"What are you doing?" Lucy hissed, shuffling closer to the edge of the bed. "Where are you going? You're not going *out there*, are you?"

"Oh, come on, Lucy." Bonnie spoke the words, rather than whispered them, attempting to bolster her own swagger. The way her voice split the silence served more to rattle her spine than to stiffen it. "It's probably just another nurse." She preferred not to voice the possibility that it was someone from the outside; less a potentially violent threat, and more a common human being.

"But what if it's *not?*" Lucy trembled, standing now herself and taking a tentative step towards Bonnie.

Even though the same thought had crossed Bonnie's mind, in this instance, she found it easier to grip tightly to rationality. Buna House was old and poorly made. It creaked and moaned at night. And, like the rest of Kenmore, it was filled to capacity with people. The footsteps were more likely to be from someone getting a drink of water than from any foul spectre or malevolent outsider. Still, she wouldn't be able to sleep until she knew…

"Wait a moment," Lucy squeaked, as she sprung for her own folded dressing gown. "Don't leave me alone, I'll come."

Moments later, Bonnie poked her head out into the dark corridor, a shaking Lucy pressed into the small of her back. The door hinges squeaked sullenly. Nothing but familiar corridors greeted them, along with the top of the narrow cedar staircase, descending further into blackness. Here in the hallway, with only the moonlight from their own window shining behind them, the dark felt even more alive. Lucy's moist, rasping breaths tickled the hairs behind Bonnie's ear and she stepped forward in irritation, rubbing the side of her head on her shoulder. Her own footfalls were immediately echoed by more footsteps below, and then came a loud crash, as if someone had run into a wall. The whole house vibrated.

"What in the—" Bonnie cut off as she reached the top of the stairs, now able to see a faint glow of warm light from below.

A door down the upper hallway opened, and Gerald's tired face popped out, her hair wrapped around curlers and secured in a net. Another crash resounded, and the next thing Bonnie knew, her feet carried her down the narrow steps.

She rounded the base of the stairs, pulled towards the warm light in the kitchen, heart hammering in her chest. The initial fear that had begun to bloom in her chest had been replaced with a heavy bud of dread. Something wasn't right, she could feel it. This wasn't just some tired nurse getting a glass of water.

"Hello?" she called as she took the final steps into the common space. "Hello?"

No more footsteps. Even the creaks and moans of the house had quietened. The silence was intense enough to crackle in her ears and solidify the air around her.

Lucy caught up to her then, almost pushing her over as she barrelled into her shoulder. "Sorry, Bonnie, I—" Lucy cut off as the two of them stumbled forward and then she let out a piercing scream. To go from utter quiet to such a shrill keening right in Bonnie's ear sent shudders throughout her skeleton. In the same moment, the horrible sight before her robbed her of breath.

Cora lay on her back on the kitchen floor. Her legs splayed, one hand clutched her chest and the other was thrown wide. Her mouth hung open in a small, surprised "o", and her eyes stared vacantly up at the ceiling. Lucy screamed again. This time, the sound seemed to sap the strength from Bonnie's legs. She stumbled the final few steps forward and fell to her knees beside Cora. A multitude of thoughts ran through her head. *This is my friend. This is my patient. How did she get out of her room? She's got out of her room before, the doors don't always close properly. My God, she's dead! I need to check if she's okay. How could this happen?! I should start chest compressions. I can't touch her. I've seen dozens of dead bodies. But this is my friend. This is my house...*

Just as Bonnie lifted Cora's wrist, feeling how cold the bare skin had already become, Gerald knelt quietly beside her. Her curlers knocked gently beneath her cap. "Oh, Cora, dear," she whispered softly, taking the hand from Bonnie. There hadn't been a pulse, though it would have been more of a shock had there been one.

"Should we start chest compressions?"

Gerald shook her head, laying the hand on Cora's stomach. "No... This isn't the first time dear Cora has had troubles with her heart."

Bonnie wanted Gerald to keep talking. She wanted to ask how Gerald knew for sure it was a heart attack and not worth trying to revive her. Wanted to ask how Cora could have got into the kitchen. Wanted to shake Cora. To shake Gerald. To scream back at Lucy. Instead, she sat back on her heels and simply nodded. A small group of other nurses and workers appeared in Bonnie's periphery vision. A silent circle of observers gathered around them without her noticing.

"Come on, then," Gerald said loudly now, getting to her feet and turning to the others. "Nurses, you know what to do. Anyone not needed, back to bed. Trainees, please collect the towels and washers and a white gown." Gerald turned to Bonnie then. "Bonnie, head to the foyer and call the doctor, love. He'll need to check her over before the boys can take her down to the morgue." Bonnie simply nodded again as the flurry of moving people broke the mirage of stillness.

She approached the entryway and the phone on a console table by the wall, thinking about how numb she felt. Her training had pushed its way to the fore and everything else aside. She wasn't feeling sad. Wasn't feeling angry. Wasn't feeling afraid. In fact, she felt nothing. She lifted the receiver to her ear and dialled for the night duty doctor. It rang only twice before a woman answered.

"Yes?"

"Good evening. It's trainee Bonnie here, over in Buna House. I'm afraid one of the patients has passed away in the night. We're calling for the doctor."

"He's in Male Four," the woman—who must have been another nurse—replied curtly. "They've had a death too. It's been a busy night. I'll call for the boys. You'll have to take her to the mortuary and he can see her there in the morning, or later tonight."

"Yes, ma'am," Bonnie trailed off as the line disconnected. She'd only been gone a minute or so, but when she padded back into the kitchen, Gerald had already pulled the white gown over Cora's head. She'd put a towel over her face to weigh down her eyes and neatly slid a rolled-up washer beneath her jaw to close her mouth. The cold would soon freeze her features in those positions.

"So?" Gerald asked when she saw her.

"He's busy. There's been a death in Male Four as well. They're sending the boys to bring her to the morgue and he'll see her there."

Gerald sighed and clicked her tongue, pushing down on her thigh as she creaked and stumbled to her feet. Bonnie marvelled at how quickly the other nurses had readied Cora for inspection. She supposed it was what they did—day-to-day—this routine. And the House was full, not wanting for hands. "Okay then." Gerald wiped her hands on her dressing gown. "You and Lucy have the day off tomorrow, correct?"

Bonnie nodded. "Yes, we just finished the day shift."

"Good. You two will accompany Cora to the morgue then. The rest of you ladies, off to bed now. The morning waits for no-one."

"B—But—" Lucy whispered, putting her fingers to her lips and chewing on a knuckle. "I've never been to the morgue at night."

Gerald's face was caught between an amused wince and a frustrated sigh. "It's the same as during the day, but darker and colder," she said matter-of-factly. She knew Lucy was afraid of the stories the other nurses told. Particularly the raucous male nurses during meals. "I need to be up in less than five hours and I'm on duty in Ward Five, understaffed." The clock above the stove ticked mockingly, driving the point home. It had just passed midnight. "The boys will be here soon. It won't be long until you can get back to your own beds. I'll see you tomorrow, ladies."

Bonnie nodded again, seeming to have lost her words along with her fatigue. She didn't understand how Gerald or the others could wander off to bed so effortlessly. The emotions may still be kept at bay, perhaps by shock, but the adrenaline kept her alert. Sleep was the furthest thing from her mind.

A drop in blood pressure, Bonnie thought to herself. *From a constriction of the blood vessels in the hands and feet. Vasoconstriction will help keep the blood pumping to my heart and other vital organs in this perceived state of danger. An automatic response from a body that fears death itself.*

It wasn't long before Bonnie and Lucy stood in the kitchen alone, staring down at the slim woman with a towel covering her face. Even though the kitchen light still glowed, the shadows at the edge of the room seemed to press further in than they should. The night, and the cold, rushed in at them.

"I don't want to do this," Lucy breathed beside her, turning her back to the corpse. "I don't want to do this..."

"We'll sleep in," Bonnie reassured, knowing it wasn't a loss of sleep Lucy feared. She didn't want to give voice to what the other woman was afraid of, but Lucy did it for her.

"You've heard the stories, though, right? The most haunted building in Kenmore. Spirits not staying dead. Doctors going mad and spraying the walls with their own blood. I don't want to go!"

Bonnie forced a laugh that sounded more like a bark or a cough than a chuckle. "You know the nurses are just trying to scare you, right?" She forced a smile and put a hand behind Lucy's elbow, guiding her through the foyer towards the front door, away from Cora's body. "There's no such thing as ghosts."

"What about *those whispers?*" Lucy started up again. Now the fatigue hit Bonnie like a wave. She was getting sick of this. "And you know weird sounds always happen in Kenmore. Not just in Buna House, but in Ward Five. And you hear what Lillian always says."

Mind the ghosts.

As Bonnie was about to chastise her fellow trainee, a loud thump sounded on the front door, making her jump. She swallowed her scolding like a whole boiled egg that caught in her throat.

"Someone called for a pick-up?" a gruff voice sounded from outside. Bonnie opened the door, letting a rush of cold night air swarm by her, tickling the loose hair at her ears. A horse whinnied when it saw her, stamping one foot against the ground beyond the door. One wardsman sat up on the cart behind the horse, the other strode past her into the room. It was the same cart that delivered the patients their food each day before taking the laundry away to be washed.

"She's in the kitchen. She's a light, small thing. You and Lucy should be fine." In a huff, Bonnie stepped into the night and up to the wagon.

Not long after Bonnie had hopped up beside the other wardsman, Cora was gently placed in the back, and the four of them—five, including the horse—had made their way out into the night. The creaking weatherboard Buna House groaned in the wind behind them. The men didn't bother to make small talk, simply hunched their shoulders against the cold as they made their way through the darkness of the well-kept grounds.

The morgue itself was small, especially compared to the sprawling grounds of Kenmore. Smaller even than the tiniest of staff cottages, its front taken up almost completely by two white doors. Its roof was almost as tall as the building was wide, giving it a squat persona.

"A'right," the first of the wardsmen grunted as the horse plodded to a stop. "You two ladies go on ahead and turn on the lights, and make sure there's a space free. We'll be right behind you."

Bonnie nodded as she got down. Lucy hugged behind her when they entered the first door of the mortuary and made for the door into the morgue itself. The dark was impenetrable. Whether it was some of Lucy's panic, or just Bonnie's own weariness, the sense of dread fell into the pit of her stomach again. Not wanting to step into the deep darkness, fearing it would somehow take her to another world, Bonnie fumbled her hand around the edge of the door, feeling along the wall for the light switch she knew was there.

Just as her hand touched the small plastic knob, another sensation descended upon her. So soft it was almost a whisper, but so cold her whole arm reverberated in shock. A hand had fallen atop hers. Distinctly human with its long, thin fingers, but too cold for any human being. At least, any living one. Like the flesh was hewn out of ice. Bonnie screamed and tried to snatch her own hand away; the dead hand held tight, yanking her forward. She, with Lucy attached as always, fell through the dark doorway, the light not yet lit. Bonnie held her hand in the other, rubbing at it frantically, desperate to rid herself of the chill that had descended into her flesh. Her eyes strained, muscles pulling in the dark, as they desperately sought to see. Glints of metal shone, but it was the white she noticed first. A sheet, laying on a slate slab, around the distinct form of a human.

Bonnie ceased to breathe. Thoughts of icy fingers long vanished as the white sheet fluttered, tensed, and began to move. The body rose up from its bed.

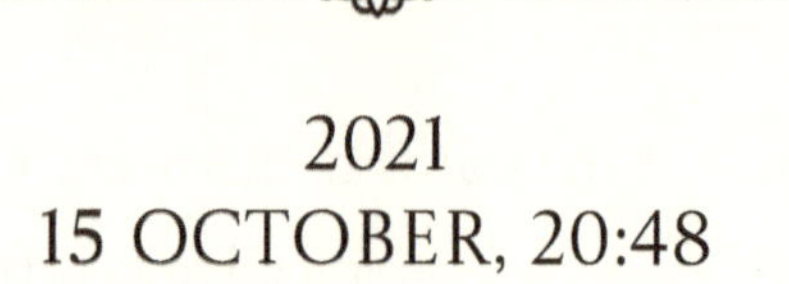

2021
15 OCTOBER, 20:48

AIDEN HAD HEARD many times people describing the dark as a living thing. He'd never quite understood what that meant until now. Holed up on the second floor of Ward Fourteen, in a corner of—what they assumed to be—one of the long-abandoned dormitories. The night seemed to breathe around them. The corner they'd chosen was relatively devoid of broken glass and plaster; across the open, empty expanse, the blue light of the moon cast shadows through the windowpanes.

Beyond the debris, the only other items in the room were old chairs of various colours and shapes. Some made of green vinyl. Others of orange fabric. Most toppled over. There were no beds, no cupboards, not even an old, blackened mattress. Even the curtains in this part of the hospital had been stripped. But not the chairs. They'd been left to clutter and rot.

"I'm fuckin' starving," Devin yawned, kicking his pack away from him with one foot. He'd switched off his GoPro for now and pulled his sleeping bag out from the side of the pack to use as a makeshift pillow. "You cookin' or what?"

Aiden half-sighed and half-yawned, his friend's drowse catching. Of *course* Devin expected him to do the cooking, too. He gently put his camera on the ground and pulled out a small butane stove from his pack. With a bit of boiled water, they'd have bowls of macaroni and cheese to tide them over before getting comfy and settling in for the evening. He silently lit the butane burner, next pulling out a small, old tin kettle, which he filled with water from his drink bottle.

"This place is next level epic," Devin said more conversationally as the flames licked up around the metal, casting a warm orange glow on the floor. It encircled the boys comfortingly, but made the rest of the room jump alive with shadows. Encroaching closer, kept at bay only by the light. "That *room*," Devin whispered, his shoulders shivering slightly. Aiden remembered. He'd probably never forget. The way the grate had slammed. And how the door had stuck… Sure, you could explain it away as an old building warped by the cold. But that grate had *slammed*. And there'd been no wind. And… "My fucking shoulder, man," Devin continued, breaking Aiden from his reverie. "It hurts like a bitch."

"Let me see." Aiden scooted closer, the cold floor attacking his buttocks again as he surrendered the small warm patch he'd made. Devin shrugged, wincing as he did so, letting Aiden pull the corner of his jersey down for a closer look. It was hard to see in the gloom, so Aiden flicked on his head torch again. Devin sucked air through his teeth, hissing slightly, as Aiden's fingers lingered lightly on the back of his shoulder.

It was red. Hot. Slightly swollen. And worst of all, three ragged, angry-looking scratches made their way across the skin. They were fresh. Not quite, but almost, drawing blood. Almost as though the scratches had been made from a hand pushing *beneath* the skin, rather than nails scraping across it. They seemed to bloom deeper and redder as Aiden watched. He picked up his camera, quickly turning it on.

"What is it, man?" Devin winced again. "What'cha doing?"

"Look at this," Aiden breathed through his teeth as the camera started recording. He zoomed in and out until the scratches came perfectly into focus. "You've got scratches on your back, dude.

Three of them. Looks like you've been fucking marked by a demon or something."

As soon as the words left Aiden's mouth, a familiar noise built around them. It shook the walls, plaster raining down on them like snow. The rumble built quickly this time, and Aiden cursed himself as he fumbled to turn off his head torch. The lights rotated from bright to dim and then flickered before finally surrendering.

"That fucking cunt," Devin growled, shrugging his shoulder back under its sleeve. He crouched forward on his hands and knees to look through the windows. Nothing yet, but surely soon enough, the caretaker's ride-on mower with its two pinprick beams of light would amble into view. "She just won't give up!"

They paused, hoping that the rumble would fade. That the ride-on mower would continue making its way past them. Instead, the whole building buzzed as it drew ever closer.

"The fucking burner, you idiot!" Devin hissed, shoving Aiden away. The kettle was just starting to boil, and those red flames—which had been so comforting moments before—now danced around them mockingly. If he thought he'd fumbled with his head torch, this was something else. He almost burnt his fingers as he finally turned the butane gas off, throwing them into complete darkness.

CHAPTER TEN

1953
AUTUMN

As the body beneath the white sheet continued to rise, Lucy let out a scream so piercing it could shatter glass. The sound pulsed through Bonnie's blood, like vibrations rippling through water. It was almost painful as it warbled through her, heightening her own anxiety until she feared her blood would burst out of her pores. Then she felt a shove from behind, from Lucy's tiny, bony fingers, and the scream faded as Lucy bolted from the mortuary. Leaving Bonnie alone. Leaving Bonnie with the slowly rising corpse.

"Hya…hya…" Bonnie gasped, panic seizing her lungs. She raised a hand to her chest, fearing she might have a heart attack herself as her ribs practically beat against her skin. *Damn… sympathetic…nervous system…* The room spun as she turned and fell against the doorway. Desperate to escape, but so terrified she could barely breathe, let alone walk. "Hya…hya…" Her stomach felt as tight as stone, and the contractions in her chest seemed strong enough to burst her heart.

Laughter erupted behind her. Deep, raucous, belly-shaking laughter. She spun, her back falling against the wall, all of her senses immediately signalling to her brain that the danger was not real. The warmth to that laugh. The mirth. The slight cough behind it that came from too much time spent in the chilly air and smoking too many cigarettes. It was all too human.

The panic released its fingers from around her lungs, stomach, and heart as her eyes fell on a young male nurse, pulling the sheet from his face and swinging his legs over the side of the slab. As blood rushed to return to her extremities, nausea bubbled in her throat. She feared to burp in case she puked all over the mortuary floor.

"Oh, you bloody bastard," Bonnie finally sighed breathily in relief, once she was sure she wouldn't vomit. The anger would come later. Right now, she was just glad to be the one back in control of her brain and bodily functions. She breathed out deeply again, letting her head fall to the wall behind her. "Oh, thank Christ."

Another cackle joined the first as a second male nurse stepped forward from behind the door, flicking on the light switch and throwing the room in bright, harsh light. "Your friend ran like the devil himself was after her. Did you see her face, Bubbles?" He wiped away the tears in his eyes as he continued chuckling.

The first man—Bubbles?—responded, "I just saw her bony ass high-tailing it out of here."

"*Bubbles?*" her voice was incredulous.

While Bonnie had never quite warmed to Lucy, she still felt the anger blooming in her stomach as their laughter continued. *Maybe,* she admitted to herself, *she also felt a little cross at Lucy for shoving her towards the apparent danger and running away!*

"James Mason," he said, throwing his sheet back onto the cold slab. "But the boys call me Bubbles. You know, cause I make everyone bubble with laughter?"

Something was bubbling within Bonnie, but it sure wasn't laughter.

"Ooh!" Bonnie grunted fiercely, clenching her hands and stomping her feet. "You childish monsters! You nearly gave *me* a heart attack, too, and then there'd be *two* bodies to deal with!"

"Ah, it's just a bit of fun," the second man said, walking up to squeeze her shoulder in apology. She flinched at the touch of his hands; those bony, frozen fingers.

"What in God's good name—" She pulled back, rubbing at her upper arm to try to return some of the warmth to it.

He wiggled his fingers at her with a devious smile he no doubt thought was charming. Bonnie rolled her eyes and harrumphed again.

"Ice bath," he shrugged, raising his eyebrows suggestively, like he was the cleverest man on God's green earth and his humour a gift to womankind.

"I don't have time for this." Bonnie ran a hand through her loose hair, thinking of how long it would take her to make it right the next day. "And a woman is dead. Come on. At least let's see her tended."

BONNIE PULLED HER cardigan tighter around herself as she stood on the open lawns, feeling every lashing of the wind on this gusty day. A small gathering of nurses stood at the far corner of the large Goulburn General Cemetery, the earth open before them, Cora's simple wooden casket already making its way down into the ground. The grass was well-kept, and its short blades barely stirred in the wind. Only the leaves of the few trees, as well as the coats, dresses, and cardigans of the nurses who had come to say farewell, fluttered in the breeze. Bonnie watched each of them now.

Gerald. Her curled hair so well-coiffed it barely stirred in the flurries. Her lips pursed; the fine creases in her skin looked like whiskers.

Patsy. Her nurse's cap sat straighter than Bonnie had ever seen it before. Her apron perfectly ironed for the first time in weeks. Her face was expressionless, but the glisten in her eyes seemed more than just a side effect from the sting of the wind.

And Nurse Hatchet. The fiercest of them all. Arms held to her side like iron bars. Head tilted slightly as if in regret rather than grief.

Lucy had not just fled the morgue that night, but Kenmore itself. Never to return. She hadn't even come back to say goodbye.

Aside from the local, balding priest—who seemed almost bored as he wound the coffin down—it was just the four of them. And Cora. Who, the doctor confirmed, had indeed suffered a fatal heart attack that night in Buna House. And that was it. No friends. No family. Just the nurses.

"I'm so beautiful," Bonnie whispered to herself, remembering the night she'd seen Cora staring at herself in the mirror.

"What was that?" Gerald whispered, nudging her with her shoulder.

"She's so beautiful," she replied slightly louder. "I heard her saying it to herself once in the mirror."

Gerald chuckled wryly, smiling and lifting one eyebrow as she watched the coffin. Nurse Hatchet's gaze flicked to them, but there was no reprimand. "Ah, yeah, she used to like staring at herself in the mirror."

"And none of her family even bothered to come?"

Gerald shrugged. "It happens more often than we'd like. Honestly, the patients sometimes get moved around so much that the family loses track of where they are. And that seems to be just how they like it. We do try to reach out, but…" She gestured her arms at the grave. "It's sometimes just us at the end. The only ones left who care. It's nothing fancy, but at least we see them off." She paused, and the two continued to watch as Cora disappeared. "Until ten years ago, we'd bury them *at* Kenmore. There was a cemetery on the grounds, you know. Now, we—"

"Mum?!"

The whole procession turned in shock as a distraught voice bellowed behind them. They saw a young man in a dishevelled suit, the hem of his shirt untucked on one side, stumbling through the grounds, blundering over old graves in his haste to reach them. He clasped a bouquet of equally dishevelled white roses in one hand— all were missing multiple petals—and held a cap to his head with another.

"Is—Is that Cora Savvas? Please," the young man motioned at the priest. "Please wait. Don't let her down yet. I—"

Nurse Hatchet was the first to recover, taking a step towards him. "Young man," she said in a firm voice, but still somehow softer than Bonnie had heard before. Like she'd softened the blow of a brick with a pillow. "This is indeed Ms. Cora Savvas. Can I assume, then, that you are her son?"

"I didn't know…" Mr. Savvas trailed off, unable to draw his attention away from the casket. He stepped past Hatchet and fell to his knees after he approached the edge of the open grave. The priest slowly cranked the coffin back up, and the man reached out a shaking hand to place it tenderly atop the wood. "Pa said she was dead. I never knew, all this time, she was so close."

Nurse Hatchet put a hand on the man's shoulder. "Ms. Savvas had been at Kenmore twenty-three years," she said gently. "The last three of which she spent living with the nurses at Buna House. She was one of the quietest, tidiest, humblest patients we've ever had the pleasure of serving."

"I was eight," Mr. Savvas said through a throat thick with despair. His lips gummed together as he fought to speak through his pain. "I was eight when she left with Pa. He said she was sick. I remember being so confused. So upset when he came home without her. I never got over it. I—" He broke down then, the roses falling from his grip as he placed his head in both hands and sobbed uncontrollably. Hoarse, raw bellows tore from him, each gasp ripping out decades of agony and trauma.

One of Bonnie's own hands fluttered to her mouth, and tears unwillingly fell from her eyes. She might not have known Cora for long, but this man's emotion was something she had known all her life. Something they all knew. Perhaps inherently. A deep part of the human psyche that emerged to both assault and comfort us at the hardest times in our lives.

Utter despair.

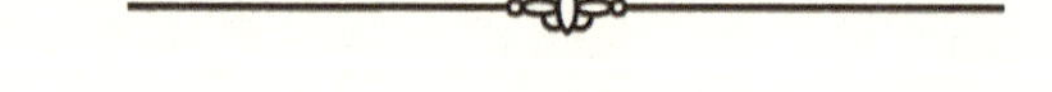

1914
ALICE: DAY 281 IN THE ASYLUM

HARRIET WAS ON her way back to the nurses' residence when she caught sight of something she'd not seen before at Kenmore. At least, not like this. On their own. At night. Not laughing on the sporting grounds, but quietly slinking through the bushes. She was sure of it: that small, timid shadow must have been a child.

She crouched lower as she jogged towards the edge of the garden, cursing lightly to herself as her small heel sank into the mud. Not that Harriet needed to crouch, with her stature probably not much taller than the child's. As she neared the darkened bush, she heard the scrambling of someone desperate to make themselves hidden. *Well,* she thought matter-of-factly to herself. *They've cornered themselves now.*

"You may as well come out," she said firmly. Admittedly, her curiosity was piqued. More than anything, though, she was cranky at being delayed from her supper, shower, and rest. Her scalp ached where a chunk of hair had been ripped out that morning. And she could still smell the bitter, acrid tang of urine on the hem of her apron. "Come on. There's nowhere else to go now. And if I have to come in that bush after you, then I've no mind to be gentle, you understand?"

There was a sniff and then the leaves shook, small twigs snapping, as a tiny runt of a boy stepped forward. His dark blazer was torn and muddied by his escapades across the garden. His matching shorts weren't in much better condition, his socks were almost black with filth, and he'd evidently lost his tie somewhere along the way. He kept his head down as he stepped forward, fumbling with his fingers.

Harriet sighed, putting her hands on her hips. She recognised the uniform as being from the small boys' orphanage that recently opened next door. St John's Boys Orphanage, run by the Sisters of Mercy. The building had barely been blessed, yet already the little scamps were out and causing trouble. "Well, what am I going to do with you? The hospital is *no place* for little rascals."

"I want me mam," the boy whispered defiantly, still not daring to make eye contact.

"Who? Speak up."

"Me mum," he said more clearly, finally looking up and glaring at her with piercing grey eyes. A lump grew and caught in Harriet's throat. She *knew* those eyes. Knew their fierceness and intelligence. How they stared straight into you, through you, understanding through sight alone much more than any human should. She suddenly realised the boy was younger than he appeared to be. He may have been skinny, but he was tall. He wouldn't even be in double digits yet. "I want me mum!"

"Who is your mother?" Harriet whispered slowly, letting her hands fall away from her hips, knowing the answer before he could speak it.

"Alice."

"Oh, not again!"

Harriet swivelled at the sound of the matron's voice behind her, and the young boy turned pale and skittish, looking about him for any avenue of escape. He darted forward but was too slow, and the matron held firm to his upper arm with her own viper-like hand.

"Come *here*, Roy."

"No! *No!*" Roy wailed, beating at the matron with his fist. She slapped him across the face, hard. The crack resounded through the garden like a whip, stunning him into silent tears.

"*Again*, ma'am?" Harriet couldn't help but ask, suddenly aware of the stains across her apron from the day's work and the pungency of her own smell. This was no condition in which to greet the iron-willed matron. Formerly a Catholic nun, the matron was the harshest woman she'd ever met.

The matron's left side of her lip twitched as it pulled up into a snarl. "*This* one has stolen into the grounds three times now, looking for his mother."

"Alice?"

"Hmgh. He claims he can *hear* her screaming from the orphanage." The matron bent down to look in the boy's frightened eyes, her snarl now a horrid smile. "That's not your mum, Roy. Where we have your mum, no-one can hear her scream."

⁂

ALICE ROCKED BACK and forth in her chair. A moan escaped her mouth before she could catch it. Her lower back was in such agony she could barely stand it. Each muscle seemed to have twisted in on itself, hardening like stone. Or perhaps freezing like ice. The room was cold enough for it, though the clothing her attendants wore hinted it was warm outside. Her slight movements caused flares of pain to shoot into her bones and down her legs. But it was *something*. A sensation, at least.

How long has it been since I've been touched? she thought. It had been so long since her mind had felt this clear, and it pleased her. *Not hosed down, or viciously rubbed, but touched? Seen?* A tear slipped from her eye. *How long has it been since I held him?* She'd tried so hard to get back to him. To get back to her boy. But the more avid her attempts, the worse her punishment. Now she'd been tied to this chair so long, she started to forget what the world looked like beyond the door. What a bed felt like. Or even how it felt to stand up. *Will I ever stand again? Will I ever see him again?*

"Roy!"

CHAPTER ELEVEN

1953
WINTER

Winter had well-and-truly taken hold. Each morning, the nurses, trainees, and patients woke to fields of white frost and oceans of mist. It had been a month since Cora passed away, and Bonnie had attended another three funerals since. Each of which had been witnessed only by the staff. Their families seemingly not only put them out of sight and mind but also out of existence. Today, while the air still had a bite and a crackle of frost covered grass underfoot, the sun shone brightly. Any mist was erased by mid-morning, and the nurses allowed the patients into the courtyard for their morning recreation time. It had been too long since any of them had breathed fresh air, so the opportunity could not be missed.

Bonnie watched Ethel wander the yard with a fascinated smile on her face and an ethereal turn of her head. She muttered under her breath continually, and when Bonnie strayed close, she heard the woman say, "The bees have sent their men to die." Bonnie wasn't sure whether it was the words, or her cheerful tone, that disturbed her more.

Maggie was out and about as well. In fact, she hadn't needed to be confined for weeks. Her angry outbursts had become fewer and fewer. She was, in fact, one of the first patients to be tested with a new medication: Largactil. Or, more specifically, chlorpromazine.

The transformation had been unbelievable. Maggie had begun life in the asylum as a woman who was constantly afraid, angry, and on edge. Who would explode into fits of rage or depression at the slightest provocation. Miraculously, while on the medication, she'd calmed down, become rational, even apologised for earlier fits of mania. She spoke more often, holding full conversations with other patients and staff. Today, she sat in the sunshine, warmly wrapped in her cardigan, with a look of utter serenity on her face. She'd even physically changed, her appearance more of a kindly, chubby grandma than a demon-fuelled monster.

It'll be a revolution, Bonnie thought, marvelling at the drug's effect.

The other patients were calm—at least comparatively—and jovial as well. Plenty of noise still echoed around the walls of the yard. Laughter, mostly. There was also the odd shout and plenty of muttering and grunting. Bonnie could now distinguish between cries of agitation and those of contentment. A sixth sense, she'd heard some of the other nurses call it. Some of the women simply needed to make noise. Constantly. In fact, Bonnie paid more and more attention to the patients' sounds than to anything else. Any slight variation could herald the start of something, either good or bad. Today, the laughter touted good things, she thought. And at least Maggie, and others on the same chemical trial as her, no longer screamed.

Lost in her musings, Bonnie was startled by a sharp spray of something wet on the back of her head. She jumped, instinctively raising her fingers to the wet liquid that ran from her hair down the nape of her neck. As she spun to see where it had come from, thoughts of spittle in her mind, another spray hit her in the chest just above the collar of her cardigan, soaking through the thick cotton fabric of her dress. No-one stood behind her. In fact, there was no-one close to her at all. Her eyes flicked over the windows and walkway surrounding the courtyard, catching only glimpses of shadows. "What in the—"

A short, surprised yell to her right was also out of place. Bonnie knew, as she turned, this wasn't a patient. Gerald wiped at her own neck, frowning at the walkway. "I see you, young James!" she said fiercely, striding towards the shadows on the walkway. Confused, Bonnie followed her. Giggles sounded then, but again, not the sounds of madness. These were deep, masculine chuckles.

Bonnie joined Gerald as she approached the walkway. The shadows gave way, revealing two male nurses aiming syringes through the windows. Bonnie gasped in indignation as one of them—the one she recognised—aimed at her and sprayed her again, right on the bosom. *Bubbles.*

"You stop that right now, James Mason. I know your mother, and I will not hesitate to phone her and let her know what a little shit her son is turning into. It's too bloody cold for this nonsense!"

The two men fell over themselves laughing at this, slapping each other on the shoulder. Gerald was probably old enough to be the boys' mother herself. If this was any sign, Master James Mason wouldn't care a wink what his own mother thought.

"Hey, watch this," Bubbles's mate said, completely ignoring Gerald and her threats. He pulled his face closer to the window and began to whistle. At first it was just a single note. It took Bonnie a moment to realise why it upset her so. It wasn't the note itself, but the effect it had on the other sounds around her. Everything became silent. In a place where sound was the only constant, the quiet felt suffocating. Then the man changed tune, whistling the opening instrumental and words to Frank Sinatra's, *I'm Walking Behind You.*

Sinatra's velvet voice played in her mind as the tune rang out: *Look over your shoulder, I'm walking behind...*

As the cinematic, soothing tones recited in Bonnie's head, bedlam broke out in the yard around her. First, one patient screamed—a high-pitched warble of terror. The patient—Janet—shook her hands by her face in utter distress. Then the pitch of all the others changed. Happy grunts turned into snorts of upset. The mumbles turned to warbled moans. The giggles to manic, air expelling "ha" noises. And then the silent ones began rocking as the screams intensified like an orchestra of Hell.

"Fuck you, Howard!" Gerald shouted as the two women split from the window, each running to the closest patient to attempt to calm them down.

Bonnie's closest was Ethel, who spun around in fear, her mutters growing in intensity. "Send the boys out to die!" she repeated over and over.

Bonnie rubbed her arm, forcing a smile. "There now, it's okay. It's just a little tune." She glanced up and was pleased to see that the other senior nurse on duty had already reached Janet. A normally quiet patient, Janet rarely caused trouble. At least, not since Bonnie had started in Ward Five. Janet was completely inconsolable now, beginning to lash out physically. She'd probably need the camisole.

A loud thump made Bonnie jump, every nerve responding to the madness ensuing around her. Nurse Hatchet had arrived at some point and strode straight to the window, where the two men cackled. She'd slapped her hand against the glass, instantly quietening them and some of the meeker patients.

"Howard White. James Mason," she enunciated venomously above the storm. "You blunderbusses. You afternoon farmers! You chuckle-headed fop-doodles!" The string of insults continued, with the men's faces growing increasingly pale after each one. This small, slightly humped, swollen-knuckled woman would hardly reach up to their chests. Yet, unlike Gerald, she utterly commanded and cowed them.

"I'm sorry, ma'am," Bubbles stuttered weakly. His friend—whether brave or stupid—still smiled broadly.

"'Twas just a harmless whistle," Howard muttered. "Just a little Frankie. I didn't know it'd cause a raucous."

"Even you're not that stupid," Hatchet spat. Bonnie focussed on getting Ethel seated on a nearby chair, but didn't spare any unnecessary concentration, utterly transfixed by the Charge Nurse's show. "You know never to whistle in an asylum. Next, you'll be off whistling in the graveyard! If I *ever* catch you doing anything so deliberately stupid again, I will *wallop* you into next Tuesday." Bubbles meekly nodded his head and jabbed his friend in the stomach with an elbow. "What are you two lolly-gaggers even doing here?"

"We just picked up the laundry, ma'am," Howard said, finally subdued.

"*Well*, there's no laundry here. Unless you want to start cleaning up the mess you've made." Hatchet gestured behind her, turning to observe the senior nurse struggling to calm Janet. "You see what you've done to that poor woman." Hatchet's voice had turned to ice. "She'll need intervention now. You two make yourself useful and go to the storehouse *pronto*. Bring us back half a dozen fallopian tubes." Bonnie's eyes widened, and she had to pinch her lips to stop from snorting in mirth. "I don't want to see you again until you have them, hear me? You'd better bring them as fast as you can. And if you don't, I'd better *never* see your faces again."

The two boys paused only a moment, confused, but then Hatchet slammed her palm against the glass again and they were off. Hatchet strode straight to Janet then, assisting in getting the woman inside. Gerald and Bonnie exchanged glances over the tops of their patients' heads, both sporting matching impressed grins. *Perhaps Nurse Hatchet wasn't so bad after all.*

2021
15 OCTOBER, 21:00

THE ROAR OF the ride-on mower continued to build as the two boys sat in terror, encircled by almost-complete darkness within Ward Fourteen. The blue moonlight, in the absence of any man-made light, rendered the shadows around them even darker. Aiden longed to reach out and grab Devin's arm. Just to *feel* that he wasn't alone in this trembling, empty ward. But he wasn't scared enough to risk being called chicken yet—even with the caretaker descending on them.

Aiden focused on the pain in his fingertips instead, from touching the hot flame of the butane burner in his haste to turn it off. At first, he thought he'd got away relatively unscathed, but he'd apparently burned himself worse than he realised. Because now, his fingers throbbed and screamed at him. He put them in his mouth, almost feeling them palpitate. The heat from his fingers even made the roof of his mouth feel warmer.

Finally, the rumbling continued past them. The caretaker was still close, but at least she hadn't stopped exactly where they hid. Devin turned to look at Aiden, the moon's glow highlighting the fingers held in his mouth. "What ya sucking ya fingers for, you baby!" His whisper grated harshly.

Aiden yanked them out of his mouth with a pop, the cold air instantly reigniting the feeling of fire. "I burnt my fuckin' fingers," he hissed back.

"We'd better pack our shit. Just in case the cunt comes back."

Aiden nodded, even though Devin probably couldn't see him in the darkness. He fumbled blindly for the butane burner, running his good hand across the dust and dirt of the floor. In an instant, something ice cold and wet stroked the back of his hand. It felt almost as though he'd been licked by tiny finger-length tongues. He snapped his hand back, panting, desperate to reach for the headlamp he wore and illuminate whatever had touched him. His fear of alerting the caretaker stopped him only just in time.

"What is it, dipshit? Keep it down!" Devin shoved Aiden roughly in the shoulder before turning back to his own scrabbling as he pulled his pack back together.

"S—s—something touched my hand." Aiden's voice trembled and he wasn't sure if he wanted to burst into tears, scream, or be sick all over the floor. Possibly a combination of the three.

Devin tensed beside him, and Aiden could *feel,* if not see, his friend draw closer and gaze into the darkness in front of them. There was barely enough light to see more than the mounds of chairs. Still, whether from false bravado or some sixth sense, Devin grunted, "There's nothing there. It's probably just debris or something."

Aiden wanted to believe him. Wanted to forget the lingering sensation that he felt more intensely than the burn on his fingers, which he'd momentarily forgotten about. "Who used to stay in this ward?" he whispered, too scared to reach out his hands into the darkness again.

"Huh?" Devin asked, before the question could register properly in his brain. "Oh, uh…the quiet ones, I think. 'Quiet and industrious'." The thought calmed Aiden, but he still flinched when Devin shoved the butane burner at him. "Come on. We might have to make a run for it."

As Devin said this, the sound of the ride-on mower cut off. It was still close; too close. Aiden felt his heart thumping so hard in his chest he could almost hear the echoes of its beats between his ears. He heard Devin scramble to his feet, so he quickly followed, pulling his pack onto his shoulders. Just like the icy hand had distracted him from his burn, the caretaker distracted him from the touch of the ghostly appendage. Together, the boys walked as quietly as they could to the windows. The silence amplified every grate of plaster and crunch of glass beneath their feet.

At first, peering through the window, they could see nothing but the dark buildings looming from the night. But then, the beam of a torch fell across the windows, shining right into their stunned faces.

WHAT IS MADNESS, really? Over the years, I suppose I've heard it all. Some fear it. Fear the insanity. Loathe the abnormality. Is that what madness is? Simply differences? A different way of seeing. A different way of feeling. A different way of being.

Some laude it. You cannot have genius without a bit of insanity, they say. The greatest creativity is found in the minds of the mad. Don't lose your little spark of madness. Is madness what makes us brilliant then? A way of seeing. A way of feeling. A way of being.

I see them all come and go. The mad. The insane. The abnormal. The brilliant. The ones who heal and fly. The ones who descend further into the dark. Which will these two be, I wonder? Do they know that I'm watching them? At least on some level. Assessing them. Measuring their anxiety. Monitoring their impulses. Testing their moods.

Listening for the sounds of lunacy.

CHAPTER TWELVE

1953
WINTER

"Careful now." Gerald smiled as she held a white plastic bottle stock-still. Bonnie grinned as she gently pulled back the plunger of the syringe in her hands, filling it with bright blue cleaning fluid. Gerald and Bonnie had come up with an idea when walking back to Buna House after their shift. A way to not only get back at the boys for their horrid prank, but also to one-up them. Nurse Hatchet had inspired their bravado, if not the method.

Bonnie giggled in a manner quite uncharacteristic for her as she pulled the final syringe clear and Gerald screwed the cap back on the bottle. "And after yesterday, you're sure they'll be back?"

Gerald laughed her familiar full-throated, mono-syllabic hoot. "Of *course* they will! Those boys are stubborn, stupid, and have an ego as big as the piles of laundry they cart out of here each day." Bonnie was pleased she'd been rostered on with Gerald the past two days. Tomorrow was her rest day, but Gerald would continue on at Ward Five one more day.

"Okay, chop-chop!" The senior nurse on duty clapped her hands together, throwing a wry look at the two women as they slipped their loaded syringes into the pockets of their aprons. "Let's make hay while the sun shines. Who knows when we'll next be able to get the patients outdoors."

Bonnie and the other trainee followed the lead of the nurses, corralling the patients of Ward Five out into the corridor for another day of splendid sunshine. If any of them remembered the whistle-induced trauma of the previous day, they didn't show it. And poor Janet—the starkest reminder of all—was still recovering in her private room. She no longer needed the camisole, but was still confined to solitary for now.

Just as Gerald had predicted, it didn't take long for Bubbles and Howard to pop up by the walkway. Bonnie felt a butterfly of excitement flap its wings in the pit of her stomach, the instantaneousness of it giving her momentary nausea. *Sympathetic nervous system up to its same old tricks again.* Tricks that worked like a charm.

In a few short strides, Bonnie stood at Gerald's side. The gastrointestinal insect returned as she and Gerald carefully drew the syringes from their apron pockets in near perfect choreography. Despite the electric tingle in the tips of her fingers, she kept a steady and sure grip on the syringe. The rising elation in her filled her up completely. *God damnit, I'm happy,* Bonnie thought to herself, not even internally flinching at the curse. And not at all surprised by the thought.

She let loose.

The cleaning fluid arced like a beautiful spray from a water fountain, through the open window frame and landing smack in the middle of Bubbles's bright white chest. Satisfaction breezed through her, beneath every inch of her skin, in warm comfort at returning the favour for yesterday's bosom attack—and for the first prank he'd ever pulled on her in the morgue. The look of shock on his face was too much, and a delighted laugh burst from her. Bubbles's indignant squawk just added fuel to the fire, and she had to grab her abdomen as she bent double in delicious, joyful pain.

Bonnie heard one of the closest patients join her laughing. They obviously didn't know why they were laughing, exhibiting the same tentative pauses as a child who couldn't comprehend a joke might. But their gusto was not pretend. It caught the attention of others, and their grunts echoed like war cries in Bonnie's ears as she fired her second syringe, hitting the second wardsman right in the hip. Retribution would be theirs. Vindication and—

"What in God's name is going on?!" Nurse Hatchet's booming voice cut through the mirth like a knife, through the sudden stillness and chill in the air. Bonnie clumsily dropped the two empty syringes into her pocket and instantly felt like a naughty child for trying to hide the evidence so ineptly. The male nurses bent their heads low and continued walking along the path until they were out of sight, hands patting at their blue-dyed uniforms. A patient guffawed tremendously at that moment, clapping her hands together and dribbling through the gap of her two missing front teeth.

"*Obviously*," Hatchet continued. "There are some trainees *and* staff who have too much spare time on their hands. Since you've time for games," she paused dramatically, "I'd say you have time to clean the ceilings in the rec room. *Today*."

Bonnie winced. She swore she heard Gerald's teeth grinding. So much for their heroics inspired by Hatchet. So much for her being on their side, after all.

Bonnie spent her remaining time in the yard in petulant silence. She smiled at Ethel when she passed. She dabbed at the drool running down Maggie's chin. She helped one particularly enthusiastic patient put her cardigan back on at least three times after throwing it to the ground. All tasks performed dutifully, but with a dark cloud hanging over her head. Perhaps it hurt worse because she'd gone from such contentment to such dark depths so quickly. From feeling the hero to feeling the fool. From feeling at home to feeling adrift. From feeling assured to feeling unreliable.

Less than an hour later, they were back in Female Five, the patients secured in their rooms. Bonnie stood side by side with Gerald, staring up at the impossibly high ceilings of the rec room. They were so tall, she couldn't even begin to see how the momentous task might be fulfilled. It was hard to even gauge how much dust there was to clean. Only the corpses of long-dead spiderwebs trailing in the corners were visible, giving any indication of the scale of their punishment.

"I don't think we even have a ladder," Gerald grunted, rubbing at her strong jawline with a callused hand. "I'll go get the duster," she muttered under her breath as she stomped loudly from the room, dragging the soles of her shoes. Bonnie barely glanced at her as she departed before returning her attention back to the room, scanning its contents for any way she might be able to reach the ceiling. There were plenty of chairs and tables, so with a deep sigh, she went about stacking a makeshift ladder herself.

By the time Gerald returned, feather duster in hand, Bonnie had placed a chair on one table and another on the floor beside it as a quasi-step stool.

"Give me a hand?" Bonnie grimaced. Gerald rolled her eyes and crossed her arms over her chest, the duster hanging by her hip. "Come on, how else are we supposed to reach?"

Gerald scoffed but acceded, letting Bonnie balance by resting her weight on Gerald's shoulder as she climbed the precariously placed furniture.

"Gonna break your neck for a bunch of cobwebs, and then I'll have to fill in all that fucking paperwork…"

Bonnie smiled to herself as she caught Gerald's muttered words. Atop the table now, she lifted a skirted knee and placed one heeled foot against the second chair. It grated noisily as it slipped slightly beneath her shoe. She gritted her teeth and leapt atop it, wobbling slightly, before righting herself and throwing both arms wide. "Hm?" Bonnie grunted happily, pleased with herself. Gerald just shook her head as she lifted the duster up to her.

As Bonnie reached up to the ceiling, feeling her torso elongate, her stomach started thumping. Almost as though her heart had truly sunk into the pit of her stomach. She was so determinedly focussed on her balance as she stretched out that her vision turned white at its edges. She ignored it, just as she ignored the dizzying sensation of being so riskily balanced.

"What in God's name…?"

Bonnie startled, shaking and waving her hands to regain her balance. The chair's legs grated dangerously across the table. She looked down at Nurse Hatchet's startled face, the duster's handle slick with sweat in her palm.

"For heaven's sake, you utter idiot. Get down!" Hatchet stamped her foot as she spoke, waving her fingers flightily at Bonnie. "*Get down!*"

Bonnie flapped her arms again as she squatted, almost falling. Gerald reached up quickly to take the duster. With a couple of quick steps and hops, Bonnie had her feet planted firmly back on the floor.

"In all my years!" Hatchet said.

Bonnie's vision was no longer white tinged, but red. *The nerve of that woman*, her inner voice spat. *How else was I supposed to clean the blasted ceilings? I just cannot win!*

1914
ALICE: DAY 478 IN THE ASYLUM

HARRIET COULDN'T HELP but look over her shoulder at the solitary door every few moments. The patients had been taken away to be bathed, and Harriet quickly stripped the beds of linen while she had the chance. Some of the other nurses made their way through the rooms on the first and ground floors, doing the same. Harriet heard them moving around below her, if not by their clicking footfalls, then by the slam of each door as they hurried to the next room. She could almost picture their route in her mind.

The ground and first floors might be more work for the nurses, being a larger space to traverse, hauling the heavy bundles of linen behind them. But the attic-level was still the worst pick of the three. It may have been less physically toiling; the beds were grouped together in an open ward, rather than segregated. The space wasn't so vast. Harriet could roll the linen down the stairs, rather than lug it through the hallways. No, it wasn't the physical stress of the attic-level that threw people off.

It was *her*. Alice.

It took a lot to unnerve the hardened psych nurses of Kenmore. Screaming, biting, scratching—these were all par for the course. Daily, if not hourly, occurrences. It was the constant "tap, tap, tap, tap" coming from Alice's room that sent shivers down their spines. The sound of that single loose, wooden leg rocking back and forth onto the hard wooden floors. They'd asked the wardsmen to tighten the bracket holding that leg to the floor, when Alice was finally released. But now it had been ten months straight of Alice sitting in that chair, and there was no sign of the Superintendent relieving her of her punishment any time soon.

Tap, tap, tap.

As rhythmic as a ticking clock. Military precision. Unnaturally so.

The thought of Alice sitting there, in her own filth, boils popping beneath the weight of her thin body, disgusted Harriet. It disgusted them all. But what else were they to do? She was too violent to set free. Even when in the camisole, she required near-constant supervision. Releasing her wasn't possible with the current staffing shortages. And even if those two things had been no obstacle, the Medical Superintendent was not convinced of Alice's remorse. Not convinced she'd do better this time. Not convinced she "deserved" to be set free. *What choice did they have?* In a place this crowded, with resources stretched thin daily, they were lucky if they could keep a roof over their heads and food in their bellies.

Tap, tap, tap, tap, went Alice's wooden chair.

Every now and then, the tapping silenced. This would almost be worse. A more unnatural void than the precision tapping. Harriet felt herself holding her breath, wondering if it had finally ended. If the monotonous rhythm had wound its course. If Alice had finally tired. Or, perhaps, finally died. She wouldn't eat enough. Wouldn't drink enough. And hosing her down was hardly any way to keep her clean and hygienic. Harriet held her breath until her lungs burst, not daring to release a sound, head cocked to the side.

The sound always began again.

Tap, tap, tap.

Tap, tap, tap.

2021
15 OCTOBER, 21:12

AIDEN PANTED AS he fled behind Devin, keeping his mate's bobbing backpack in close view. Plumes of dust puffed up around them as they ran through the long-abandoned halls. The first to disturb the quiet in years.

The caretaker had almost caught them. She'd actually entered the building. They'd been too cocky. Thinking she'd be too afraid to chase them into the ward. Aiden mentally kicked himself for thinking that the burner, which had allowed them to cook their now abandoned meals, would go unnoticed. He wondered for a fleeting moment if the food he'd left open on the floor would eventually rot. And even more fleetingly, how long uncooked instant macaroni cheese took to decay. Perhaps it would outlast the building itself.

The echo of their footfalls finally faded as they got to a concrete staircase. Aiden was relieved to finally be past the squealing hardwood. He chased Devin down the sharp descent so fast that he feared he'd lose balance and topple down the stairs.

He jumped the last five steps almost too aggressively, painful zaps shooting up his legs from the soles of his feet. But he couldn't—wouldn't—slow down. On the ground floor, the two of them ran full pelt towards an emergency exit door, breathing a sigh of relief as it gave way and they burst out onto the grounds. The open sky yawned above them. The sight was so contrary to the narrow, darkened corridors, that it made Aiden's stomach tighten queasily. Every star twinkled as if in celebration of their escape.

Aiden paused, gasping, hands atop his knees. He peered behind him at the recently vacated ward, his adrenaline-primed eyes taking in every detail of the darkened windows looming over them. Every strip of peeling paint. Every broken shard. Every splintered piece of wood. He imagined he could still hear the caretaker in there, stomping through the abandoned hallways, ears pricked and eyes wide for any sign of intruders.

Devin didn't stop, however. He sped across the grass, not even turning to look over his shoulder to make sure Aiden followed. Aiden sighed again as he took after his friend before he became lost in the gloom. A muscle cramp below his right rib cage protested at the sudden resumption of physical exertion. *That was too close*, Aiden repeated over-and-over in his head with each footfall. *That was too fucking close.*

CHAPTER THIRTEEN

1953
WINTER

"SHE'S PUNISHING ME," Bonnie grumbled into her mug of lukewarm coffee. Lillian had burnt the pot—unbelievably, as she was normally the coffee queen—and it tasted even more acrid and bitter now that it had chilled. She could almost feel fur sprouting on her tongue after each sip.

Patsy pinched Bonnie's shoulder firmly, but affectionately, as she stood. She then patted down her pockets in search of matches, a cigarette hanging from her mouth. "If she's punishing you, then she's punishing herself, too," Patsy mumbled around the end of the fag. "Your shift isn't the only one to have changed."

"Great," Bonnie groaned, letting her forehead flop onto the table and putting both hands on top of her head. "Not only am I moved to night shift for the next month, but I get to do it with *her*."

"Perk up, love." Patsy finally had her cigarette lit. She puffed with what looked like relief as she sat and stretched back in her chair. The nurse paused, letting the swirl of white mist curl around her. The smell instantly struck up a craving within Bonnie and she lifted her head. "You'll get a solid ten days off after, *and* I think it's a sign you're doing something right. There's not as many nurses on duty at night. This means Hatchet at least trusts you enough to leave you to your own devices."

Bonnie hadn't thought of that. She felt some deeply buried nugget try to push its way to the surface. *Pride?* That emotion didn't last long here, although it did feel satisfying to briefly relive the sensation that had driven her so far in life. *Maybe I am doing something right…*

"Mind them ghosts, though."

Bonnie twisted her head to watch Lillian re-enter the room, a cigarette dangling from her own mouth. The weatherboard floors had been lacquered with kerosine again recently and it probably wouldn't take much for Lillian's cigarette to light the place up. It was a miracle it hadn't happened already. Bonnie watched as the fag swayed dangerously back and forth. She waited for Patsy to chastise Lillian, but the other nurse simply inhaled deeply on her own cigarette.

"What, no comeback? No 'there's no such thing as ghosts'," Bonnie teased, finally sitting upright and patting down her pockets for her box of Craven As. One cloud of passive smoke had been hard enough to resist. Now that the sweet burning mist encircled her, she had no choice but to give in to the lure. Maybe it would even help warm her up.

"That's not me," Patsy spoke around the cigarette, both hands resting on her stomach, her eyes loosely closed. "That's Gerald who's always shutting down talk of spirits."

"Yessum." The chair beside Bonnie squeaked as Lillian eased her small frame into it. "Patsy's had enough experiences to know better than to pretend these walls don't hold more than screams and secrets." The beauty, depth, and darkness of Lillian's observation startled Bonnie. No matter what she saw or heard here, there were still surprises around each corner.

"Ha! Even Gerald will tell you she doesn't believe in ghosts, but with the same breath add "that one time though'…" Patsy finally opened her eyes and leant forward, giving Bonnie a long, fierce stare.

"What?" Bonnie tried to shake it off with a timid laugh, drawing deeply on her ciggie as a distraction for her hands and mouth. "You're saying it's real, then?" She thought of Lucy and the whispers beneath her window. She thought of Cora—God rest her soul—looking into the mirror in the dark and whispering. And she thought of the creaks and groans of Buna House. Nothing at Kenmore was ever fully silent. "But what? What happens?"

"Footsteps mostly," Patsy whispered, stubbing out her cigarette, repeating what others had told her already. "When I *know* there are no patients up and about. You just—you get used to *human* sounds. Whatever these footfalls are, they're not human anymore."

"And tappin'," Lillian added, reaching for the burnt pot of coffee to pour herself a fresh cup. "Some say the tappin' is from *inside* the walls. Others say it's comin' from *her* room."

"Her?"

"Alice," Lillian and Patsy said in near unison.

Of course. It's always Alice.

Patsy nodded at Lillian to continue, closing her eyes and leaning her head back again.

"Let's just say a lotta strange things happen in Ward Five at night."

THE NEXT TWO days, Patsy and Gerald tormented Bonnie with jibes that she was Hatchet's new favourite. That the decision to put her on night shift, with herself, wasn't punishment at all. It did more to solidify the feeling of penalty in Bonnie than anything else. Tonight—her teeth chattering from the cold, her fingertips numb, and her nose and ears well past freezing to practically burning—

was her first shift. She'd worked it up so much in her mind she felt physically ill. A headache pounded in her right temple and cheekbone. Her teeth on that side ached, too; no doubt from the good grinding she'd given them while lying in her bed the night before.

Bonnie shivered violently as she pulled Ward Five's door closed behind her. Her breath expelled from her lungs in a guttural burst. She stamped her feet, pushing her icy fingers into her armpits to warm them. It was barely any warmer inside than out. It was barely any lighter, for that matter. So deep into winter, the sun had set nearly a full hour ago, and the patients were already tucked into their beds before 6:00 p.m.. Bonnie had been on the *other* side of this routine the past several months. At the end of the day, the day staff would have fed and changed the patients, put their clothing into bundles for the next day, tucked the patients in, and then stood outside their doors in neat and immaculate uniforms. Waiting for the Charge Nurses or one of the Superintendents to inspect the Ward for perfection.

Up until now, Bonnie had been one of the women frantically tugging at her soiled apron, ensuring her cuffs were in place, and only the requisite two inches of hair showed under her cap. She'd been the one forcing the patients into their beds, sometimes while they screamed, before rushing to stand outside their doors, pretending all was well for the routine inspection. Tonight, Bonnie would trail behind Charge Nurse Hatchet and the Superintendent as they made their rounds. Watching her colleagues have strips torn off them for a wrinkle or a loose lock of hair. And then she would be left there, alone, until it was time for the next circuit of rounds.

"Come along then, trainee!"

Bonnie flinched at the sound of Hatchet's voice calling from beyond the entryway. The Charge Nurse had obviously heard her enter. The disembodied, all-knowing voice beckoned her to the next chapter in her Kenmore life. A darker, quieter, colder chapter.

"I haven't got all day!" A pause, and then Hatchet repeated as though she'd not spoken earlier, "I haven't got all night!"

It was only Charge Nurse Hatchet and one of the other senior nurses leading the handover that night. The Superintendents had evidently been called away to other tasks. Bonnie trailed ten steps behind them, as far behind as she dared. Lights shone at odd intervals, but everything had been dimmed. The hallways seemed larger in the darkness; their corners hidden, and so seemingly expanded, in the night. The path had faded to grey, its edges blurring to black. The extra chill in the air didn't help Bonnie's anxiety. She perceived that she had entered another world; a whole new dimension within the asylum. She'd been there at this time of day before, of course. But that was the end of her shift. She had been leaving. Now, it was only the beginning, and she couldn't help but notice all the details that had escaped her tired gaze.

Patsy stood before the next door, her hands twisting gently into her apron. At the sight of Bonnie, the corners of her lips tilted up in just the hint of a smile. It was enough encouragement for Bonnie, who continued forward, closing the gap between herself and the Charge Nurses. A large bang sounded from the room behind Patsy and her fingers tightened in her skirts. She grimaced, looking up at Hatchet. Not so much at her, but through her.

"Your charge doesn't seem to be in bed," Hatchet said matter-of-factly, her head tilted to the side. "Unless she's having a particularly vicious nightmare."

Bonnie recognised this as Janet's room. They'd been in and out of there often over the past several days, still trying and failing to calm her down after the whistling incident. Janet screamed, slamming her hand against the wooden door.

"Trainee," Hatchet said firmly, gesturing her head towards the door, shaking her own key loop to indicate what she wished Bonnie to do.

"Ma'am…" Patsy started, cut off by Hatchet's steely glare. "I—I wouldn't…"

"*Trainee.*"

Bonnie moved forward, key in hand, and entered it into the lock. The noises behind the door quieted immediately. She tilted her head forward slightly, concentrating, focusing on any noise that might give warning as to what she might find. There was *perhaps* the quietest of scrapings. She paused before twisting the handle, her forehead now so close to the wood she almost leaned on it. Hatchet cleared her throat loudly and Bonnie thrust open the door. It was pitch black inside, and it took a moment for her eyes to adjust. Just as the grey shapes of furniture began to loom within the dark, something else streaked across the room. Too small to be a person, and far too fast.

She wanted to scream, but sensing the object that torpedoed towards her, she pinched her lips closed instead, then drew in a sharp breath through her nose that whistled as it flooded into her. A cold and hard sensation struck her, immediately forcing out her held breath. The shock of the impact reverberated through her chest. She had no time to focus on the brief pain before the warm, wet, and slippery contents of the hurled chamber pot exploded across her chest, up her neck, and over the bottom half of her face.

The hot, acrid smell weaved its way inside her nostrils, forcing another burst of air from her mouth. She gagged, throat muscles squeezed tight. Janet burst into laughter before taking up her screaming again. Bonnie tried not to think about the trickle of thick faecal matter snaking down her neck and beneath her dress. She dry heaved again, this time managing to keep her mouth closed and her retching noises to a soft whimper.

"You infernal, wretched, foolish, useless girl!" Hatchet's insults stank almost as bad as Bonnie now did. "Ugh!" Bonnie's eyes stung and watered, and she couldn't tell if it was from the stench, the anger, or the hurt.

I was right, she thought forlornly, hands twitching at her sides, desperate to swat away the larger clumps of shit on her chest but equally repulsed at the thought of soiling her fingers. *I was right. This is a punishment. She doesn't think I have what it takes. She just wanted to move shifts to keep an eye on me!*

"The two of you clean this mess up. *Now*. Then, Patsy, you get your charge *into* bed like you were supposed to. And trainee, you get yourself cleaned up and back here as fast as you can. If you're not back by the time I finish my rounds, God help you…" Hatchet left the threat unfinished as she turned and continued down the passage. Bonnie hated that she was impressed by how the two oldest nurses had avoided the spray. A sixth sense she herself had yet to develop.

"I'm sorry," Patsy mouthed-whispered as she turned and pulled an old towel from inside her apron pocket.

I should have run away with Lucy…

1915
ALICE: DAY 602 IN THE ASYLUM

Harriet watched Alice carefully for any signs of distress. Even when she had to turn her attention to other tasks, she found her gaze wandering, seeking the patient out from the corners of her eyes. She'd lost track of how long Alice had been in the room, and in the chair, this time. It had been months, though. The poor woman had to lie on her side in the bed, unable to put any weight on her backside. Early-stage pressure sores had formed on her upper back and the undersides of her arms. The skin had thickened, with large, overlapping patches of dark reddish-purple and white. Older sores had healed, regressed, healed, regressed; the damage left behind deep cracks and huge, patchy scars.

Alice's bottom, however, held the type of sore that sunk through every layer of skin. A deep crater with blackened edges, bubbling red debris, and white flecks of infection. The wound *stank* of decay. The rest of her body had withered so much that she looked sick, near death. Like the pressure sores were from some horrid disease that had sucked the life, fat, and colour from her. Alice hadn't just turned pale from lack of sunlight, but a phantom grey. An unnatural shade for the human body. It unsettled Harriet, and the other patients and staff, greatly. Like they looked at something that *pretended* to be human. Something sinister and dangerous. Not a woman at all.

Harriet realised she was staring again and shook herself, mentally and physically, trying to break the spell Alice held over her. It was just her and Alice in the room at that moment. The other patients had been permitted to enter the courtyard. After what had been a long, cold winter, the sunlight finally held a bit of warmth that stretched all throughout spring. She finished making the bed in front of her and stepped towards the next one, slowing partway and frowning as her gaze grazed the windows. A commotion started up outside, near the front of the building. Two nurses struggled with something.

A patient? Harriet thought, standing up on a chair so she could see through the tall windows. *No, not a patient, too small. A child?* She put a hand on the glass, squinting. *Roy…*

She turned in panic, her heart beating frantically in her chest, to check if Alice was still in the bed. Of *course* Alice wouldn't know;

Harriet had only just realised herself. But Alice was the type of patient the nurses took *no* chances with. Harriet wouldn't have been surprised to learn the woman could read minds. Could see through Harriet's own eyes that her son was just beyond the window. Older, taller, larger than she would remember. But still her son. So close. *Too close.* "The closest you've ever got…" Harriet whispered to herself under her breath as she turned back to the window to watch.

The shouts from the garden intensified as the first nurse picked up the young boy, leaning backwards to maintain her balance as she clenched him in her arms. His little legs kicked violently, preventing the second nurse from getting close enough to assist. Roy's voice echoed in the courtyard. Harriet frantically closed the small windows to block out the sounds. Blood rushed to her head, drowning out everything but the pounding in her ears as the latch finally caught.

She turned again, stepping down from the chair. She gasped when she saw that Alice now sat up in bed: putting pressure on that horrid bedsore, staining the sheets pink with her infected fluids. Those piercing, keen, intelligent eyes fixed on Harriet. Her face, the shade of wet cement. She didn't even flinch from the obvious pain of her open sore. She looked like a corpse. A horrid spectre risen from the grave to haunt her. To haunt them all.

"Roy." Her voice, barely more than a whisper, came out cracked, hoarse from weeks of disuse. Despite this, it held all the emotions of the world. Agonising hope. Tortured longing. Ragged despair. Harriet couldn't even tell if Alice still breathed.

She fumbled at her waist for the chain that linked to her whistle, desperate to call for help. Its cold, smooth surface felt like a lifeline. Would anyone come in time? Would she be able to fend the woman off long enough on her own? How much stronger might Alice become if she's *this close* to her son—closer than ever before?

"A-Alice…" Harriet's own voice came out bare and breathy. Powerless as her patient rose up to her feet. Even wobbling, the woman held a fierce determination that would make the most seasoned veteran pause in their war charge.

Roy let out one more yell, loud enough to break through the shuttered windows. Alice joined him, screaming as she launched herself at her nurse.

Harriet blew the whistle.

2021
15 OCTOBER, 21:41

AIDEN HELD HIS camera steady, aimed at Devin as they climbed a creaking metal catwalk. He found it easier to watch where he was going *through* the viewfinder, despite the slight unevenness to their path. Even though the view was grainy and washed with green, it still revealed the details of the walkway with more clarity than his own eyes could offer. And, if Aiden was being honest with himself, it kept the crazy world contained. Held within the set parameters of the tiny screen. If he looked around him, he'd suddenly feel adrift. Lost within a night that never ended.

"We've lost the caretaker, for now," Devin whispered in his trademark horror-rasp. "But it was a close one. We heard her mower power up about ten minutes ago and head away from us. It sounded like she was heading back towards the front gate. Let's hope—" Devin paused, panting. He looked around, uncertain. His face might have been covered in that stupid skull bandana, but those grey eyes betrayed enough of his emotion. Terror. A breath shuddered out of him and he focused on Aiden. "Fuck. *Fuck!*" He shook out his hands and bounced on his toes. "I need to go again."

Aiden just nodded and kept rolling, motioning for him to start, his eyes still fixed down on the viewfinder.

"We've evaded the caretaker," Devin said with more confidence in his on-camera voice. "An epic chase through the wards has led us *here*." He motioned behind him, pausing for dramatic effect. "Like fate, to the infamous Ward Fifteen. Not even the caretaker will follow us here. The most haunted ward in the most haunted asylum in Australia. We're completely alone now. And we're going inside."

CHAPTER FOURTEEN

1953
WINTER

THE ONLY LIGHT that glowed in Ward Five was the small office in which Bonnie sat, cardigan wrapped tightly around her shoulders, two layers of stockings barely keeping the winter chill from her legs. She blew on her hot cup of sweet tea, letting its steam attempt to melt the ice-tip that was her nose. Unlike the patient areas, the office did not have a heater. Bonnie had just finished her first ever midnight round with Charge Nurse Hatchet. Only two patients had wet the bed this time, *not* including Edna, miraculously. Hatchet said Edna usually needed a change at least twice a night. This meant she'd need a change at 4:00 a.m., for sure.

Bonnie sighed as the last of her tea slipped down her throat. At this rate, she'd be racing Gerald for the title of who could skull hot beverages fastest. She meandered to the corner of the room where a small phonograph sat on the edge of the desk. Curious, she lifted the dust cover off the case and saw that a small 45 record still sat on the turntable. She lifted it carefully, squinting through the gloom to read *DECCA GOLD LABEL SERIES, BLUE TANGO, LEROY ANDERSON, "Pops" Concert Orchestra, 16020.* Bonnie replaced the vinyl on the turntable, glancing over her shoulder as though to check if she were truly alone. She yawned widely, the sweet tea not strong enough to fight her internal body clock. She hoped that as the nights wore on, she'd get used to this new rhythm.

"What's the harm," she whispered to herself, turning the black knob on the side of the phonograph, which set the turntable spinning. She kept the knob only just turned, so the sound that came through would be softer. She checked the speakers, too, to ensure they wouldn't suddenly blast noise through the completely silent ward. Flicking the golden switch, the record fell down into place, the arm clicking as it lifted automatically to place itself on the spinning vinyl. The entire orchestra immediately leapt to life in the small room, filling up the silence.

The music helped both her heart and her jaw unclench slightly, and her eyes sprung open a little wider. Her body clock wasn't the only thing that needed adjusting; her heart wasn't used to the eerie silence of night alone in an asylum, either. "Do-do-do-doo-dooo," Bonnie half hummed, half sung to herself, just as the strings took over. She sighed as she sat back at the desk, her brief tea-break over. The paperwork sitting on the desk beckoned her, seemingly having doubled in size during her brief distraction with the phonograph. A lot in her day often came unexpectedly; she never knew what might happen from one shift to the next. *Except* for the paperwork. That was an ever-constant guarantee.

She pushed her first small pile of papers to the side just as the song finished and the phonograph started clicking, readying to drop the next 45 onto the turntable. In the brief interlude, another sound rattled, seemingly from the ceiling above her. She pushed the remaining pile of papers away from her and placed the fountain pen neatly in its holder so it wouldn't spray ink. An upbeat version of *China Doll* started playing on the record before she walked the few paces over to switch it off.

Bonnie tilted her head in the sudden silence, looking up at the plaster ceiling. It *sounded* like it had come from above her. But that was impossible. No patients were currently bunked in the attic. Occasionally, yes, when the staff needed the overflow space, they'd use the attic like a dormitory. But not tonight.

Sounds echo in a place like this, she thought to herself. *It's probably just reverberating from the ward. Please don't let one of the patients be out of bed…*

She'd heard night shifts were even more taxing than the ones during the day. The structured rounds happened only four times a night, but the patients rarely followed routine. If one of the patients became distressed, Bonnie knew she wouldn't always be able to help them on her own. Their doors may be locked, but that didn't stop them getting out of their beds and hurting themselves, risking waking the others. She held her breath as the silence continued.

Knock.

She let the breath out in a long, hard sigh. Shuffling followed the knocking noise, then the odd tap, which indicated footfalls. The sound was faint, but undeniable. Its echo made it hard to pinpoint where it had originated from, but someone was up and out of bed. Patting her belt to make sure she had her key loop, Bonnie reached for the large flashlight sitting on the shelves by the door. Its red colour made it stand out clearly even in the dim lights, so she had no issues clasping her hands around its handle and lifting it up. It was said to be a "big beam" flashlight; as such, it had a good weight to it and its huge bulb instantly lit up the hallway in a wide, high ray.

The only parts of the hallway that remained gloomy were the corners, which gave the space the illusion of rotundness. Bonnie realised this was her first time walking the halls at night, alone. She hurriedly stepped past the wide windows to her left, the ones that yawned over the gardens. Clouds shrouded the moon and stars tonight, leaving utter darkness to beckon to her from the corner of her eye. Howard's silly whistle ridiculously started playing in her head, and she really felt as though someone was walking behind her.

Sinatra's smooth, but warbling, voice taunted her again with the lyrics to his song, *I'm Walking Behind You*. She may have forgotten about Frank for a while, but was she still on someone—or something's—mind?

Once she knew she was past the windows, additional office doors now appearing to her left, Bonnie spun to shine the light behind her. Of course, the hallway was empty. Still, entertaining the trivial lyrics in her head had been enough for her heart to start thumping. The torch light reflected off the windows with a sinister sheen, and she turned forward again before her mind could play tricks on her, distorting the refractions into something more supernatural.

Another scraping sound came from in front of her. Bonnie paused. She told herself she just needed to hear where the sound came from, over her own footfalls. Her gurgling stomach seemed to laugh at her lie. In reality, she was afraid to move. The sound seemed to have come from the darkness just beyond the edges of her light.

She cleared her throat and called in a voice barely above a conversational tone, "Nurse Hatchet? Is that you?"

Only silence responded. Bonnie drew a deep, slow breath, filling up her lungs until her chest heaved and her stomach extended uncomfortably. She blew it out as fast as she could, imagining her jitters speeding out with it, and started forward. Once again, she heard only her own shoes clacking on the wood floors. She reached the door to the main recreational hall, pulling her keys from her belt and fumbling the correct one into the lock. Cold air greeted her when she pushed open the door. She felt the hairs on her arms raise underneath the sleeves of her cardigan. The fires in the communal areas had been doused for the night, and the heat escaped quickly through the massive high ceilings. The same ones she'd nearly broken her neck trying to clean for Nurse Hatchet.

Bonnie's torch beam reflected off every surface. The well-polished floors. The marble columns in the centre of the room. The shiny piano in the corner. And the many, many windows. The room wasn't quite a hall of mirrors, though in her present state of agitation, it very well could have been.

Some of the other wards had two nurses working shifts together each night. At that moment, she envied them; they attended to louder, noisier patients, or the ones prone to fits and falls, no matter the time of day. She thought she might prefer that over the empty silence or strange, abstract echoes which seemed to come from all over, yet nowhere, at the same time.

Bonnie quickly locked the door behind her and hurried across the room, her footfalls reverberating even louder in the open space. She breathed deeply in relief when she reached the door on the opposite end and jammed the same key (which hadn't left her fist) into the lock. It gave instantly. She entered another hallway, the temperature immediately warmer and the sounds muffled. The patients' rooms began here, so she steadied her legs as she pushed the door shut behind her. She took careful, measured steps, attempting to keep her footsteps soft. She pinched her lips as she strained her ears, listening as she passed each door for any sounds that indicated she'd found the patient who was out of bed. In the maze of hallways, doors, and the occasional bathroom, all was silent. All but her own breaths and steps.

Just as she thought she might give up, a bang sounded directly above her. No mistaking it this time: the noise did not echo down the hallways. It wasn't faint, either. The sounds from earlier had been almost whisper-like. These were undeniable—they certainly came from the attic.

Bonnie put her hand on her chest and felt her heart thumping desperately, as if seeking an escape. For a moment, she considered escape, too. Imagined rushing back through the recreation room, down the hall, and into the office. Closing the office door behind her and ignoring any further noises. Hell, even fleeing Ward Five itself and hiding under the covers of her bed in Buna House.

"I'm not like Lucy," she whispered to herself as she gritted her teeth and turned down the hallway she knew would take her to the attic stairs. She couldn't fathom how anyone would even have got into the attic. That door, too, would be locked. Even if a patient had managed to escape their locked bedrooms, navigated the maze of passages in the night, and ascended the stairs… Even then, they would find the attic door locked. "I'm not like Lucy…"

1915
ALICE: DAY 889 IN THE ASYLUM

Harriet had been given scant details about the new patient. She knew her name: Helen. She knew that the woman was *not* to spend any time in the reception house, but to come straight to Ward Five. An almost unheard of decision. Even if Helen's insanity was not in question, the Medical Superintendent would still have to observe her to determine which ward would house her until she recovered. Or, Harriet supposed, for the rest of her living days.

In Helen's case, there was no denying she needed to be at Kenmore. The nurses whispered that Helen was well known in the town of Goulburn. The wife of a well-to-do man, who often travelled for work. The neighbours had spied her parading around her gardens in her wedding dress. As gossip would have it, she'd even been known on occasion to walk the streets in the gown.

The only thing Harriet knew for certain was that Helen had been admitted following a miscarriage. Well, not quite a miscarriage. A stillbirth, as the baby had died during the midpoint of the pregnancy. Helen had gone into labour far too early, and quickly birthed the already dead infant. The tragedy instantly descended her into lunacy. Refusing to dress or to eat. Violently throwing things around the house. Neglecting her hygiene in favour of utter filth. Her husband had been quite firm at the time of her admission: she was not to be released. He no doubt gave a sizable donation to ensure this special treatment. Why else would Helen come straight to the wards?

Harriet broke from her reverie as the new patient came into the ward through the side door. Tangled knots of hair obscured her face, and Harriet decided at once to shave her head. Black stains from faeces and urine ruined the hem of her nightdress. Harriet was used to the smell by now. Her eyes barely watered as she met the wardsmen who guided Helen into the ward, one arm on each shoulder. Harriet finished sizing her up and sighed, turning to lead the men through.

"This way, if you please, gentlemen." She didn't bother addressing the woman, who was obviously drugged out of her mind on opiates. She'd developed a quick sense of which women were dropped at the asylum by their husbands simply because they'd tired of them, or they'd aged—or God forbid, started menopause.

Helen already felt different. Almost as though an energy buzzed about her. Subdued, for now, by opiates, but unmistakable all the same.

They reached the bathroom and Harriet removed her arm cuffs, enabling her to push her sleeves up high around her armpits. Helen looked up at her, blinking dully. "I think I can take it from here, gentlemen. Though wait by the door, please, in case I should need you." They nodded silently and released Helen so Harriet could shepherd her into the bathroom. As soon as they were in relative privacy, Harriet removed a pair of scissors from the belt she'd fashioned for her waist that held an assortment of useful instruments.

"I'm…I'm Helen," the woman whispered. Some part of her former life resurfaced briefly, demanding courtesies be observed for this first meeting.

"I know." She circled the woman and gently patted her shoulder. "I'm Nurse Harriet. I'm going to have to cut your hair now."

Helen didn't answer, but dropped her gaze to her feet. Harriet let her hand trail across the top of the woman's back and then scooped up the hair. Helen didn't react, and so Harriet moved quickly, chopping the locks free. She didn't bother to do a neat job. She'd have the junior nurse finish shaving her the next morning. It was too close to the end of the day to bother with neatness. The other patients would finish up dinner soon and be readied for bed. Helen simply watched the tresses fall around her feet, as calmly as if she watched autumn leaves fall from a tree.

"I—I'm Helen."

"Mmmhmmm." Harriet brushed the final strands of hair from the woman's shoulders. "I'm Nurse Harriet." She was used to repeating herself. In fact, she found this to be a nicer interaction than some of the others she'd already had that day. "I'm going to cut your dress free now, dear. Then we can get you washed, into some nice clean clothes, and ready for bed. For a nice rest."

Helen fell silent again. As Harriet began chopping the nightgown free, she could see tears fall from the woman's eyes in great big drops. These weren't quiet, silent tears that politely dribbled down her cheeks. These were fat as rain drops, splashing through the dirt on her face. The gown joined the hair on the floor, and Harriet could see from the deep purple stretch marks on the woman's still slightly swollen belly that it hadn't been long at all since she'd lost the baby. Days, at most. Her breasts were still plump, and she made a mental note to watch for signs of infection as the milk dried up.

Harriet didn't take her eyes off the patient as she turned the water on, waiting until it reached just the right temperature. She tested it with her own elbow, as Helen might have done for her infant, if things had turned out different. "Come on, now." She guided the woman to the water and began the mechanical task of washing her down, scrubbing away the dirt and muck that no-one else had dared to touch. It made no difference to her.

As Harriet reached for the towel, the tears on Helen's face finally dried beneath her puffy eyes. "He's going to keep him chained up," she muttered as the nurse towelled her dry. Harriet merely grunted and nodded as she finished her work. "My husband, he keeps our son chained in the basement. Muzzled, like a dog." Harriet had heard worse. An Italian grandma had once told her she'd chopped her neighbour's balls off to serve as meatballs and spaghetti to her own husband.

Harriet reached for a fresh nightgown. It would swamp Helen's frame, but would have to do for now. Just like her awful hair. "I'm going to take you to bed now, dear. Do you think you might like to have a good sleep?"

"He was going to do the same to me, but I escaped. Will you help my boy escape, too? He could stay with me."

"We'll see what we can do."

Helen exhaled deeply and smiled for the first time since she'd entered Harriet's care.

"You two can go." Harriet nodded at the wardsmen as she helped Helen into the hallway. "Though I'd appreciate it if you could clean up in the bathroom before you do."

"You'll be alright with her?" the first wardsman asked kindly, though with an obvious mind to Harriet's diminutive stature. She may have been small, but she was strong as a pit bull.

Harriet took one more look at Helen, then nodded sharply. It wasn't just the patient's looks or behaviour that told her all would be well. It was a feeling. And Harriet had come to trust her gut most of all.

The walk up the stairs was easy and fuss-free. Harriet had no qualms about settling the woman into one of the beds in the attic. She doubted she'd cause trouble for the other women here, either. And Harriet would let the night staff know to check-in on her regularly. As she tucked her in, a gentle tapping sounded behind her. It sent a small trill up her spine in a way Helen's words about chained children never could have.

Alice is welcoming her here, she thought to herself. She couldn't help but picture the woman with the dark, calculating eyes, staring through the wood, staring into Helen's soul. Leaning on that one loose leg to tap-tap-tap her greeting.

Welcome to Kenmore.

THERE ARE SO many spirits here. So many souls that haven't merely passed through, but are stuck. Not just lingering, but tethered. Just like me. Anchored to the grounds as I am. Thousands have passed through. Dozens have passed away. But only a handful have never passed at all.

What is it called when this happens? What does it mean, when so many congregate in one place? Are they all even aware of each other? Aware of me? Are they haunting me? Or am I haunting them? Perhaps...just perhaps, we are haunting each other.

CHAPTER FIFTEEN

1953
WINTER

Bonnie put her foot on the first step and glanced up. With her bright torch, she saw where the steps, the banister, and the wall all curved up towards the left. But she couldn't see what waited around the corner, and that set her sympathetic nervous system into overdrive again. Despite the cold, her palms sweated where they gripped the handle of the light. Her heart continued to drum not just in the pit of her chest, but also in her temples, her legs, and even her forearms. She breathed through her mouth as if in exertion.

Another bang sounded directly above her, and she pictured some ghoul rushing down the stairs, unseen until it rounded that final corner. Of course, that wasn't possible, even if ghouls were real. The door at the top of the stairs was locked. But still, if she listened hard enough, she could hear that scraping sound again. As if feet dragged across the wooden floorboards. Soft, tired feet.

I'm not like Lucy, Bonnie reminded herself as she put her foot onto the next step. A bolstering mantra that repeated in her head with each ascent. She poked her head forward as she rounded the first corner. Empty. Another blind corner awaited her at the second landing. She switched the flashlight to her other hand so she could wipe her sticky palm on her apron. She imagined she felt the blood rushing into her limbs, readying her for fight or flight, driven by its cortisol masters.

Reaching the final turn, poked her head again to shine the light up at the closed white wooden door. A whimper escaped her lips unwittingly as another bang thudded behind the door.

"Whoever is out of bed," she called in a slightly raised voice, careful to not rouse the other patients, "I don't know how you got upstairs, but it really is time to head back to bed."

She paused in front of the door, one hand aiming the light, the second firmly gripping her key loop. The pulsing in her palms increased in tempo. She scraped the key into the lock. The chill that rushed out from beneath the door almost seemed to have personality as it caressed her ankles. Teasing her.

"In I come!"

The door swept open gracefully, dramatically, as though it were curtains unveiling a theatre. The room almost reminded her of some stretched-out spaceship, like a scene from the 1951 hit movie *When Worlds Collide*. The room was not rectangular. The corners seemed to have their own corners; a squat, but lengthy, 3D octagon. A large column took up the middle of the room, and each wall held brackets that looked *just like* the ship she remembered from *When Worlds Collide*. Almost like triangles, but with their pointy tips meeting at the exterior walls. Everything was white and undeniably empty.

Bonnie flashed her light across the room, the odd shapes of the beams and central column casting long shadows in which a patient might easily hide. She couldn't see behind the fat central column either, nor to the door she knew waited at the far end of the hall. Whatever had been banging around up fell silent as she'd entered. They knew she was here. They were hiding.

Whatever had been banging? Bonnie thought to herself. Surely, she'd meant *whoever.*

Mind the ghosts of Ward Five. Lillian's words came back to her unbidden. She trembled, letting her key loop fall to her belt so she could grab the light with both hands. She knew she was supposed to lock the door behind her, but she just couldn't bring herself to do it. To lock herself in here with the invisible phantom who had been making those noises.

"Come on out, please," she said in her calmest voice. A slight waver warped her final words, but she still impressed herself by keeping her composure. *Surely, they're behind that column.*

Bonnie ventured deeper into the room, her heels smacking loudly with each step upon the wooden floor. She froze when another noise echoed behind her. Not her own footfalls, but a creak. Quick and clacking. She spun, breathing through her mouth, her chest rising and falling in panic. Her beam of light fell on a second door, stationed to the left of the one she'd just come through. A door she hadn't noticed before now. White and wooden as well, but undeniably unlocked. Her light passed across just in time to see the door swing outwards ever so slightly, the space behind it just a strip of black visible against the doorframe, too deep for the light to pierce.

She held her breath, and the door moved again. Inwards this time, as though whoever had peeked out at her now attempted to pull it closed again. The change in air pressure as she'd entered the attic might have been enough to explain the door swinging outwards, especially if it hadn't been latched. But what could explain how it closed again? Painful heartbeats strained the muscles in her chest. Bonnie released a breath and flicked the light away, just for a moment, to see if she could spy anything in the corners behind her.

The door groaned again, now pulled almost shut. The darkened slit was no longer visible.

"Hello!" The word burst from her. "Who's there?!"

With all of her senses on overdrive, Bonnie noticed something slightly peculiar when she trained the torch light back on the door. It had a key lock and an external bolt, two layers of protection that locked away whatever might be inside. Except this time, both the door and the bolt were unsecured.

Pounding feet echoed again. Not her own. Not from in front of her. From behind, heavy and menacing.

She spun around and saw a flash of white as a large figure swept towards her. The threat within that little room was instantly forgotten as she stumbled back towards it, screaming shrilly. She'd always laughed at how women screamed in the movies. Totally unrealistic. Except now, having emitted a sound just as sharp and ringing, she may never laugh at those movies again.

The white figure descended upon her. However, just like it had been in the morgue, little details started to pop the bubbles of fear that enveloped her heart, lungs, and throat. The white flash was a *white sheet*. The heavy footfalls came from large boots poking out from beneath said sheet. And there were *chuckles*. Chuckles she recognised all too well.

"God damn you, Bubbles!" Her voice still came out high-pitched. Bonnie laid a hand on her chest to feel how swiftly her heart fluttered, how violently her lungs made it rise and fall. Breathing in deeply through her nose and out her mouth, she tried to settle them. "Heavens to Betsy…"

Bubbles pulled the sheet completely free, his laughter fading to fits of giggles. "Your *face*," he wheezed, rubbing tears from his eyes. "I about nearly wet my pants!"

"Oh, put a lid on it!" Bonnie busied herself wiping her dress down, just for something to do with her nervous hands. "You nearly gave me a heart attack! Again! And what if you'd woken one of the patients?" She cocked her head then, relieved to hear that silence had descended once again. *Thank God he hadn't woken anyone with his foul prank.* "How did you even get in here?"

"The catwalk," Bubbles said and shrugged, his huge dumb grin still plastered on his face. Bonnie maliciously lifted the beam of her light. His wince as it struck him in the eyes gave her momentary pleasure. "It connects to Ward Sixteen," he continued, holding a hand in front of his face. "We had another body to pick up next door. They didn't need all three pairs of hands. I'd heard it was your first night, so I thought I'd better check in and see how you were doing." He smiled in what he no doubt thought was a charming way. His sandy blond curls fell over his forehead in a way that probably made some ladies swoon. Right now, she just wanted to slam his head into the column he'd hid behind.

"And who did you bring with you then, hm?" She spun back to the creaking door, shining her light on it. "Come on, out! The jig is up!"

All was silent, aside from Bubbles sauntering closer. His heavy footfalls weren't dragging or shuffling now.

"There's no one with me."

"Oh, get bent!" She roughly pushed on his chest. It did little more than make him sway, though the physical act of "attacking" him still made her feel better.

"No, seriously." He reached into his back pocket for his own flashlight. A long, simple silver cylinder much smaller than Bonnie's, with a beam that didn't light up the space quite so brilliantly. He clicked it on and walked to the door. Just as he reached out to push it open, a feeling of dread landed in the pit of her stomach again.

There's no-one with me.

Words of warning caught in her throat, but she was too late. The door creaked again as Bubbles yanked it open. Bonnie took a tentative step forward and shined her light inside.

Empty. The room was completely empty.

"The door was creaking," Bonnie muttered, striding over to Bubbles's side. With a push, she looked over his shoulder and confirmed what she already knew.

"See, I was doing you a civil service, really. Making sure you took those ghost stories seriously."

"Honestly, get lost, Bubbles." She was in no mood for further taunting. The adrenaline was wearing off, leaving her feeling even more exhausted than before. She still had all that paperwork to finish, and the rounds would start again in a couple of hours. A dull pain throbbed again in her temples. "If you ever try anything like that again, I will seriously push you down the stairs."

2021
15 OCTOBER, 21:55

WARD FIFTEEN ECHOED in a way the other wards hadn't. It had its similarities with the previous buildings they'd explored: the bone-deep chill in the air, the sounds that seemed to have no origin, and the creaks and groans of the wood that seemed to be living things themselves. Sounds with bodies that slithered around the floors and walls, coming from all directions.

But unlike Ward Fourteen or Sixteen and the rest of the buildings, the sounds didn't seem natural. Aiden had trouble describing it. The only words in his head were *deliberate. Malicious.*

"It's like the walls are breathing, isn't it?" he muttered under his breath, giving voice to the thought he couldn't shake. If Devin heard him, his friend chose to ignore him. "This is the attic, isn't it?" he said a little louder, shining his torch on the oddly shaped walls. The wall brackets threw elongated triangle patterns across the hardwood floor. The paint peeled, though it looked more like it rotted away than simply faded with time. The whole place was both alive and decaying.

"Yeah, I recognise it from those pictures on the library website." Devin's voice was faint and timid. A rare combination. "They kept patients up here when they ran out of room downstairs."

Both boys jumped at a loud groan of old wood. A white door, just to the side of the staircase, hung ajar. Paint peeled from the surface, exposing the splintered wood below. Aiden trained his camera on it, watching through the viewscreen for any movement. He gasped as the door rocked slowly open and shut; only by an inch or two in either direction at a time, but unmistakable. The black slit of whatever waited beyond widened and then thinned ever so slowly.

Devin strode over to the door and slammed it shut with the palm of his hand. They both heard it click as it latched. "Hey, bring the camera over," Devin instructed, standing back. "There…" He pointed at the bolt secured on the external side. No doubt put there to keep someone inside. "They must've locked people up in there. What do you reckon is in there?"

"I'm not curious enough to find out," Aiden whispered back. For once, Devin didn't respond by calling him a "piece of chickenshit". There was just something about the place, and Devin wasn't rushing to object either.

"Come on, let's get a bit more filming done up here, then find somewhere to crash. I'm beat!"

Aiden swept the camera back towards the large attic. He remembered seeing the photo Devin had mentioned. The beds had faced with their heads to the walls and their feet to the centre of the room. There'd been nurses posing for the photo, and each bed had been perfectly made. But there'd been something off-putting about how fake the poses had seemed. It had made him doubt their smiles. *I can splice the photo in with the footage*, he thought to himself, as he got his angles just right.

A squeak and soft tapping, as if weightless fingers rapped on glass, became audible in the stillness. Devin headed towards it, and Aiden followed wordlessly behind. With every second step, the planks of wood groaned behind them as if in delayed protest. Or as if the building itself reminded them it knew they were there. Aiden frequently found himself swivelling the camera to look behind them. It felt like a morbid game of Mr. Wolf, with him the targeted wolf.

What's the time Mr. Wolf?

Two O'clock!

Step. Step. Spin. No-one behind him.

What's the time, Mr. Wolf?

Four O'clock!

Step. Step. Step. Step. Spin. No-one behind him.

Even though, according to the schoolyard game, it was the wolf who was eventually supposed to yell *Dinner Time!* and start chasing the other players back to the starting line, there was always the chance the wolf would lose. Invite them too close and they'd tap you on the shoulder before you could spin, ending the game.

"It's a curtain," Devin said in hushed tones, beckoning Aiden forward and pointing up at one of the high windows. Too high for him to reach, and much too high for any patient who had once resided there. Devin stood back to allow Aiden a better shot with his camera, and he panned up. The small, thin, white curtains were more holes than fabric. Their elastic tethers squeaked and tapped as a light breeze from the broken window caused the fabric to sway. In the dark, the fabric almost looked scorched around its holes. More like a tissue burned by small cinders than a cloth that had slowly rotted away.

The groaning wood sounded behind him again, and Aiden swivelled so fast he nearly lost his stomach. The dizzying sensation made him sway slightly. His camera's viewfinder pointed back at that white door. Once again, swayed open.

"Are you seeing this?" Aiden whispered, despite knowing that Devin was observing over his shoulder. "Are you fucking seeing this?"

"I latched that motherfucker," Devin breathed.

The whispering wind silenced Aiden swore his eardrums vibrated in the empty air, feeling for sound the way a blind man felt along the walls. All he heard was his own blood rushing in his ears.

"Come on…" Devin took one step forward, then waited for Aiden to continue forward together.

Aiden's brain screamed at him to run. Every nerve ending zapped a signal to his muscles. *Run. Get out.*

But his heart, despite how fast and hard it beat, called differently. Aiden felt drawn to the black, gaping door. A discovery like this was what they'd come for, after all. A moment to peer beyond the veil, to reach past it and touch something incorporeal. A feat no-one else had done before. And then bring the money rolling in since they were the ones to capture it.

Aiden shivered as he remembered his own reason for coming. Stardom, yes. Royalties, Hell yes. Proving himself to his friend, undeniable. But for Aiden, there was a deeper reason. A family connection. Aiden had joked about his Dad dropping his Uncle at the front gates in the 80s as a "new patient". But that wasn't his only link to this place. His whole family had been born and bred in the area, and every single one of them had a story. His youngest Uncle reminisced about the parties in the wards in the early 2000s, shortly after it had been abandoned. His eldest Uncle liked to tell stories about stealing fruit from the orchards when it was in season. A school mate who grew up in a house on the property often complained about being made to sleep on the veranda, even in the winter. Everyone had a connection, in some way.

But Aiden's Dad went further. This place had always fascinated him. More than any local. *Obsessed.* Aiden had grown up hearing stories about Kenmore. The old man normally ignored him, unless it was time for a beating; only when his Dad told these stories did Aiden get any of his attention. His Dad had gone on the old ghost tours at least a half-dozen times before they stopped, coming back with stories of rattling windows, footsteps, dimming lights. At age ten, Aiden discovered the full truth after his Grandma had died. His Dad's Mum. His Grandma had been a patient at Kenmore in the 1950s. Ward Fifteen, in fact. His family never told him what was wrong with her. All he'd been able to find out was that medication finally fixed her up and she'd left, going on to get married and pop out his Dad and Uncles.

Insanity runs in my family. Runs in my blood. This place *runs in my veins.*

The boys crept closer to the creaking door. A hard knot formed in Aiden's throat. He tried to swallow and gulped instead, almost choking. Aiden's Mum had only moved them to Canberra after his Dad passed away four years ago. *Fucking cancer.* He'd been friends with Devin—and obsessed with abandoned places—ever since. Obsessed, like his Dad. A man he'd promised himself he'd never turn into. And yet, that obsession pulled him towards the door.

He reached the handle first and tugged it open sharply, before he could think better of it. The door didn't groan but squealed when Aiden yanked it backwards. The room had an odd L-shape due to a large, raised platform in one corner. It was tiny, damp, and *freezing*. A couple of toilets stood in one corner, one missing its lid, the other its entire seat. But this place wasn't meant to be a bathroom. He didn't know how he knew that. Not that it looked nothing like any bathroom he'd ever seen, but that he knew it wasn't its original purpose.

"It's empty," Aiden breathed, even as his panic-filled brain screamed at him that this statement was, in fact, a lie. *It's not empty. It's in there. Run. Run. Run. Run.*

"Let's get out of here…" Devin pulled him roughly back by the shoulders and again slammed the door shut. This time, he hauled on the handle a couple of times, rattling it in its latch to make sure it held steady. "Let's set up for the night."

Aiden nodded as they turned back to the stairs. He doubted either of them would sleep a wink.

As they descended to the lower levels, their shoes tapping and clapping with each step, Aiden's mind wandered again.

What's the time Mr. Wolf?

How close were the ghosts behind him now? Should he keep counting? Should he let them continue to creep up on him? Closer and closer until they tapped him on the shoulder and it was game over? Or was it, as his brain still screamed at him, time to run? Time to chase while he, the big bad wolf, was still in charge.

1953
WINTER

Bonnie tried not to think about what had happened that night as she trudged across the gardens, fog thick in the air, the clouds hanging low in the early morning sky. She'd returned to her office to find the phonograph still playing. She could have *sworn* she'd turned it off before she left. But no matter how hard she racked her brain, she just couldn't remember. Perhaps she hadn't, after all? Perhaps she'd gone straight to investigate the noise?

And the noises hadn't stopped. At least, not for very long. Groans and the odd clack or squeak continued throughout the night. Worst, there'd be the odd *shuffle*. That same noise she'd first heard. Despite not wanting to mull over the same unnerving thoughts, they kept repeating as she trudged back towards Buna House.

Bubbles's feet didn't shuffle like that, she finally realised. *His feet were loud, heavy, clacking. I never heard him shuffle.* That thought unnerved her the most.

"We did not fulfil our destiny…"

Bonnie stopped at the whispered voice. Its grating rasp came from the bushes directly in front of her. Directly in front of Buna House.

No, Bonnie groaned in her head. She did not have the mental stamina for any more craziness today. At least, not any more than usual. And not any crazy that might only be in her own mind. Her heart couldn't take it. She paused, cocking her head. More whispers, though indistinguishable. She looked up and saw the window to her bedroom. The one she'd shared with Lucy. *Whispers beneath the window?*

Something rustled in the bushes; before Bonnie could react, a man stepped free from the shadows. His features lit up in the early morning light. He was a slight man. Only her height, if that. He was also thin and worn-looking, for. His clothes swamped him. And something was wrong with his hands. They were too big. Too thick.

"They're real, you know?" He took another step forward, and Bonnie breathed in relief as she realised his inhuman hands were, in fact, gardening gloves.

"Oh, you gave me a little fright!" she said, immediately donning her "patient voice". She hadn't expected to see anyone walking the grounds so early. Most patients would still be locked up in their rooms. "I'm Nurse Trainee Bonnie. Are you okay?"

The man paused for a moment, rubbing his gloved hands against his large trousers. "I'm Alfred," he mumbled. Obviously not quite used to conversation, at least not with real, living people.

"Do you tend the garden here, Alfred?" Bonnie asked patiently. Her eyelids felt like they were suddenly turning to granite, and her body quickly followed suit. Heavier and heavier by the moment. It had been a *long* night.

"These are my gardens…" Alfred whispered so softly that Bonnie almost couldn't hear him. "Francis lets me out."

She recognised the name of one of the other male nurses. So this is Lucy's ghost, then.

"They're lovely." She paused for a moment, yawning widely and rubbing at her jaw. "Are you okay, Alfred?"

He nodded timidly, taking a step backwards, as though meaning to return to the bush.

"Well, I'm heading off to bed now. But it's nice to meet you. I'm sure I'll see you again tomorrow morning."

"I'll be here…" he whispered, turning back to the bush. He bent to the ground, scratching in the dirt, then stood and pressed his hands against the stems of the bushes. "We didn't fulfil our destiny…" he whispered at the bush, his string of unidentifiable murmurs starting up again.

Bonnie passed close by as she headed to the front door. Alfred bent again, lifting something and turning to the bush in a repetitive, rhythmic motion. *He's trying to put the leaves back on the bush,* she realised.

CHAPTER SIXTEEN

1953
SPRING

Two months after her first night shift, Bonnie became accustomed to the strange shuffling, creaking and footsteps that echoed the hallways and—particularly—in the attic at night. Her days at Kenmore blurred into weeks. In turn, those weeks blurred into months. A new, rhythmic cycle. Ten days on night shift. Ten days off. Then three days on day shift, one day off, for the rest of the month, before returning to the nights. Many nurses hated the nights, refusing to work them unless they literally had no choice. Gerald and Patsy, cases in point. Patsy openly admitted to being too disturbed by the ghostly sounds. To her nerves being constantly on edge. Gerald wouldn't confess as much, simply complaining she was "too old" to adjust to being awake all night.

Bonnie had started the night shift again the night before. Edna had needed to be changed *every single round*. It wasn't uncommon for her to wet herself twice a night, but this had been extra, even for her. Bonnie's upper arms ached from carrying the bundles of wet linen from Edna's room to the top of the stairs, throwing it down, and then hauling it out for collection the next day. Twice, she'd been unlucky enough to "spray" the polished wooden steps and had needed to take precious more time scrubbing them, praying they wouldn't stain.

"Good morning, Alfred," Bonnie said pleasantly as she approached Buna House. While the sun had started to rise earlier each day, it was still too dark to make out the elderly patient when he was bent beneath the bushes. And even then, he did an excellent job of hiding from view.

Alfred shuffled out slowly, a couple of leaves held in his hands. Once he finished with the bushes, the wardsmen told her he'd wander over to the trees, attempting to stick their leaves back on as well.

"Mornin'," he whispered in his usual tone. Bonnie had quickly become used to his soft raspings and his odd turns of phrase.

"How are the voices today?" Bonnie wasn't actually *worried* about Alfred, or his voices. He'd been tending the gardens for ten years now without incident—or so she'd been told after enquiring around. He was strange, no doubt about it, but harmless. In Bonnie's new routine, this question about voices in Alfred's head was as benign as asking after the weather.

"They're not voices…"

This was new.

"They just want me to *think* they're voices. They want us all to think they're voices. They're *real* creatures." He tightened his fist around his leaf and winced as it crumpled. "Argh…" he groaned, using the fingers of his other hand in a vain attempt to smooth out the new creases. "See? See what they made me do…"

"It's okay, Alfred," Bonnie smiled, patting him on the shoulder as she passed him. She knew there was no point arguing. It would only rile him up more. Instead, she deflected. "You're doing a wonderful job with the garden." Alfred perked up at this, turning back to his work, muttering under his breath again. Most of it illegible, as it always was, though she caught snippets of what he said. "Failed my destiny… We all failed… Now she's causing havoc. Causing mayhem up there. In the walls… It's in the walls…"

Bonnie gave him one final look, then pushed open the door to Buna House with a loud creak, stamping her feet to loosen the dewy grass and dirt she'd tracked inside. She kicked her shoes off, leaving them close enough to the stairs that she'd remember to bring them up with her after breakfast. She'd taken to eating breakfast in Buna House every day. In fact, when she was on the night shift, dinner was the only meal she'd have in the staff dining hall. Another *fun* task of working nights was being on kitchen duty. She thanked her lucky stars—all their lucky stars, really—that she worked alone in Ward Five. All the trainees and junior nurses who worked in pairs not only had the more difficult patients, they also had the job of preparing meals for all the nurses working a shift. Bonnie was no cook, despite her fine Italian ancestry on her Dad's side. Her nona was appalled.

Bubbles seemed to work *every* night shift. One of the few happy to do so. His whole family lived in Goulburn, and as an Italian himself, he loved to spend time with them. *All* of them. And from what he told her, there were *dozens*. It wasn't the nights he enjoyed, but the ten days off afterwards. So, she'd find herself chatting to him most nights they shared shifts, and he increasingly brought her meals to her himself. His meal, too, which they'd eat in companionable silence in the Ward Five office. Well…as silent as Ward Five ever got.

While Bonnie was still determined to repay Bubbles for his atrocious humour, she had to admit, when she heard stories about his pranks on *others,* it was enough to elicit "bubbles" of laughter from the pit of her stomach. Yes, Bonnie was quite content.

"Me trainee!" Lillian shouted loudly, throwing her arms wide as Bonnie stepped into their living area. She was another "patient" the nurses were happy to let loose early in the morning. Lillian's pot of coffee sat proudly on the table, with rolls and jam waiting beside it. The coffee was half empty and the crumbs across the table also told her the others had already imbibed. Probably on their way to handover from the night shift. But lately, Lillian always waited for Bonnie before drinking her own coffee and eating her own rolls.

"Morning ladies!" Bonnie echoed their gusto, grabbing the proffered cup of liquid gold and making a beeline for her favourite recliner, next to a lightly snoring Bertha. Lillian followed behind, a plate of rolls in her other hand, already buttered (generously) and lathered in fresh jam. "You are a gem, Lillian." She kissed the woman's dry, leathery cheek, feeling the woman's wrinkles deepen in a grin as she did so.

"How'd ya go last night, dear?" Lillian spoke in conspiratorial tones, and one of Bertha's eyes popped open. "D'ya mind those ghosts?"

Bonnie slurped from her coffee, then said, "You know I did. No more adventures into the attic for me."

"Hmgh," Bertha grunted as she sat upright, reaching for a roll. "And how 'bout that Jimmy fella. Did ya mind him as well?" She gave Lillian a knowing look as she grinned, losing her thin lips behind those gorgeous pillow cheeks.

Bonnie felt her own cheeks flush, and she buried her face in her coffee. "You know I hate Bubbles," she lied. When the silence stretched, she continued, "Okay, hate is a *strong* word. But I certainly don't *fancy* him. He's a rascal. You never know what you're going to get with that one!"

"Ah, but aren't they the best kind?" Lillian winked, carefully picking out her own roll. "The ones who keep you on your toes. Keep you entertained. You'd never be bored."

"Ha! That's for sure." Bonnie shook her head at the roll Lillian proffered. "No, I'm not too hungry this morning…"

"You're starting to waste away, me love. Ya need to keep those hips plump for Bubbles."

"Lillian!" Bonnie didn't mind the mothering that Lillian bestowed on her. In fact, so far from home, she rather enjoyed it.

"Who's plumping who's hips?" Gerald wandered into the room without anyone noticing, and her arrival elicited the same raucous welcome from the inebriates as it had for Bonnie. Gerald hadn't just grabbed a mug, but the entire coffee pot, and brought it with her to their small circle.

"*No one,*" Bonnie emphasised, lifting her mug to her lips only to realise it was already empty. She grabbed the roll from Lillian, if for no other reason than to have something to distract her mouth.

"I smell gossip," Gerald teased. She was dressed in jeans, the cuffs rolled up, and a long-sleeve shirt she'd tucked in at the waist.

After a pleasant half hour or so, Bonnie yawned widely, her hand unable to cover the gaping maw of tiredness. "Well, I'd better get on with the laundry." Lillian groaned as she stood, her own hips creaking loudly. She reached over for Gerald and Bonnie's empty coffee mugs without asking.

"And I doos the polishin'," Bertha said. Her trademark catchphrase. Bonnie sat for a moment after they'd shuffled off, building up the energy to grab her shoes, head to the bathroom, have a much-needed shower, and fall into bed.

"It's a shame their sentence is nearly up," Gerald muttered as she stood, collecting the now empty plate of crumbs.

"What do you mean?" Bonnie suddenly had the energy to stand up and anxiously follow behind Gerald.

"They were only given a six-month sentence this time," Gerald explained. "You know, they choose. Either six months in jail, or six months at Kenmore. They always choose Kenmore. Then it's back to the streets."

"But…but…"

"It's not fair, but it's the way of it. Don't worry. They'll be back. Those two always are."

"Back?" Perhaps it was the fog of much needed sleep calling her, but Bonnie struggled to follow.

"They'll be found drunk-and-disorderly at some point. Make a raucous. Get picked up by the cops, end up back in court, and then they'll be sentenced again. Usually just before winter. And back they'll come. For 'the cold times', to see themselves through the winter."

Bonnie felt her contentment take a small hit. She'd only just fallen into a routine that pleased her. And already, just like that, it'd be over all too soon.

———◦◊◦———

1915
ALICE: DAY 900 IN THE ASYLUM

HARRIET CLOSELY WATCHED Helen in the rec room. Only a small group had gathered today. Many of the girls had been confined to their rooms. With everything going on in Europe, staff levels were even more strained. As were resources. *Thank God we have our own farms and orchards, and we can trade with the nearby orphanage for bread…*

Any patient who caused too much trouble found themselves confined to their rooms for longer and longer stretches. Harriet felt awful, seeing the trend of defiance among the women being met with an increasingly vicious pattern of punishment. She couldn't quite put her finger on why it upset her so. It's not like the asylum staff had a choice. Worrying and complaining wouldn't bring more

153

pairs of qualified hands to help. And it certainly wouldn't suddenly cure their patients.

Helen paced the rec room, back-and-forth, back-and-forth. Her condition had become worse. At first, she paced only when anxious, and only during the day. Now, she paced any moment she was out of bed. Any moment she wasn't forced to sit and eat. She'd need a private room soon. Somewhere she could be safely restrained. Not just for the other patients' sake, but for Helen's own. As soon as a room became available, she'd ensure Helen took it. She just needed to find a moment with the matron or the Medical Superintendent to sway them. Both of them if she could.

A noise sounded from the attic. So faint that it was easy to miss. But this was another noise that Harriet had subconsciously trained herself to hear: the rhythmic tap-tap-tap of the chair leg in the only solitary room upstairs. A space that was half the size of the other patient bedrooms, hidden behind a white door. Though there was no need for a bed in that room. Just a chair.

Alice, Harriet thought, looking up at the high ceiling. *How long will they keep you in that chair this time?*

Tap-tap-tap.

Harriet glanced down and saw that Helen had paused to look up at the ceiling as well. As soon as the tapping faded, she resumed her pacing. Shivers ran their way through Harriet, from the pit of her stomach, to the tips of her toes, and all the way to the top of her head. *You listen for her, too,* she thought in shock and fear. *Is Alice the reason you're deteriorating so fast, Helen? Does she whisper to you at night, up there, in the attic?* The thoughts were irrational, but demanding. Insanity was *not* contagious. Besides, Helen was already a lunatic.

Harriet thought of a recent journal article written by an American doctor that she'd read in the staff library. From Nebraska, she thought, if memory served her well. George Elliott Howard, his name was. One of those proponents of "social psychology". *Insanity is not contagious*, Harriet thought firmly to herself, watching as Helen paused again each time the subtle tapping noises resumed. It felt like watching something monstrous. Like Alice was somehow transmitting her instructions—*her infections*—to Helen via morse code.

Insanity is not contagious.

And yet, parts of the journal article began to recite itself in Harriet's head against her will.

Social mind, social consciousness, inter-mental phenomena: these and similar terms convey a practical meaning sufficiently well understood… They imply a social-psychic life which transcends that of the single personality… In fact the isolated or absolute individual is a myth. The more keenly we scrutinize the genesis of personality the more the purely individual factors—if there be such—shrink in the vanishing perspective of human evolution. In the spectator-crowd, how very much of the relatively undisciplined social instincts or desires of forgotten generations wells up from the abyss of the unconscious or the subconscious?[1]

What is welling up from your abyss, Alice? Harriet found herself pondering. *What powerful springs of emotion and social action are you unleashing, just by your mere presence in the ward? What dramatic spectacle is Alice—the mere spectator—spearing us towards? And how will poor Helen survive?*

As Harriet turned back to her work, she couldn't help but mutter under her breath, the one line of Howard's that had plagued her most since she'd read that damned paper:

"The spectacle which the spectator molds, in its turn molds the spectator. The spectator is a being which feeds on its own offspring."

---

1   George Elliott Howard, "Social Psychology of the Spectator," American Journal of Sociology 18, no. 1 (July 1912): 33–50, https://doi.org/10.1086/212057.

2021
15 OCTOBER, 22:13

THE BOYS FOUND themselves in the largest room of Ward Fifteen. A broken piano sat in one corner, and debris and broken chairs filled every corner. The marble columns would once have gleamed brightly, but now they stood sadly in the red light of the torches, completely coated in dust. Here, six tall windows gaped over the outside world. The boys had pulled the red blinds closed as best they could. But inevitably, light still glimmered through the cracks. A beacon for the groundskeeper to help find them. They only had one torch lit, dimmed to its lowest setting, and even that paltry amount of light made Aiden's heart hammer.

He wasn't sure what was worse: the fear of being caught by the caretaker or the darkness beyond the dim glow that threatened to engulf them. The nagging thought that they weren't alone. That *things* waited in the corners. *Creatures.* That if they turned their lights off, they'd become infected by the spirits. Tagged, marked, and unable to flee. Aiden wished he could dull his vivid imagination or shut his brain off completely. They'd have to go to sleep soon.

"This'll do," Devin whispered, putting his pack down against one wall. He didn't remove his sleeping bag this time, instead slowly sat down, using the pack as a makeshift pillow. Prepared to run. Devin nodded at Aiden, encouraging him to sit as well. Aiden didn't even remove his pack, feeling the need to be primed to move even more keenly. "Switch the light off," Devin instructed. His voice wavered slightly, as though not sure himself of the sanity of that command.

Aiden's breath caught in his throat. The torch shook in his left hand, the other still clutching the camera. "I can't, man…" he began. "It'll be black as shit down here without the light."

Devin reached across and wrenched the torch from Aiden's limp fingers. "Fucking chickenshit." But he held no conviction in his voice and faltered as his fingers found the off switch. "Keep your camera on. We can see through the night vision mode, aye?" Devin nodded and the torch flicked off, plunging them into complete darkness.

Aiden held his breath until his eyes adjusted. The reflections on the windows glowed to life first. Then the edges of the windows and the columns. The dark gaping holes of the doors were next to emerge from the gloom as his pupils widened. He fumbled as he raised the camera up, panning it across the room, Devin's eyes fixed just as firmly on the screen as his own. Through the blurred green and grey image, they saw clearly enough. They were alone. Yet still, the feeling of intimidation refused to lessen.

Just as Aiden prepared to lean back against the wall, a sound rang out above them. Clear as day. Footsteps, in the attic. The camera jerked as he flicked it up towards the ceiling. Of course, he could see nothing but the green glow of the plaster. The footsteps continued. Slow. Methodical. *Pacing.* He could almost picture the feet, starting at one end of the attic and making their way to the other. Back-and-forth. Back-and-forth.

"The caretaker's inside," Devin hissed. "*Fuck!*"

CHAPTER SEVENTEEN

1916
ALICE: DAY 1,008 IN THE ASYLUM

Harriet sighed in relief as she followed her fellow nurses outside the door of Female Five. It had been a *long* day. Alice had been released from her solitary cell for the first time in months. With the wards still overcrowded, she'd gone straight to a bed in the attic, alongside Helen. Harriet had heard the two of them whispering after they'd been tucked into bed, while she waited for the Superintendent to complete his final rounds for the day. Helen, talking about how her husband was torturing their son. Alice, talking about how she knew Roy was at the orphanage next door. How Alice *knew* this, Harriet couldn't begin to fathom. Perhaps other nurses had careless tongues? Certainly, Roy had been caught on the grounds twice that month alone. But Alice had been in solitary. There was no way she could have known.

"I'm going to take him home," Alice had whispered to Helen. *"Don't worry. I'll take them all home. All the lost children."*

As if thinking of the boy had somehow summoned him, Roy's little face suddenly appeared in front of Harriet. Stark white in the night, reflecting the light of the moon in pasty hues. Shocked, she gulped air and blinked several times, in case this apparition she'd summoned might disappear. It didn't. In fact, it became more and more real by the moment. His gasping breaths grew in intensity as he stared at her, terrified. Frozen in place like a rabbit caught in the glare of a predator. He was bigger than the last time she'd seen him.

"Please…" the boy mouthed silently, his lower lip trembling long after he'd finished whispering the word. Rational little Harriet baulked. Did she delay because she was just tired from an already long day? Or did she delay because she truly felt sorry for the wretched thing? Perhaps the latter, because she knew it would make no difference what she did. He would never stop coming. Not so long as he knew his mother was there.

Before Harriet made up her mind, the little boy started bawling. He threw his head back, curling his hands into rigid fists at his sides, as though having a seizure. The sound of the air expelling from his tiny lungs sounded similar enough to the ethereal, bone-grinding moans that the patients with the falling disease sometimes emitted in their own moments of rigour. Harriet felt a brittleness in her sternum from the utter and complete sadness that coalesced there.

"Oh, for heaven's sake! You *bloody* nuisance!" Drawn by the sound, the on-duty Charge Nurse swept out of the darkness and roughly grabbed the boy by his arm.

The Superintendent emerged straight behind her, talking firmly, but without real conviction, "Off you go, you larrikin. Back to St John's! We've no time for you tonight."

"Matthew, we *can't* just leave him…"

"Hush, it'll be alright. This is the only time we've had since—" He cut off as Harriet cleared her throat.

The sound had been almost involuntary, and her face bloomed crimson under their scrutiny. Apparently, she and Roy had interrupted a nighttime rendezvous. The boy, none the wiser, continued snivelling, wiping his sleeve to catch the snot that dribbled down his face as freely as his tears.

"And you are?" Matthew said tightly; the night wasn't so dark that he couldn't recognise a woman he'd *literally* just seen on his rounds.

"It's Nurse Harriet Davies," the Charge Nurse said flatly, her own cheeks a slight shade of pink. She gazed between Roy and Harriet, and a small smile lifted up one side of her face. "Harriet, perfect. You can take this boy to see the matron. At once."

"I—" Harriet sighed, pushing her fatigue deeper into her bones. Any resistance against her two superiors was futile, no matter how tired she was. "Yes, ma'am."

It didn't take long for the two midnight lovers to depart, thus continuing with their evening affair, leaving Harriet holding Roy's sticky, grimy hand alone. It looked like he wore the same clothes as every other time she'd seen him. Not just the same uniform, but the exact same set, now too short at the wrists and ankles. She sniffed, wondering if the clothes had been washed at all. She guided him through the gardens towards the administrative building. He looked over his shoulder at Female Five at every second step, stumbling and yanking at her arm.

"Mama's in there," he finally said, just before the ward fell from view. Harriet stopped, grasping the boy by both shoulders and turning him to face her.

"But how do you *know*?" She squatted down to his level, not so much to make him feel more at ease, but so she could drill into his eyes with her own. Her curiosity demanded an answer, even if she refused to give him affirmation. Because Alice always seemed to know as well. "What makes you so sure?"

"I just feel it…" he trailed off. "She always said we could feel each other, in our hearts, no matter what happened. No matter where we went. No matter what Daddy did…" The boy's piercing eyes were so akin to his mother's. So deep and dark. In the dim light, his round, black pupils nearly filled him up, making him seem even more inhuman. Even more alien.

"I *don't* understand." She stood up and grabbed his hand again. "But you can't keep coming here, Roy. You'll never find your mother. You can't feel her. That's not how the human body works."

Roy just sniffled and began crying again. At least this time, instead of bellowing, he just sobbed every now and then as his breath caught in his throat. And snorted, too, when his tears became too heavy for him to breathe through his little nose.

Harriet exhaled deeply when they finally arrived outside the matron's office door. Unsurprisingly, light still shone beneath it. The matron had a reputation for starting work early and finishing late. Who she was outside the asylum—if anyone—was a mystery.

"You be on your best behaviour," she whispered between gritted teeth. "None of that horrid sniffling. Real boys don't cry."

Harriet pushed the door inwards after the matron called for them to enter. The matron's face darkened the instant it fell on the boy. And this was a face that was *always* dark. Always pinched. Always scowling. The old woman took on the features of a wicked witch when her eyebrows furrowed low enough to obscure her eyes.

"*Again*, Roy?" the matron spat. "What will Sister Margaret have to say? How many lashings did you get last time, hm? I think we'll at least have to double it!"

"I want my Ma!" Roy wailed, his grip tightening on Harriet's hand, his nails painfully digging into her palm. "I want her! I want her! I want her! *I want her!*"

The matron emerged from the other side of the desk as Roy's tantrum erupted. A deafening crack split the air as her hand fell across the side of his face. Again. The boy instantly fell silent. He wrenched free from Harriet and fell to the ground, stunned. It took a moment for him to turn and face the matron again, his mouth gaping, face slack, and eyes vacant. A large red mark already bloomed on his cheek.

As Roy's eyes finally came into focus, the matron, still staring down her nose at him, whispered venomously, "Your mother is *dead*." She let the words sink in for a moment before repeating. "Your cow of a mother is *dead*. She's not here anymore. She's food for the worms."

Roy's mouth still hung open as he struggled to comprehend the lie the matron fed him. Harriet, who'd thought herself immune to having empathy for the runt, felt something break inside her.

"But…but I *feel* her. In my heart," he sobbed. He held a small fist over his left breast.

"You feel her *ghost* haunting you, young man. Now, if I ever see you here again, you mark my words, I'll send you to the mines. The world will *never* see you again. Am I clear?"

And she was. Like crystal. Harriet could see his acceptance, his devastation, reflecting clearly in those piercing black eyes. The lie had worked.

2021
15 OCTOBER, 22:59

Aiden and Devin sat as rigidly still as statues, listening as the footsteps paced above them. It lasted five minutes, perhaps, and no more. Yet it felt an eternity. By the time the feet finished tracking their path above them, Aiden picked out a pattern to it. The feet were lightweight; definitely a woman. They followed the same path from one wall to the other at the same slow pace. Unlike the groundskeeper's, though, these feet *shuffled*. As though dragged forlornly. These didn't sound like the steps of the determined, self-appointed policewoman of Kenmore, Hell-bent on finding intruders. No, these were something else. Something depressed, even grieving—no matter what Devin said.

Just as the footsteps faded, the battery icon on the digital video camera flashed angrily at Aiden. "Fuck, the battery is going dead…"

"You got the spares, though?" Devin's voice sounded nothing like his usual bravado. He didn't even attempt to hide his fear. Aiden nodded, the movement barely visible in the gloom of the darkened building. He pulled his pack off his shoulders to rummage through the contents. "We keep the camera on at all times," Devin continued. "I don't care how many hours we need to cut in the edit. This place is *fucked* at night." He shivered, his voice shaking, too.

"It's like it's alive," Aiden agreed, fixating on that same metaphor, his fingers fumbling as he ejected the depleted battery. "Not just haunted, but *fucking alive*. And pissed off."

"Wouldn't you be?" Devin's whisper became frantic. "This place is trashed. Everything's been stolen, or broken, or just fucking rotted."

A noise broke the silence. Aiden fumbled and dropped the fresh battery, his fingers numb from shock. It sounded like something heavy and plastic being placed roughly on the floor. Only a stone's throw away from them. The sound was *too real*. Their senses heightened, the two peered through the dark for any unseen person. After a brief, breathless pause, the sound of wheels rattled loudly across the floorboards.

Aiden and Devin leapt to their feet, frantically pushing up against the wall and each other for purchase. Every detail sharpened. The edges of the columns. The blinds flapping gently in the breeze. Aiden's heart thumping. The cold sweat that trickled down the centre of his back.

A sploshing noise followed, as though something wet rubbed across the floor. *A mop?*

The two boys took a tentative step forward, still clutching at each other. The source of the sound materialised before them. Aiden's mind tried to deny what he saw just as quickly as his eyes sent pictures whizzing up to his brain. A *shadow* formed within the darkness. Incredibly round. Huge—a monster of a being, in human form. It *was* mopping, dragging a shadow bucket along behind it. Cleaning the dusty floor with invisible water.

"Argh—Ah—Aaah!" Devin clawed at Aiden's arms as though trying to hold on to something real, anything living, to drive away the impossible images lingering in front of him. He trembled so badly that he shook Aiden's entire body. Though, perhaps, Aiden did a good enough job of that himself.

The figure glanced up at the noise, bright white eyes blinking at them through the darkness. As if by unseen hands, Aiden felt his breath snatched away, leaving him feeling raw and violated. It had *seen* them. It was *seeing* them. And no matter how many times Aiden blinked, wishing this nightmare over, wishing this illusion or hallucination finished, the creature continued standing there. Staring.

"I doos the polishin'," the voice suddenly grated, deep and thumping. So much bass in it that it disturbed the dust hanging in the air.

Devin screamed again, pushing at Aiden in his attempt to run. He didn't even bother to pick up his pack from the ground. Aiden didn't pause to grab it, or the battery he'd dropped, either. His own pack was still slung over one shoulder, and his hand gripped the camera tightly. They didn't even look where they ran, simply headed for the closest door and out into the hallway beyond.

1953
SPRING

"I HAVE A story that will shake you out of your knickers," Bonnie said conspiratorially, leaning across the dining table to whisper to Gerald and Patsy. The two older nurses had the day off together for the first time in a *long time*. And Bonnie, who'd just finished her night shift, was eager to soak up the company before her weary body demanded she return to Buna House to rest.

The hard, yet watery, scrambled eggs and cold, dry toast placed before her did nothing to whet her appetite. She thought of Lillian and Bertha again, a twinge of longing hitting her chest as she remembered them fondly. They'd been gone close to a month now and *how she missed them*. She often wondered where they were, what they were doing, and if they still ate buns and jam. It wasn't just the coffee and the buns she missed, but their company. They would have loved this story, too.

"Go on, then," Gerald said as she sipped from her second cup of dark, bitter brew.

"I heard noises again last night." Gerald rolled her eyes at Bonnie, but she continued regardless. "Not just the footsteps this time, either. I heard a tapping and scraping, as if it came from *inside* the walls. Like someone was trapped inside."

"I've heard that, too," Patsy murmured, twirling her fork through her own breakfast. "So have the others." This earned Patsy her own eye roll from Gerald.

"Well, I followed the noises out to the rec hall. And you won't believe it, but I *saw something*. A dark, black figure crouching inside the fireplace. I'd pulled the cover back so I could sweep the ashes out, you see. The figure had white, shining eyes that glared at me like the devil. And then it screamed like only a demon could, higher pitched than any human. Like it was Lucifer summoning the army of Hell to his side."

"You *did not*," Patsy said, whilst reaching out a hand to clasp Bonnie's, leaning in further for the next part of the story.

"I did. I was *terrified*. I thought this was the end of me, for sure. And then it came *out* from the fireplace, writhing along the ground on all four limbs. I thought I was going to faint! But I turned on my flashlight, and…" She paused for dramatic effect. Even Gerald's interest had been piqued. "It was a possum."

A moment's silence, and then Gerald burst into her monosyllabic guffaws of laughter. Patsy joined in after a moment, wiping away a tear.

"Oh my *Lord*, child!" Patsy chided, a hand over her heart. "You about nearly scared me to death! A *possum*! You've been spending too much time with Bubbles, getting us all worked up like that."

"It must be living in the chimney," Bonnie shrugged, bringing her own cup of coffee to her lips, deflecting the Bubbles comment. The drink was weaker, and yet somehow more bitter, than Lillian's brews had ever been.

"I thought you'd seen Alice," Patsy sighed, pushing her plate away from her and leaning back in her chair.

"Alice? You've mentioned her before. What *is* her story? The full story?"

"Well…" Patsy drew a breath, readying to rival Bonnie's own storytelling. "Plenty of nurses say they've seen her in Ward Five. Or at least heard her pacing the floors. They describe her as a black shadow, a wisp of a human. They usually see her in the attic."

"Why the attic?"

"Because that's where she spent most of her time here at Kenmore. Mostly in that little room they have up there, tied to a chair, for months at a time."

Bonnie remembered the room. The one with the white door that had creaked open and closed the night Bubbles had tried to scare her. "Why was she here?" she asked curiously, pulling at one of her sleeve cuffs.

"Story goes, her husband dropped her off here when he got sick of her. He had a young squeeze on the side who he wanted to make things right by. So he ditched his wife so he could remarry the new, pretty young thing. He even abandoned their son in St John's orphanage next door. Wanted a *full* fresh start. Claimed both of them were bonkers. Wanted nothing around the house to remind him of his first wife."

"I've heard that story before…" Bonnie started, thinking of Cora and the many other women she'd heard were left at the asylum when they became a nuisance. Thankfully, it happened less and less as the decades went on, but still…too many forgotten wives walked these halls.

"But *Alice*…" Gerald tsked, leaning back in her chair dramatically. "There was something wrong with that one. Something violent. Something *inhuman*. The way she died, all—"

"That's quite enough."

The three of them turned to see Nurse Hatchet standing over their backs, her face entirely darkened by a scowl, the likes of which Bonnie had never seen before. Even though it looked to be a relatively warm spring day, ice suddenly descended on Bonnie's shoulders at the realisation that the woman had been standing right behind them. And for how long?

"I'll tolerate no more gossip. *Especially* not about patients. You lot need to have some respect. Nothing good ever comes from antagonising the dead."

CHAPTER EIGHTEEN

1916
ALICE: DAY 1,122 IN THE ASYLUM

ALICE HAS SETTLED, hasn't she? Harriet thought to herself as she watched the woman circling the yard with Helen. Not only was she quiet, listening, even contrite, but she was also able to *eat* with the others, *wash* with the others, *walk* with the others. It was like she'd transformed into an entirely different person. *Ever since Roy stopped coming,* she thought, not for the first time. She still didn't believe in psychic connections between two people, no matter how close they were. There was no basis for such fanciful claims. Even as she denied it, though, unease continued to roil in her blood, and her thoughts flickered, as they often did, to something else she'd recently read that had also stuck in her mind.

Her Father had bought her a book for her birthday that year. Told her it had been written by a fine Englishman who'd spent the better part of a year travelling Switzerland, returning to England to publish his collection of twenty short stories in 1910. *The Lost Valley*, by Algernon Blackwood. Her Father no doubt thought it was a collection of memoirs, travel journals, or European history. If he'd known what it was, she doubted he'd have given it to her. Perhaps he might have burnt it. The book had been fascinating, yes, but foul, too. Dealing with loss and horror, the supernatural and the macabre. Yes, it had offered glimmers of hope and redemption, but it had been the ghoulish and unknown that had stuck with her.

As she thought of Roy and Alice, *The Lost Valley* recited itself again in her head. "*…they were not so much one soul split in twain, as two souls fashioned in precisely the same mould…*" This was exactly how she felt about the mother and son. The same dark, piercing eyes. The same, singular intent to reunite. The same passion that bordered on madness. Or, perhaps in reality, it was their madness that bordered on passion. *The Lost Valley* was a story of two brothers so strongly bonded that one had given up his life so the other might live and love without him. "*One of us has to go…*" It had been a long and torturous farewell that had lingered beyond the grave. It made her think of Alice and Roy. Perhaps the lie the matron had told Roy about his mother had allowed him to let go, finally. To give up, and in doing so, to free Alice as well. "*One of us has to go…*"

Harriet shook herself free of the thought, refocusing on Alice and Helen. Pacing. *That* had only got worse for Helen since Alice was set free. And while the other staff claimed to have cured Alice with their chair-bound torture, nothing *inside* Alice seemed to have broken. She was thinner, yes. Looked older, yes. Knew when to put her head down, and when it was safe to hold it high.

Her eyes, though, still held that dark depth and fiery intelligence. She still veritably buzzed with energy. If Harriet was being truthful with herself, the thought of Alice loose in Female Five terrified her. She couldn't shake the belief that nothing they'd done had actually helped. Only Roy's absence had shifted something. Inconceivably. *How does she even know he doesn't come anymore…?* It felt like they celebrated too soon. It felt like the insanity had merely been covered by a loose, moth-eaten sheet that might blow free at any moment. And the winds were building. She couldn't shake the feeling that Alice hadn't let go. She was merely *waiting.*

2021
15 OCTOBER, 23:16

THE HALLWAY WAS much darker than the open recreation room. Aiden and Devin couldn't adjust their eyes with such little natural light, and they banged into walls and into each other just as often as they progressed forwards. Rounding one corner, panting and frantic, they saw a beam of moonlight strewn across the deep blue carpet. Without having to give notice to the other, both boys scrambled for it. Aiden reached it first, and Devin barrelled into him from behind, nearly toppling him in his terror to get inside.

They both spun back towards the door, which opened to nothing but blackness. Devin raced forward, hand outstretched to slam it shut, and Aiden managed to halt him just in time. "No! Wait! You might lock us inside!" Relief burst within Aiden's chest as Devin grabbed the door right at the last moment, ensuring it didn't quite close all the way. A strip of darkness still welcomed them. Whether to freedom, or to whatever else lurked out there, was yet to be seen.

Aiden realised they'd entered a patient's room. A flower-patterned curtain still hung from the window, badly torn, and flung open to allow the moon to shine through the thick-pane windows. The type of window that had only small squares of glass—the type they couldn't climb through. *Designed to keep people in*, Aiden thought, as his eyes flickered back to the thick, heavy door and its large lock. *What if Devin had trapped us inside?*

A bed frame was still in the room, devoid of any mattress or sheets, sagging as though it still held the weight of all its patients over the years. A wardrobe stood against one wall, both doors firmly shut. A thick layer of dust covered everything.

Both boys listened. It was hard to pick up any sound over the noise of their own hearts grinding against their ribs, or of their breaths panting.

"I don't think it followed us," Devin finally said. Perhaps more to convince himself than from any genuine conviction. "What the fuck… Did we—did we just see a *ghost?*"

The two had their YouTube channel up and going properly for only a couple of months, but they'd done a fair bit of exploring in that time, as well as in the time before its creation. They'd seen and heard weird things. Unexplainable things. Felt them, too, like cold spots or nausea. Once, they'd even caught a glimpse of a shadow from the corner of their eye. On camera, they could almost see it if they enhanced and brightened it enough. That had all been exciting, compelling. Just a teaser, a taste, enough to encourage them to keep adventuring.

What they'd just seen had been something completely different. Something all too real. And at the same time, maddeningly false. A contradiction their brains struggled to process.

It may have had the shape of a human, but it had been pitch-black as well. Darker than the surrounding night. Sucking up the light. Its proportions had been slightly off. At first glance, it appeared too small; the next, larger than any humanoid had any right to be. It had moved too quickly, too inhumanly. And its voice, the sounds it made, were so clear, but incredibly loud. Like it *intended* to capture their attention. It wasn't right; Aiden felt like they'd stood right next to the creature—not across an empty hallway.

"We weren't filming…" Aiden mumbled, looking down at the camera he still clutched in his hands. He wasn't going back for that battery, ever. He didn't care that they cost more than $50 a pop.

Devin gave him a quick glance, then turned to the window. He walked slowly to it and looked back and forth across the gardens outside. "I can't see the groundskeeper… She's either still upstairs or fucked off."

"If that even was her in the attic before," Aiden gritted his teeth as he said it, flopping down onto the cold floor with his legs crossed. He let the camera fall into his lap so he could put his head between his hands. "I just want to get the fuck out of here."

"I'm not going back that way," Devin said firmly, pacing, one eye always on either the window or the door. "It was *right* in the path to the doors. Like it was there on purpose. I'm not fighting my way past a fucking dead cunt."

Aiden shivered from the cold. He couldn't stop shaking.

"Did you get any building plans of this place?" Devin continued. "When you found the maps?"

Aiden shook his head in answer. There'd been nothing. At least, nothing online. They'd entered the building through the catwalk, via the attic, so that was still an exit option. Except they'd heard those footsteps. And if it hadn't been the caretaker, then maybe it was one of *them*.

"I don't know all the ways out," he said, realising the gravity of the words as he spoke them aloud. "I don't know all the ways out…"

1953
SPRING

Bonnie whooped as the hard, red leather cricket ball whacked into the wickets. Patsy cheered on one side of her, with Bubbles on the other. The local Goulburn men's cricket team had taken up the Kenmore team's challenge of a friendly game, and their side was *whooping* them. The Goulburn team batted first and had scored only ten runs with three wickets down. It was enough to make Bonnie consider joining the women's cricket club. "Take that, you chicken-hearted fop-doodles!"

"My, my," Bubbles chastised sarcastically. "And I thought I was spending my day with a lady." Patsy glared over Bonnie's head at him. "Sorry, *ladies*." He gestured widely, also taking in the patients who had been allowed to join them in the stands. They also applauded, in their own way.

"Who said us ladies wanted to spend our afternoon with *you?*" Janet teased, her whole body loose and relaxed as she leant forward, flopping her arms at him, laughing.

"*Touche.*" Bubbles smiled and leant back, kicking one leg up over his knee as he turned his attention back to the game.

With a sly grin, Bonnie swivelled to Janet and winked. Janet really had taken a turn for the better. Not just a turn, a full 180. Her medication had brought her back from the brink of mania to the edge of civilisation. Barely a year or so older than Bonnie herself, she found Janet to be some of the most pleasurable company on offer in the asylum as of late. She couldn't reconcile this witty, calm lady with the same skittish creature that had hurled her chamber pot at her. Bonnie would be pleased to see the woman eventually sent back to her family, perhaps well-medicated indefinitely, but free. Still, it would be yet another person she would miss terribly.

"Ref!" Bubbles cried, cupping his hands around his mouth. "The batter is *damaging the pitch!* Look at him!" He turned to gesture at Bonnie. "He's guarding from the centre. Rubbish."

Bonnie scoffed and turned her attention to Patsy and Janet, not so worried when the game was slowing pace as it was. "I hear you're going on nights tomorrow, Patsy." She had a sly, teasing tone to her voice. No doubt buoyed by the infectious company and atmosphere of the game. Of being surrounded by patients and colleagues who she thought of more as family. A strange family, albeit, but one she loved deeply.

"Oh, don't even remind me!" Patsy spoke in short, clipped tones, stamping a foot as she did.

"It's not that bad, Patsy," Janet said and smiled, patting the woman on the wrist. "We're a pretty well-behaved bunch…for the most part…" Bonnie could tell from the slight hollowness to Janet's eyes and tone that she *was* looking forward to leaving Kenmore soon. And so she should. The asylum was no place for the cured.

Patsy tsked as she answered, "It's not *you* I'm worried about, dear."

"It's the ghosts in the attic," Bonnie whispered. Not a conversation she'd have with just any patient, but the others were distracted enough. And Janet had become more of a friend than a charge in her mind.

"Oh, yes, we know all about them." Janet's tone fell serious. "And *not* the ones with flesh and blood and pulses." She glared at Bubbles as she said this, who remained fixated on the game. "It's Alice, isn't it? The one who paces upstairs in the attic and bangs around sometimes."

Patsy shivered head to toe, despite the gentle warmth to the day.

"And as soon as one patient hears her up there, they all go off, don't they, Bonnie?"

Bonnie thought about it a moment, then nodded half-heartedly. "Sometimes, yes. Sometimes it's hard to know what might be a ghost and what's just a patient having a night terror or some other small episode. It all seems to happen during the same night. It's either quiet, or it's not."

"They kept her chained up for *months* at a time, did I tell you?" Bubbles picked up the conversation—one of his favourite topics— and couldn't help but weigh in. The ladies rolled their eyes in almost perfect unison. "Okay, so you've heard that one. But did you know that she was so crazed because she was trying to get back to her son, Roy? He was dumped in the boy's orphanage next door and always tried to get back to his Mum, too, but never could."

"How do you even know all this?" Bonnie tried, but failed, to keep some of the respect and awe at his resourcefulness from her tone. Patsy seemed awed by something, but not his apparent inside knowledge. Her pinched mouth and rolled eyes demonstrated disbelief at his horrid imagination instead. There was more white than anything else to her eyes as he continued talking.

"I have my ways." He tapped the side of his nose. "Anyway, the matron finally told the boy rascal that his Mum was dead, and he stopped coming. And Alice *killed herself*. Like she knew he'd given up on her. I reckon Alice is the Grey Lady people see walking the halls some nights, hey? Still looking for her lost son."

"You need to dye your white sheet grey, then," Bonnie mocked.

"Hey! I'm a struggling artist. I do my best with what I have. There's also stories 'roundabouts of a stunted boy, muzzled and chained, somewhere on the grounds."

"Oh, that's just poppycock!" Patsy's tone had become angry now. "Who would even think up something so awful!"

"That's not the worst of the stories you'll hear over on the male side."

"Hm?" Janet leant towards him, both elbows resting on her upper thighs. She'd maintained calm indifference through the whole conversation thus far.

"Well…" Bubbles looked around conspiratorially, dramatically so, before whispering. "One of the doctors went *nuts* himself. Before my time. Probably even before old Patsy's time too." She scoffed. "He couldn't take it anymore. All the insanity around him, and he went loopy himself. One day, they found him in the morgue. He'd cut himself open and sprayed his blood all over the walls!"

Patsy had enough then. She pulled her square shoulders up to their full height and smacked Bubbles with a rolled-up *Women's Weekly* magazine. His mock cries of pain just encouraged her to keep smacking him as hard as she could, the occasional sharp whipping noise interspersing as her makeshift weapon hit him at just the right angle with just the right wind behind it. *Then* the cries he emitted weren't mocking.

Bonnie, ducking, shifted seats to sit beside Janet. Chuckling, she accepted the woman's hand as it reached out to her, and they sat in companionable silence—well, they were silent amidst the mini-riot beside them—watching the game.

Bonnie's mind wandered, thinking of something both Bubbles and Janet had said. Janet, that the patients always riled up when the supposed ghosts did. And Bubbles, that the doctor (if that story had even held remote grains of truth) had been infected by insanity himself. *Is madness catching?*

The staff library contained plenty of materials on this subject. Or at least, on a subject vaguely similar. The earliest books in the library talked about social psychology—the psychology of the group rather than the individual. More recent articles talked about behavioural contagion; she'd devoured anything she could get her hands on about that topic.

An article published in 1950 by Polansky, Lippitt and Redl— leaders in the field of psychology—had been particularly compelling. *An Investigation of Behavioural Contagion in Groups.* They'd become interested in the subject themselves after observing the behaviour of patients during group therapy sessions. Bonnie had written favoured phrases down, re-reading them in her room in Buna

House on the days (or nights) when her shifts hadn't overlapped with her friends. She thought back to them now…

"The spreading of a mood, an attitude, a behaviour from one person to another, or through a whole group, is a phenomenon long familiar to the social psychologist…always with a sense that something rather important was happening in the communications between the individuals concerned, and always with a sense that what was happening was instantaneous, unpredictable, and somehow rather mysterious."[2]

The words recited in her head like poetry, rather than a medical journal. It certainly seemed a little fantastical. That just the sense of something mysterious could compel one's emotions and very beliefs until an entire group altered their behaviour. Thereby making that mystery, that fable, into truth.

Like ghosts? Fear was certainly a contagious emotion. *But are the ghosts contagious, or is it the insanity? Which sets off the patients of Female Five at night? And which precedes the other?*

Another thought struck Bonnie as she watched the batters running from wicket-to-wicket: *Whatever happened to Roy?*

THE GROUNDS OF Kenmore have never been quiet, not really. It's not just spirits that haunt its walls, closing and opening doors, pacing the floors. It's the stories. Their stories. My story. Twisted, sometimes. Turned into something new. Taking on their own forces.

Stories have power. They're catching too. Almost as catching as madness.

---

2   Norman Polansky, Ronald Lippitt and Fritz Redl, "An Investigation of Behavioural Contagion in Groups", Human Relations, Vol 3, Issue 1, January 1950, p.319, https://doi.org/10.1177/001872675000300401

CHAPTER NINETEEN

1953
SUMMER

BONNIE, GERALD, AND Patsy flew down the highway, the windows rolled down and the breeze attacking their hair with desperate, clutching fingers. For the most part, their well-fixed hairdos remained safe beneath their bandanas, pins, and several layers of hairspray. Gerald was behind the wheel, a cigarette dangling from her mouth and her well-coiffed curls not budging an inch. They drove Bubbles's Holden. One of the first 48-215s to roll off the production line during the preceding decade. Bonnie could almost hear then-Prime Minister Chifley's words ringing in her ears as they sped down the roads: *"She's a beauty!"* Like the rest of her family, she'd sat in front of the neighbour's TV, utterly transfixed, as she'd watched it happen. That historic moment when Australia's car industry was born. Bonnie couldn't help but agree with Chifley, patting the pale-green metal fondly through her open window. *She's a beauty!*

Not far out of Goulburn, they'd passed many a truck, their loads of boxes, sacks, or milk jugs jiggling pleasantly. They'd even passed a nomad pulling his cart with four donkeys abreast, which had elicited squeals of delight from Bonnie. Quite uncharacteristically, admittedly, though she didn't care. As soon as the three friends realised they all had the same weekend off, the excitable squeals had begun building inside her. No doubt existed in her mind—or within the minds of her friends, really—that this weekend would be something special.

It had almost been enough to take my mind off Alfred, she thought to herself, tucking a stray strand of brown hair back behind her ear. She gazed out of her window, but didn't really see what flew past her. Alfred had disappeared completely just a week before. She hadn't even noticed the first couple of days, just thought he must have taken ill, or tended to another part of the garden. Only when someone had asked her about the last time she'd seen him did she realise something was amiss.

He'd apparently left his bed early one morning, as he always did, and never returned. Never even made it to the garden. Bonnie had wracked her brain for any clues, trying to remember what he'd said. He never said anything that made much sense, though. Just carrying on about the voices and the walls. Like he always did.

Gerald and Patsy's chuckling brought her attention back, and she focussed once more on their road trip. As they approached the Hume Highway to Sydney, potholes replaced the dust, and their speed reduced to a more measured pace. The larger, more modern trucks on the roads had rutted the sides of the highway. Now, approaching the outskirts of Sydney, the roads were black and glistening, and *full* of noise and traffic. Men and women called loudly above the din; women in sundresses, men in suits, blue-collar workers in nothing but their shorts. Their sun-tanned bodies glistened from sweat. Buses, motorcycles, and other cars sped around them. The odd green and yellow tram clacked by, an advertisement displayed on its body reminding everyone that the latest *Women's Weekly* magazine was now available for purchase. They would take the tram later, Bonnie remembered with glee, after parking the car at Gerald's Aunt's house, where they'd stay the night.

Less than two hours later, well-fed by the elderly Aunt and dressed in their evening finest, the three women bounced along the tram into the heart of Sydney. Bonnie stood, holding onto the seat for balance, to look out of the window at the lights flicking by them. *So much light*, she thought, comparing the life and roar of the city to the darkness of Kenmore. *I'm not tense*, she thought, finally labelling this feeling of hers. *I'm finally relaxed.* She stood more erect as Patsy pulled the wire above them, dinging the bell to indicate they wanted the next stop.

Her heart beat fast. She swung her hips, enjoying the sensation of her full-bodied skirts swishing around her knees. She'd sewn the dress herself. Made from a lovely navy fabric with white polka-dots, well-fitted at the bodice, and with a delightfully daring V-neck that went all the way to the tips of her shoulders. Gerald had taken her attire one step further, exposing both of her shoulders with thin spaghetti straps. Her bodice also fit snugly around her waist, but bloomed over her bosom, giving the illusion of fullness. The bright yellow with patterned flowers almost matched the tram. Only Patsy, with her heavy-set shoulders, dressed more modestly, wearing a sleeveless green dress with a rounded collar and a skirt that reached almost all the way down to her ankles.

Bonnie felt like she'd emerged into some kind of adult playground as her heels alighted on the bitumen. Lights glistened *everywhere*. Streetlamps, strings of bulbs draped above them, and giant signs advertising cigarettes, soft drinks, bars, restaurants and more illuminating the towering buildings. Her senses were immediately overwhelmed by the thick smell of cigarettes and densely congregating human bodies. A stench of restaurant grease and car exhaust—and somewhere amidst it all, a sick that smelt of vinegar and wine—was made even more heady by the heat.

The pavement and buildings seemed to sizzle with it, flushing her cheeks.

"Isn't it marvellous!" Bonnie beamed, grabbing Gerald's hand. "Where should we go first?"

"I hear The Roosevelt has topless servers now," Gerald yelled over the din, winking at Patsy, who scoffed and crossed her arms across her chest.

"*Really!* Next thing you know, they'll have full strippers, just like they do in America."

"I've seen enough topless women to last me a lifetime," Bonnie yelled back, only half in jest. No matter the apparent novelty of a topless restaurant, *that* wasn't a sight she wished to see. And she doubted they'd be allowed into such gentlemen's establishments, anyway.

"I know just the place." Gerald grabbed Patsy with her other free hand and navigated across the busy road. "A wine bar I've heard of has cheap booze, good music, and even better company."

Gerald quickly manoeuvred them away from the bright, shining lights and into the darker corners of Sydney's King's Cross. The crowds thinned, though the cigarette smoke in the air remained just as full and hazy. Perhaps even more so.

"*How* did you hear about this place?" Patsy asked suspiciously as she stepped over a puddle that looked —and smelt—suspiciously like the wine vomit Bonnie had picked up on before.

"From the inebriates, of course. Who else knows the best place in town for a drink?"

Bonnie's heart fluttered even more at the thought of seeing that crowd again. They were so far from Goulburn, yet she'd certainly heard Lillian talk about Sydney often enough. In fact, she knew she'd heard one or two tales about a wine bar in its dark corners and the characters who frequented it. Gerald had obviously gone

one step further and secured the address. The acrid stench of regurgitated vino suddenly didn't seem so off-putting.

"Ladies!"

The three of them spun at the sound of the gruff, worried voice. A tall policeman in his dark navy suit with gleaming buttons jogged to catch up to them, a torch swinging from one hand. His thin black tie hung slightly askew against his white shirt, but his cap was well-placed on his head and his face was well-shaven. *He must only be about my age*, Bonnie thought to herself as he came to a stop before them, his shining black shoes mere inches from the spew puddle.

"Ladies, are you alright? Are you lost?"

Patsy chuckled in her deep, breathy way, but Gerald gave her barking "ha!" laugh that took the officer aback. She said, "No, no sir. We're quite alright. We're here to see if some friends of ours are out for the night. Just at that wine bar on the corner."

The officer looked over their shoulders, puzzled at first, and then with increasing concern etching the youthful lines around his eyes. "Male friends, then, is it?"

The chuckles soured, and Gerald's thin lips pinched in a way that would make Nurse Hatchet proud. Her tone was harsh from decades of cigarettes as she replied, "No. Some *lady* friends, actually."

"Ma'am, I take it you're from out of town. You mustn't know this part of Sydney too well. There are some rough sorts about. I can escort you to a much more pleasant bar for your evening drink."

"Perhaps later," Bonnie said in her best youthful, fresh, and wistful voice. Eager to move the conversation along. She knew her normally tanned skin had paled from her months at Kenmore, and that her bosom—on full display—heaved and glistened softly in the minimal light. Creamier, brighter, and more youthful than it ever had been before, under the harsh sun of Gundagai. She played into it. "I really want to see our friends. We'll only have one drink."

He paused for a moment, sizing them up. "I'll be waiting for you out here," he finally said gruffly, straightening his perfect hat and leaving his crooked tie. "One drink, right? If anything goes awry, just come straight back to me, you see?"

The three nodded and practically shoved each other in their haste to make it to the door for a chance to peek behind the curtain of Lillian and her comrades' lives.

Even though Bonnie knew just from the seedy smell and the officer's warning to not have high standards, the establishment still smacked her in the face on entry like an old, wet toilet brush. She supposed the carpets had been blue, once upon a time, but they were now so dark, damp and sticky, it was hard to tell. The lights seemed even dimmer inside, if at all possible. Perhaps the dark wood sucked away the light. At first, she thought it glimmered from polish. Then she realised it was more of the same sticky substance that coated the floor.

If she'd thought the smell outside had been bad, the inside literally made her eyes water. She was grateful for the heady smoke and immediately fumbled in her bag for her own box of ciggies and a lighter. At least breathing through the cigarette meant she'd breathe through a filter!

"*Me nurses from Kenmore!*" A voice boomed above the din of noise, the cry both welcomed and welcoming.

Bonnie recognised that voice, that yell, and that laughter anywhere. Everything else fell away, as she turned, eagerly, to see Lillian's gap-toothed grin. Slightly more lop-sided than the last time (courtesy of the booze), but just as eager as ever. Her arms were wide, like she invited them into her very own home. Perhaps, in a way, she did.

"Lillian!" Bonnie bounced towards her, the other two women following at a more measured pace behind. "We hoped we might find you here. How have you been? How are the others?" She lightly gripped one of Lillian's old, worn hands in hers. Just as sticky as the floor, unfortunately. Lillian's nails dug firmly into her palm. Hygiene had, apparently, been something only acceded to at Kenmore. Perhaps that was even the last place her nails had been trimmed?

"You can ask 'em yourselves! Bertha's out back at our table. And Connie, Daff, and Mildred." Bonnie vaguely remembered the other three names as the "white trash" Lillian so often called them. The women whose pale skin wasn't so forgiving from suffering decades of booze and abuse. More wrinkled and stretched, more stained and scarred.

Lillian led them to an even darker corner of the badly lit wine bar at the seedy edges of Kings Cross. To evade the stench, Bonnie breathed deeply from her cigarette every chance she could. *I would have thought I'd be used to any smell after Kenmore!*

A gaggle of half a dozen women sat around a dingy corner booth, the fabric torn at the edges; at least the light was too dim to see the stains clearly. A carafe of red wine sat in the table's centre, and each woman had a small, mismatched glass in front of them with varying levels of fullness.

"Come on, come on." Lillian pushed the newcomers forward and into a couple of empty chairs. Bonnie and Patsy perched on the edges, though Gerald practically lounged on her own stool. "Have a glass, have a glass!" The women smiled their crooked, gap-filled smiles at them as they offered a few empty glasses. Well, empty aside from the rings of wine stains. Bonnie repressed a shudder; even in the poor lighting, she could pick out a lipstick mark.

Connie only just had syphilis, Bonnie thought to herself, not regretting the company, but perhaps regretting the situation she'd put herself in. *What other diseases will these women share along with their wine? Hepatitis? Gonorrhoea?*

"Oh, I'm not too thirsty." Bonnie politely declined, waving a hand at them. "I really couldn't." Patsy squirmed in the seat next to her, obviously worrying about the same thing.

"Come on, me loves!" Lillian perked up, pouring some wine into the lipstick-stained glass. "It's the least we can do for you after all you's done for us."

Bonnie stared at the glass like it was filled with poison. Not the kind to kill you quickly, but to sap your life slowly, painfully. Like a potion that might magically transform her into one of the women sitting opposite her. A witch's foul brew. She stole a glance at Patsy, whose own eyes bugged out of her head spectacularly, arms frozen by her side.

"Yes, come on gals!" Gerald clapped her hands, leaning forward. "But let us contribute, hey? Come on ladies, up to the bar for one more carafe. The night is young!"

1916
ALICE: DAY 1,381 IN THE ASYLUM

HARRIET SAT FOR a moment on the edge of Helen's bed in the attic. She'd just finished making the dozen beds all squeezed into the spaces between the columns and beams. The asylum had grown even more crowded in the previous weeks. Despite this, she'd finally secured a private room for Helen. This *should* be her last night sleeping in the attic's open ward with Alice and the others. She watched Alice now, moving in stiff, jerky movements across from her as she swept the fireplace. Well, what passed for a fireplace.

It was more of a wood burner, hastily constructed, joining into the flue of the fireplace below to provide warmth for those now occupying the highest level.

The other staff referred to it as that: *"the highest level"*. Harriet still couldn't help but think of it as anything but an attic. She looked over her shoulder at the small room with its white door. Alice's room. Now used for storage more often than not, though, that chair had been left bolted to the floor. A reminder to Alice of what fate awaited her if she messed up. Or stood up to them again. Alice may have convinced the others she had recovered enough—safe enough—to be given a bed, a broom, a modicum of freedom, and set to work. But she hadn't convinced them to give up the chair.

As if sensing her thoughts, Alice looked over her shoulder at Harriet and grinned. Those piercing black eyes saw too much. Understood too much.

Yes, Harriet thought with more conviction than ever. *You haven't changed. At least not for the better. You're smarter than ever.*

"Can you hear it?" Alice asked conversationally, tilting her head. She'd grown gaunt in her years at the asylum. What had once been dark, shimmering hair now hung limp, streaked with more grey than brown. Even in three years, it had barely grown back down to her shoulders. Her skin stretched over her bones like thin, bumpy papier mâché. "In the walls." Alice sighed, turning back to the fireplace, one skeletal hand stroking the plaster, the other grasping the broom. "There's someone in the walls, I think…"

The words were visceral, like fingers stretching from Alice's mouth and down Harriet's throat, grasping. Forcing her to hold her breath. Alice's words, though softly spoken, not only reached inside Harriet's throat but also rang in her ears. Until she *could* almost hear it: the sound of scratching within the walls behind the fireplace, as if from long, thin fingers gently scraping. The same fingers that tried to choke Harriet. Alice continued sweeping the fireplace. The swishes were almost rhythmic, paced in time with those scratches.

Insanity is not catching. Harriet tried to imagine a possum or rat behind the plasterboard instead of those fingers. Maybe it was just the sound of the broom. *I see you,* she thought stiffly, refusing to answer Alice's taunting. *I know you… I know your games. You can't fool me.*

2021
15 OCTOBER, 23:31

THE AIR GREW colder as the night dragged on. Aiden checked his phone compulsively, watching the time tick by in agonising, languishing seconds. *It's only been ten minutes,* he thought forlornly. It felt like hours. It felt like *days.* The temperature had dropped faster than he'd thought possible in such a short time. His breath fogged in front of him, and his ears and nose burnt painfully from the chill. Thankfully, the throbbing of his burnt fingertips had finally abated. He jealously stared at Devin's beanie. Wriggling around to warm his bony bottom only woke up the nerve-endings, reminding him he sat on blocks of ice.

"We c-can't stay here forever," Aiden whispered. Devin had barely moved since they'd entered the room—the cell—his eyes focused on the black gap between the door and its frame.

"I can *hear* something out there," Devin finally whispered, still not breaking concentration, as though he were in a staring contest, to the death, with the darkness. "Something's scratching, scuffing… It might be in the hallway."

Devin's voice was so low that Aiden's ears throbbed with how hard he tried to listen. As if reinforcing Devin's fears, Ward Fifteen groaned around them, settling. The wooden frames creaked. The plaster cracked. *It's sighing.* Aiden's shivers intensified, and he picked up the camera from his lap so he could pull his knees in tighter.

It wasn't a ghost, was it? Aiden thought. Even after such a short time, the memory had become distorted. Replayed a short, one-second loop over and over again. That voice and a black figure stretching in the gloom. Stretching too tall, too fast. *It wasn't real. Ghosts aren't real. Not like* that, *anyway. Too real.*

He looked back over at Devin. While Aiden's brain desperately tried to rationalise events to keep him safe, Devin seemed to be going in the opposite direction. He seemed to obsess over every sound, as if determined to see the supernatural danger first. *Is this insanity, then?* Aiden closed his eyes and pressed his forehead down onto his kneecaps, relishing the biting sensation. It reminded him he was alive. *Insanity is not catching,* he repeated in his head like a mantra. *Insanity is not catching. It's not. It's not. It's* not.

But it's in the walls…

Aiden quickly lifted his head as the intrusive thought dug into his mind. Like the talons of some horrible creature gripping deeper and deeper into the fleshy parts of his brain, refusing to let go. *This place has been filled with madness for years. For decades. For a century. Surely, some of that lunacy had leached into the walls. Into the plaster. Into the wood. Into the stone.* The cold within the floor seemed to intensify. He pulled himself into an even tighter ball, determined to touch the floor as little as possible. He shivered so hard it must look like he was seizing.

A light entered the room. Not a supernatural orb, but the distinct yellow beam of a torch as it shone through the tattered and worn curtains. Aiden and Devin both gasped. Devin's eyes finally tore away from the door. The entire room glowed, the curtain fabric so thin and full of holes that the light was nearly blinding. Aiden's breath came out in short, shaky gasps. Devin motioned to him, Aiden knew this, but he couldn't tear his gaze away from the window.

Even as Devin scrambled into the corner, wedged between the window and the wardrobe, Aiden couldn't tear his gaze away. Just like Devin and that fucking door. Only through his periphery did he see his friend desperately motioning for Aiden to scoot back into the opposite corner. To *hide*. Breathless, Aiden finally did as commanded, his feet scraping as he thumped into place. The torch ceased shining into the room like a beacon.

It's the groundskeeper. Even Aiden's internal monologue trembled and pitched. *Has she found us? Did she hear me?*

The distinct crunching sound of boots walking across gravel followed, coming closer to the window. A hand struck the glass with a dull thud. He couldn't see it, through the torn drapes, but surely that's what it had been. The torchlight shifted, then came another thud. Perhaps she pressed against the glass?

As if to taunt all three of them, the curtain suddenly moved. Aiden held his breath, feeling his muscles struggling against the pain. He flicked a wary glare towards Devin, but his friend was nowhere near the curtain. It moved on its own. Fluttering towards the cell door as if caught in an absent, slow-motion breeze.

If Aiden hadn't been frozen in fear, he might have leapt to his feet right then. *Is it in here with us?!*

The door slowly creaked open, the barest crack. He felt like passing out. His heart beat too fast, sending too much blood away from his brain. He felt the whiteness coming, the blurring of the edges around his vision. The caretaker obviously seemed entranced by the motion as well. She waited, torch held still. The boys waited, trembling. Whatever had moved the door, and the curtain, waited.

Finally, they heard the crunch of her boots moving away. Perhaps she concluded that she had startled the air in the room, which then moved the curtains. Either that, or maybe this wasn't abnormal. *Was she used to curtains and doors moving on their own?*

Aiden and Devin looked up at the ceiling. More creaking. Shuffling. Those same repetitious footsteps. Someone was in the attic. Some*thing* was in the attic. And it wasn't the caretaker.

THERE'S NOTHING QUITE like fear. The emotion defies rationality. Makes the blood rush from your brain to your limbs, so you can run or fight. But in doing so, it removes capacity for thought, for careful planning. It risks a loss of consciousness or, at the very least, a loss of faculty. Such primitive instincts. And I love it.

Sometimes, I want them scared, I've realised. I want to see them shake. To see the blood drain from their cheeks, leaving them pale as ice. And cold, always cold, no matter the season. I want to see their pain. Because sometimes that's what they come for. To break. To shatter. To smash. To cause pain. So why should I spare them from the same?

They don't realise it, but I can smash, too. I can break them.

CHAPTER TWENTY

1954
SUMMER

BONNIE STOOD IN the dark, empty hallway of Female Five. She watched as the external door locked behind the Charge Nurse on duty. Not Hatchet this time, but someone as equally blunt and cutting. Three patients had needed changing, and one had hid under her own bed, scared of the shadows. Of course, this had elicited a telling-off for Bonnie. Like she was somehow supposed to know that a patient had silently squirrelled out of bed and burrowed her way beneath the mattress.

She shook her head, then brought a hand up to rub her temples. *Only two and a half more hours*, she thought to herself. The 4:00 a.m. round was the last of the night until it came time for handover.

I'd better get that linen, Bonnie reminded herself. She'd thrown it down the stairs but hadn't had a chance to move it to the laundry heap that Bubbles or one of his friends collected the following morning. The longer it sat, the greater the risk it would stain the floors, and she'd spend hours of her own free time polishing it.

For reasons she couldn't explain, Bonnie decided to walk back through the rec hall. Not the most direct route, but perhaps she just felt the need to move. Either that, or her sixth nurse's sense had developed in her, after all. As Bonnie unlocked the door to the rec room, she heard a sound. So faint it would have been easy to miss, even without her own footsteps and breaths to camouflage it. A sound that barely tickled the hairs of her ears.

She walked towards the disturbance, holding her Big Beam torch in front of her. At first, it appeared to be a scratching sound. Like tiny claws etching into the wood. *The possum is back?* she thought. But this sound was too soft for a possum. That creature wouldn't be so subtle. *Mice, then?*

The sounds came from the fireplace, she realised. She *had* seen a possum crawling down from there once, after all. Perhaps it just attempted a modicum of respect or sneakiness, for once. Normally, it scratched as hard as its claws would let it. Bonnie shone her light on the fireplace, but this time, no white eyes glared out from between the gaps of the fireguard. The sound trickled, and the light caught a flash of something reflective on the back of the fireplace. *Water?* she thought in disbelief, her clicking heels now bringing her to the edge of the grate. She gripped the torch under one armpit as she grappled with the protective cover, clenching her teeth at the sound it made as it came free. She tentatively reached out her hand and placed it on the brick. It was wet. And cool, though still warmer than the bricks themselves. Even in summer, the stones stayed cold.

She brought her fingertips to her nose, but she smelled only the ash from decades of fires. She tried to shine the light up the chimney, but the darkness was too thick, even for the Big Beam. Even though the possum had chewed its way through the flue, the narrow space was still mostly barricaded. The fluid still trickled through, however. From upstairs. From the empty attic. She thought again of Bubbles and his pranks, but it had been weeks since he'd last tried to scare her. And he wasn't on duty that night. *Not that I keep tabs on when he's on duty.*

Wiping her hand on a hanky she kept in her apron pocket, Bonnie walked decisively to the opposite door. Her heels clacked just as determinedly. Either there was a leak, or something fishy was going on in the attic. It hadn't rained in weeks, so it wasn't the roof. Perhaps it was that dodgy plumbing that had been installed in the old white room. Quite a few renovations had taken place all over Kenmore, including in Female Five, in the recent weeks. They'd started the fortnight before their road trip to Sydney. New plaster. New walls. New floors, where necessary. Though *why* the water would seep through the fireplace, she couldn't begin to fathom. Although…she supposed the contractors had removed an entire wall upstairs. Doing *something* before re-plastering it. Perhaps they'd nicked a pipe? Just a small hole that had finally given way. If she had to call for maintenance so late into her shift, she thought she might scream. *If only it had held out another few hours, it would have been somebody else's problem…*

Locking the door behind her, she headed down the hallway, navigating their lengths until she reached the stairs that led up to the attic. Once again, her light was unable to capture what waited round the corner. Tiny bubbles of fear popped in the middle of her spine. She clicked a heel a little too briskly on a step as she shoved her way forward. At the top of the landing, her key in the door, she couldn't help but pause and listen. She turned her head, almost pressing her ear against the attic door. A slight crick in her neck told her just how stiff and tired she was. How ready she was for this night to be over, to return home, wash herself clean, and crawl into bed.

Silence. Not even the sound of trickling water.

Bonnie clicked the key in its lock, pushing the door inward, shining her light across the beams. *I've always hated attics*, she thought. *No matter how renovated they are or how often people claim this is an open ward. I hate them.* She took two small steps inside, the shadows looming, reaching fingers out towards her every time she swivelled the torch, retreating only when the light swung towards them.

Now she heard a sound. Beyond the pillar, near the fireplace. She heard *something*. The trickling wasn't continuous, but rather, came in spits and spurts.

"Hello?" she couldn't help but call. As she took a few more steps around the right side of the column, her breath caught in her throat. There *was* someone up here. Pale and shining in the beam of her torch. A gown fluttered about them. "Agh—" The shout caught in her throat, turning to a gurgle of shock. "Wha—" No man hid beneath a bedsheet. This figure was fully formed.

The figure turned slowly, facing the light. Its features became washed out by the glow.

"Ethel?!" Bonnie breathed in disbelief, her grip on the torch loosening slightly. "What in heaven's name?!" She peered around the woman to the door that led to the catwalk. Shut and, at least presumably, locked. She'd also remembered to lock the door she'd come through. "Ethel! How did you get up here?" Even if the patient had somehow sneaked out of her room during the recent rounds, there was no way Bonnie and the Charge Nurse wouldn't have seen her. Or heard her. They locked *every* door behind them. Ethel wouldn't have been able to get out *or* sneak by them.

Even if she had, how did she get into the attic? Silently navigating the stairs in the dark and then sneaking through a *locked* door. And for what? What was she doing?

Ethel turned fully around. Her hands clasped her nightdress, which had caused it to billow around her. She held it aloft, revealing more of her frail, drooping body than Bonnie desired to see. Especially now. The woman was *urinating*. A sputtering stream, but one that rushed nonetheless.

How had she urinated so much? Bonnie found herself wondering, her feet still frozen in place. The oddities unnerved her, refusing to let the eeriness and shock of finding someone in the attic dissipate. Her brain felt like it rushed to catch up, but only ran in frantic circles.

"Ethel?" It was all she could bring herself to say, the word choking its way out.

"I have to put the fire out," Ethel explained calmly, softly. Her old vocal cords scratched over the words. Bonnie waited for the woman to add a random fact about bees, as she so often would. But she didn't. She just let those seven words linger, as though they were the most important sentence in the world.

The woman released her nightdress then and took a few padding footsteps towards Bonnie. Her naked feet slapped on the wooden floor, making the boards groan. *I would have heard her come up here…* The thoughts continued their flight around the hamster wheel of her mind.

"Ethel, sweetie. How did you get up here?" Bonnie was proud of how calm she'd managed to make her voice sound, despite the rising panic and shock that clutched her breast.

The elderly patient blinked a few times, as though suddenly coming back to herself. She looked around her, at the attic, at her bare feet, at the slight stain of urine on the front of her gown. "Did I have an accident?" she asked in a voice much brighter than before. "I think I was dreaming."

"Ethel…" Bonnie stopped short of asking the woman again. It was no use. She hated to admit it, but she knew it decisively. There would be no answers. "Come on, dear, let's get you cleaned up and back to bed." Her own feet finally allowed her to take the last few steps to Ethel. She placed her free arm around her shoulder, the other holding the light. She shuddered. Ethel was *freezing*. It had been a warm, dry summer. Even though Kenmore was normally cool inside, no matter the season, this chill was something else. Like the woman had stepped out of a snowdrift. "Oh, you're freezing!" Bonnie repeated the phrase out loud in shock.

"Am I?" Ethel lifted a soft, wrinkled hand and lightly held onto the tips of Bonnie's fingers. The old woman's fingers felt deflated. Like raw sausages that hadn't been filled quite right. "Do you know what? I think bees do dream."

Bonnie grunted in reply as she shuffled Ethel forward, all of her focus on the door within the opposite wall. She wanted to get them out of that attic and willed the old woman's legs to move faster.

"You know, they think that bees *learn* in their sleep? I wonder what I was learning about in my dreams."

They finally reached the other end. Bonnie reached a hand out to unlock the door and pull it all the way open so they could both fit through, side by side. As she stepped over onto the landing, finally releasing a deep breath, another sound rattled behind her. Just as faint as the trickle of Ethel's urination. A soft, gentle tapping. A rapping of knuckles. As though someone were knocking on the walls of the fireplace.

❧

2021
16 OCTOBER, 00:09

AIDEN AND DEVIN stayed in their corners long after the sound of the groundskeeper's boots had faded. Long after the curtain had returned to its stillness in front of the window. The door was still cracked open a little more than it had been, though nothing seemed to stir beyond it. The footsteps above them had faded as well. So slowly that Aiden suddenly realised they were gone. That he'd repeated their pattern in his head long after the sound had diminished. How long the sounds had filled in his head, he couldn't be sure.

Time had dragged on before the groundskeeper found them, but now it seemed to rush by. The light of the moon shifted as the orb slowly moved through the sky. Had he been in that room for an hour now? Two? Did it matter anymore? Aiden wasn't sure what disconcerted him more: the sounds rattling through the ward or this absolute stillness.

"It was in the walls…"

The whisper was so faint, Aiden barely caught it. The sounds tickled his ears long before his brain could make sense of the words.

"Huh? What do you mean?" he asked his friend, turning his head to stare at Devin. Devin, too, hadn't moved since he first huddled in that tight corner between the wardrobe and the wall. Aiden wondered if he'd ever get him out of there again.

"I didn't say anything," Devin replied so breathily the words almost didn't carry.

"You have to speak up." Aiden stretched out his legs, almost groaning as the tightness in his knees released. He'd been balled up for too long. He flexed his fingers and arms next, one hand always held tightly to the camera. Their only way of seeing through the darkness without giving themselves up to the groundskeeper. Sooner or later, they needed to get out. To make it back through the pitch-black hallways, then the gardens, under the fence, and back to their car. He didn't care if they didn't stay the night anymore.

"We didn't fulfil our destiny…"

"Hey, it's alright man," Aiden spoke a little louder, buoyed by the fact he hadn't heard the groundskeeper for some time. "We got more footage than anyone else I've seen. Some of it is really creepy. It's enough, man. We can go, yeah? It's got quiet, anyway."

"What're you going on about?" Devin's voice was harsh, grating. He sounded like he needed a drink of water. Or a lozenge. Something to soothe the chaff to his vocal cords.

"Hey, you're the one going on about destiny. I'm just saying, it's not that big a deal." He fished his phone out of his pocket, the bright white digits revealing the time. They'd passed midnight. "See, it's Saturday already. We made it to tomorrow. Technically through the night. Let's just go, man."

Devin paused a few seconds, then scrambled out of his corner. His lips and eyes drawn, the skin pulled taut as though by invisible hands. He grunted as he got to his feet. "Why would you say that, dude?!" His voice was barely a whisper. Spittle sprayed as he approached. Aiden struggled to his feet as well, hopping around as blood returned to one numbed leg.

"Fuck, Devin. It's just a YouTube channel. We've got enough footage!"

"No, not that!" Devin shoved him in the shoulder, his voice an octave higher. Aiden struggled not to fall, one leg still a blanket of pins-and-needles. "About the fucking walls. You're fucked up, man."

"What?" The chill that had settled on Aiden's skin as he'd sat in this cold prison started to leach inside him. Through sinew and flesh, right into his bones. Running the length of his limbs until it settled in the pit of his stomach. "What did you say about the walls?"

"What *you* said, man. That you're trapped in the walls. That's sick, dude. We're not trapped."

"I—I didn't…"

Aiden suddenly realised the tone of that whisper he had heard wasn't at all like Devin's voice. His brain had auto-corrected, not identifying any other plausible source for the words than his friend.

Light, slow tapping came from the window. Both boys turned their heads to gaze at it, noticing that once again, the curtains reached out to them. Agonisingly sluggish. Aiden could picture a single finger gently knocking against the glass. Then came a squeak, as though that finger slowly traced its way down.

"Do you hear that, too?" Devin asked, his voice returned to a hush. He'd obviously surmised the same as Aiden, that neither of them had whispered cryptic things to the other. Who knew what other previous whispers Devin had falsely attributed to his friend?

"It's in the walls…" The whisper came again, this time unmistakably from behind the glass. A rasping that sounded as cold as the air felt around them. *"The whispers told me to find it. They told me to do it. The voices told me to climb into the walls."*

Aiden's breath matched Devin's staccato gasps, the air hopping in and out of his lungs.

"Told me to stay quiet. Alfred is always quiet."

"Fuck!" Aiden yelled, pawing at Devin with his free hand. They both stumbled backwards, eyes transfixed on the rising curtain and what it would soon reveal.

"We all failed our destiny. I tried to fix it. To fix her. The voices spoke about her all the time."

The exit was right behind them. They needed to run. Get out of the room before whatever was outside came *in*. The curtains lifted enough to reveal the shadow of something rapping at the glass. A gnarled hand, its pointer finger raised, caressing the window.

"It got into the walls…"

Aiden felt the edge of the doorframe digging into his shoulder as he backed up towards the door. His eyes remained transfixed on the window, but his hands still moved relatively freely. He fumbled, feeling for the edge of the door, his fingers curling tightly around the wood.

"So I got into the walls too…"

A huge thump rattled the wall to their right, hard enough that dust and plaster sprayed into the air like a fine mist. Both boys screamed. Devin's a harsh, grating groan. Aiden's several pitches too high. The type of shriek that would make Devin tease him about his girlish wailing for aeons to come. Yet the thought didn't even cross Aiden's mind as he thrust the door open and the two of them stumbled into the dark hallway.

They stood there a moment, disoriented. They peered into the black pitch, then back towards the open room, where the curtain flapped supernaturally and the moonlight cast an eerie blue light. Neither knew what to do. Aiden fumbled with the camera, turning it on, hitting record, and setting it straight to night vision mode. He panned the camera left and right haphazardly, gasping in the air like it was an alien substance, suddenly suffocating him.

He turned side to side as if on auto-pilot. He desperately wanted to keep still, but he couldn't. He was a puppet to the cortisol and adrenaline pumping through him. Look left, look right, look in the room. Look left, look right, look in the room. It was compulsive.

In those split seconds, the rational part of his brain tried to give credence to his body's automation. But the internal narration didn't help. *It's dark. So dark. Look left. Make sure the hallway is empty. It doesn't feel empty. It's creeping closer. Look right. It's encroaching. That darkness. Pulsing at us. Look in the room. Has it got through the window yet? Is its hand still there? Still tapping? Or…is it to your left?*

Each time he swung the camera, the panic swelled a little higher. It felt as if the darkness reached out to him. Coming closer and closer. And if it reached him, it would sink its claws into him and become a part of him forever. Never letting go. Even if he managed to make it back into the light.

BANG!

A thump reverberated through the wall behind them, off to the left. It rattled the walls louder than physically possible. "Ah—Argh—Ha—Ha—Hargh!" Aiden lost control over the sounds that tumbled from his mouth. Half screams, half panicked grunts. He barely registered the feel of them leaving his throat.

"Run!" Devin roughly grabbed Aiden's arm and jerked him through the hallway, away from the sound. They ran blindly, Aiden never able to stop and hold up the camera for long before another bang shook the wall beside them, urging them on, chasing them, hunting them through the abandoned corridors.

Aiden wasn't the only one who wailed. Devin screamed, too. The thumping in the walls beat a drum to their chorus of terror. And it built to a climax. To a cinematic crescendo. Faster and faster, surrounding them on all sides. The boys burst through the closest door and stumbled straight back into the rec room. The place they'd seen that first ghost, the one that loomed large from the shadows, speaking to them.

"*Fuuuuck!*" Devin yelled, slamming his hands onto his knees and bending over to catch his breath. The thumping in the walls had finally stopped, having done its purpose of shepherding them back into this space. Aiden swung the camera, recording everything, looking for anything that might come after them next.

"It fucking chased us back in here," Aiden muttered, his mouth thick from exertion and fear. His words gummed together as he spoke. "It wanted us back here. It—"

A knock. A booming echo, as though it came from a large bass drum at the end of a deep, long hallway. He felt it in his chest. In his stomach. Trembling down his fingers. It sounded almost ceremonial. They both looked up to find its origin.

The fireplace. Another knock, distant this time.

"It's in here too…" Aiden sobbed. He realised he was crying when he tasted salty tears. He didn't fucking care anymore. Devin gripped his forearm tightly. The pain was welcome.

"*Let me out…*" A voice just as resounding as the drum, coming from the fireplace. Building in intensity as it channelled its way through the walls and then out from the hearth. "*Let me out… Let me out!* LET ME OUT!'"

I've lost track of how long I've been here. Time has been meaningless for as long as I can remember. That's funny, isn't it? As long as I can remember, I cannot fathom time. Ha!

Do any of us truly fathom it, though? Its passing mars us, sinks into us, draws us thinner and thinner. Etches its lines into us. Yet we don't notice it. Don't feel it, until one day, it's too late. We have turned, crumbled, disintegrated. Time is silent, creeping. A thief. The most competent killer of us all.

So who am I to say it is meaningless? Just because it has lost meaning to me?

We'll see… We'll see who I am. Perhaps I am the one who has escaped time. Who time will forget. Perhaps I am the meaningless one, after all.

CHAPTER TWENTY-ONE

1954
AUTUMN

"You touched it?"

"Yep!" Bonnie replied to Patsy across the table. Both of the women sat in the staff dining hall. They'd resorted to having breakfast there ever since the inebriates had left more than six months ago. Gerald promised her it wouldn't be long until they were all back, once the weather got cooler again.

Patsy burst out laughing, her fits falling into contented murmurs as she drew enough self-control to pull a spoon of porridge to her mouth. Her spoon scraped at the edges of the green-rimmed bowl. The "ring of confidence", the older nurses had called it. A green ring that differentiated the nurses' crockery from the patients'.

"I thought it was water. I thought something had sprung a leak with all those renovations they've been doing. I don't even know how she got up there."

Patsy swallowed and nodded her head slowly. "Yes, that I can't figure out either. We may never know. I wouldn't trust anything Ethel has to say on the matter. She'll probably tell you she turned into a bee and flew there."

"And that's not the only strange thing that happened," Bonnie continued. "Where did Alfred go? He did a magic disappearing trick just as spectacular as Ethel getting out of her locked room and into the locked attic. How did he get over the walls? How did no-one see him leave? How has there been no trace of him since? It's not like he'll blend in out there. Surely the police would have picked him up by now, trying to stick the leaves back on all the trees in Goulburn."

"I'll admit…it's strange. But there's *always* strange things going on around here."

"And you don't want explanations?"

Patsy sighed, pushing her now empty bowl away from her. Bonnie's eyes flicked to the large clock. Ten minutes, at most, until Patsy had to go back to Female Five. Ten minutes before Bonnie should go to bed, trying to get her body ready to start the night shift again that evening.

"If you ask Gerald," Patsy continued in a measured tone, "she'd no doubt have a rational explanation for you. Or at least tell you there would be one if we could find it. She'd tell you to ignore it. Me, I'm happy sitting on the fence. I've seen enough here, heard enough, to believe there must be some things we just can't explain. Now you…you seem to be falling in with that lot who believes with all their mighty hearts that ghosts and magic exist in these walls."

Bonnie went to interrupt her, to defend herself and her theories, but Patsy raised a hand and stalled her.

"Don't deny it yet; let me finish. If you want to go poking about looking for answers, just don't be sorry if you find them, right? I'm content not sticking my nose into anything paranormal. You know the saying, curiosity killed the cat."

"So you do believe in *some*thing then? What else do you know about Alice? Maybe it'll help me piece things together."

Patsy stiffened. "Everyone likes to talk about poor old Alice, but she's not the only woman who experienced terrible things both before and after she came to this hospital. Not the only *person*, full stop. I won't label it, but…" She sighed deeply, looking up at the clock herself. "It's the usual, isn't it? Cold spots near the fireplace. Humanoid shapes out of the corner of your eye, but when you spin around, there's nothing there. Finding doors or windows open that you *swear* you locked behind you. And those damned footsteps. Always those shuffling feet in the attic, even when you know damn well there's no-one up there. Not even those feckless male nurses and wardsmen playing pranks."

"Ha!" Bonnie laughed, stretching back in her chair, extending her arms and fingers to wake up the muscles. "Yeah, Bubbles got me good. You know, I've considered sitting on those stairs at night, in-between rounds. Waiting, ready to fling the door open and spring whoever's up there, making all that noise."

"I've thought about it too," Patsy admitted. She stood, picking up her bowl to signal her intent to leave.

"Then why haven't you?"

"Because I was too scared. Too scared that it wouldn't just be a jack-arse prankster. Terrified I'd find something worse. Something unexplainable. Horrified at the thought I'd find out Kenmore is actually haunted."

BONNIE SAT HUDDLED on the top stair of Female Five, leaning against the wall to her right. Every now and then, she'd flick her eyes to her left, watching the door to the attic intently, wondering if this was the night when things would be silent for once. She'd tried turning her light off to draw out the spook, but had felt too exposed. Sitting there, in the dark on the landing, unable to see who—or what—crept up the steps towards her.

She'd already fit her key in the lock, ready to turn it and pounce on whoever was up there. Prankster. Possum. Spectre. Whoever it might be. Her heart thumped in her chest and she longed for a cigarette to calm her nerves. She'd go downstairs for one in a few minutes. Just a few moments longer. Her fingers impatiently tapped on her knee.

Bonnie finally stood, tiring of waiting in the cold. As she did, she swore she heard the imitation of her own footfalls. Like Kenmore itself—or whatever waited in the attic of Ward Five—mocked her. She froze, eyes wide, ears pricked.

A definite grating sound, as if a foot scraped heavily across the floorboards.

She sprung to the door and turned the lock, her hands so flooded with blood and adrenaline she could scarcely feel them. As she rattled the door open, her torchlight flooding the room, the supernatural sounds were overcome. Emptiness lay beyond. She took a few steps into the room to check behind the pillar and ensure the door to the catwalk was secured. It was, and she was most definitely alone. She froze, waiting, unsure if she wanted the sounds to return or to remain absent.

After a few moments of agonising silence, she retreated back to the landing, locking the door behind her. *There was definitely a sound,* she thought to herself as she resumed her perch. *It wasn't just an echo...*

Bonnie stayed there, repeating the same cycle. Just as the cigarette's call became too hard to ignore, the noises started up again. Shuffling. Tapping. Even a grunt. Each time, she waited just a moment to ensure it was a real sound before she'd burst into the room. Each time, her detective *ah-ha* moment had been ruined by disappointing emptiness. She'd even checked the little white room. Rattled the handle on the far door *again* to double-check it was locked. Made sure every window was fastened, to account for any breeze that might mimic a human being. *Nothing.*

Nothing. Nothing. Nothing, she thought disappointedly, angrily. After the third false start, she flopped onto the stairs, head in her hands, torch by her hip, and sighed deeply. It was like some sick game of hide-and-seek that she'd never win.

"*Is* it you, Alice?" she mumbled through the palms of her hands, exhausted. A strong black coffee and a ciggie would clear that right up, surely. "Are you the one up here causing all this noise? Why did you stick around so long? Are you—" An idea struck her, one she wished she'd thought of sooner. Jogged by something Bubbles had said long ago. "Are you waiting for Roy?"

Bonnie startled as the door to the attic, with her key still dangling from its lock, slowly creaked open. Inwards, into the attic. She slowly got to her feet, one hand on the wall for balance, the other clutching the torch like a weapon.

"I locked that door…" Bonnie whispered through teeth clenched tight enough to squeak as they rubbed together.

I did. I'm certain of it…

Bonnie took a tentative step into the attic. It looked just the same as the past three times. Aside from the motes of dust sparkling in the light of her torch, nothing stirred.

She took one more heeled step into the room.

Step. Tap.

She spun. Had that been an echo of her footfall, or something else? She turned back to the room, both hands fisted around the Big Beam.

Step. Tap.

She looked over her shoulder again. There it was, once more. Mocking her. Taunting her with imitations of her own footfalls. *Is it coming from the little white room?*

She stepped lightly towards the room this time, the tapping echoing each footfall. "It's okay if it's you, Alice. I just wonder why you're still here. How I might be able to help you…"

The tapping picked up, even in the absence of any movement from Bonnie. A rhythm that was precise. Perfect. Like a pendulum or a metronome.

Tap. Tap. Tap. Tap. Tap.

Her breaths shuddered in and out, but this was what Bonnie *did*. What she was trained to do. She helped people who were disturbed. Who weren't quite there. Who'd suffered things most "normal" people could never begin to even comprehend. Sure, this one happened to be deceased, but perhaps that meant she needed her most of all. She'd found no respite, even in death.

"Alice—"

The little white door to the little white room blew open in a rush of cold air. Bonnie stepped back, bringing her hands up and coughing as the dust swirled into her face. In that moment of disorientation, the door slammed shut again, loud enough to rouse the entire ward. Hell, to wake the entire hospital!

The door repeated it over-and-over, just as the tapping had, but faster. More aggressive. More desperate.

Slam. Slam. Slam. Slam. Slam. Slam.

Bonnie didn't just hold her breath; she couldn't breathe at all, her lungs completely robbed of air. In the intervals between the door rushing open and slamming shut, Bonnie imagined she saw the figure of a hunched woman with limp, shoulder-length hair. A woman with entirely black eyes; devoid not only of colour, but of light. An intimidating woman who vibrated in her chair as fast as the door swung. Even as Bonnie's brain denied it, the image etched itself into her mind. A supra-human form, arms outstretched behind the door.

Bonnie ran. In her mind, she tried to convince herself she needed to check on her *living* patients. Ensure they hadn't been disturbed by the racket. In her heart, she knew she was terrified. Despite her recent bold conviction that she'd help the tormented spirit, she was really a coward. Willing to flee, to never set foot in that God-forsaken room again.

She pulled the attic door closed behind her, feeling as though she pulled against a fierce, gale-force wind. The door resisted. Sucked inwards, as though in a vortex. With a final grunting cry, the door slammed shut, and she twisted the key in the lock. This time, she jiggled the handle, making damn sure the thing was locked.

"I'll find Roy," she mumbled, as she ran down the stairs, two-at-a-time when her long legs allowed it. "I'll find Alice's son…"

⋯⋯◆⋯⋯

2021
16 OCTOBER, 00:43

Aiden huddled next to Devin in the furthest shower stall of the bathroom they'd stumbled into. As soon as that whisper had turned into a scream, demanding that they "let me out", the two bolted. Back through the door they'd come through, the banging resuming within the walls. They were followed—pursued—by those wails as they raced down the darkened halls.

"It herded us again," Aiden whispered, shuffling slightly closer again to his friend. Devin had taken the corner, leaving Aiden exposed on one side. There were no curtains in here. Looking up at the ceiling and noticing the lack of any railing, he doubted there ever had been. These were patient bathrooms. Devin had switched his headlamp on, casting the windowless room in a red glow. The imitation terrazzo tile floor looked dirty, rather than modern, with its random splotches. Cracks ran through the white tiles and tarnish coated the silver handrails. The impact of what the boys had done—sneaking into an abandoned, decrepit, *insane asylum*—hit home like an anvil.

Devin didn't respond, so Aiden kept talking, needing to fill the silence. "It stopped screaming and thumping as soon as it chased us in here. It's a dead end. We're cornered." He looked at Aiden squatting in the shower. "*Literally* cornered."

"Fucking shut it, man. I know. I fucking *know*."

Even knowing that the entity had treated them like sheep, they hadn't been able to fight it. Hadn't been able to resist their impulse to escape. They'd been driven to this room so easily. Just one bang sent them running in the opposite direction.

"What does it want?" Aiden breathed again. He couldn't "shut it", just like he couldn't force his legs to move the direction *he'd* wanted to go. *Out.*

Devin sighed, exasperated, defeated. "You know as much as I do." He trailed off, then nudged Aiden to give him some personal space, stretching his legs out, settling in. "It wants fucking out!"

Aiden shuffled over slightly, though he left his arm touching Devin's shoulder. He needed to maintain some contact; a reminder he still had his friend. He wasn't alone. He looked at his hands, both still tightly holding onto the video recorder. Without thinking, he flicked the screen open, turning the camera on and navigating to the recently saved files. Small voices floated out from the camera's built-in speakers after he selected the first file: their first moments when they'd entered this place.

"*Okay, ready when you are.*" Aiden's recorded voice sounded so carefree and excited. He hated himself for his tone.

"*I'm here at Kenmore Asylum, the largest luna—*" The audio cut off when Aiden fast-forwarded, searching through the footage.

"What're you doing, man?"

Aiden didn't answer, concentrating on the video that sped at four-times normal speed. "There!"

"*Yeah, fucking epic,*" Aiden's miniature voice yelled. The camera pointed down a gloomy hallway, rooms spilling down the left side, a staircase further ahead and to the right. It was the first building they'd entered. A galah shrieked through the camera and both boys jumped. Aiden felt Devin's bicep tense against his own. He remembered this. He knew what came next. Devin had been behind him during this shot, wandering into one of those rooms. And the door had shut behind him, leaving Aiden alone just for a moment.

Tap tap-tap tap. There it was. Behind-the-scenes, Aiden had looked over his shoulder at that moment, and…

"Holy fuck," Devin breathed. During the moment when Aiden had looked away from the viewfinder, the camera caught something. Something dark and sinister, walking across the hallway in front of him. A woman, her long hair tangled over her face, but not enough to hide those black, piercing eyes.

Aiden rewound the footage, pausing it on her. There was no mistaking it. The longer he looked at her, the more real those eyes became. Goosebumps pricked Aiden's skin from the top of his scalp, down his arms and to his fingers. A thousand cold needles drawing his skin rigid.

"They were there, right from the fucking start…" Aiden barely got the words out.

"Keep going! Keep fucking going!"

Aiden did as he was told, fast-forwarding almost blindly until he reached the church. The two watched in silence as the camera played their route through the large open hall, caught the rumbling of the ride-on mower, and followed their frantic scramble to the stage and up the ladder. Amid the jostling of the camera as Aiden climbed, they saw it again. Just for a few frames. Aiden paused, rewound, paused, rewound, and paused again.

"It's the same fucking one." Syrupy fear filled Aiden's mouth, his words thick as he spoke them. The woman, with her dark eyes, glared at them from the open doorway of the room filled with junk. Her face was so covered by hair, so blurred, that they couldn't make out her expression. Nevertheless, Aiden knew it could only be menacing. The emotion practically vibrated out of the camera at them. "Fuck…fuck…fuck…"

They continued winding their way through the footage. She appeared in every building, at every turn, caught within the moments when they'd looked away, or were distracted. The worst had been the shot in the solitary cells, after the grate had slammed and the cell door had jammed, locking Devin inside.

"*Let me out, dickhead!*" Devin's miniature voice screamed. The camera jostled to the ground, landing on an odd angle that faced the floor and part of the hallway. They heard Aiden grunting as he struggled to open the door. A foot stepped into view. Pale, almost blue in the dark, despite the green night-vision filter. Then a second foot. Both bare, ragged, worn, thin—the tendons and veins almost bursting through the skin. The tattered bottom of a nightgown shifted past, and then her face—its face—appeared. One dark eye took up the centre of the shot as it looked at the camera lens. Seemingly looked *through* the camera at them.

The goosebumps returned, this time pulling Aiden's skin taut across his scalp. A tear broke free. Not one of sadness or anger, but of pure terror. At that moment, he couldn't do anything but cry. His own eyes remained transfixed on the screen.

How had they not seen her? How had they not heard her?

Devin sobbed as well, great bursting, snotty bellows as he gulped for air like a drowning man. "It—it—it c-can't be fucking real!"

He pushed the camera away. Aiden lost his grip and the camera clattered to the floor, just like it had in those cells. He snapped it up quickly, closing the screen, and turning the power off. "I need to get *the fuck* out of here!"

"It was watching us the whole time…" Aiden bumbled, his words flowing out of him like water bursting through a dam. "She followed us the moment we got into this fucking place. Shit! I wish the caretaker had found us in the church. I wish she'd dragged us out of there kicking and screaming. It must be in here too. With those other *things*. How many of them are there? Fuck, *how many—*?"

"Shut it!" Devin lurched to his feet, screaming. He frantically looked around him as though a new door might appear with an "exit" sign flashing green above it.

"The—the caretaker—" Aiden muttered as he stumbled to his own feet. Somehow, he'd kept hold of his backpack, and it rubbed on his back as he pressed against the tiled wall. A part of it snagged on a broken tile, ripping slightly. He didn't care. If he wasn't too terrified to try, he'd have flung it off himself. Free himself to run faster.

"We need to get to the caretaker. Hey!" Devin screamed as loud as he could. "Hey! Help! *Help! HELP!*"

The caretaker didn't answer. But the walls of Kenmore did. Echoing, mimicking, groaning back at them.

I'VE HAD SO much time now, to watch. To listen. To learn. They claim insanity isn't catching. But I know better. Mental conditions aren't catching, but fear is. Joy is. Sadness is. Longing is. The emotions are so powerful, they almost become their own entities. These are the infections that jump from person to

person. That linger in the walls, in the floor, in the air, long after the last living soul has gone.

And not just emotions. Suggestion is catching as well. It just takes one… One other person to believe the murmurings, and then that suggestion grows. It's given power. It spreads. Theories become truth. Hunches become indelible. Dreams become memories. Fiction becomes fact.

And what happens if you give these myths, these murmurs, your attention? Like sun to the flowers, or rain to the fields, they grow. They blossom. They bloom. Taking root in your mind.

So you see, insanity is catching. Fear is the contagion. And I am the host.

CHAPTER TWENTY-TWO

1954
AUTUMN

Bonnie approached the imposing building of Goulburn's Boys Orphanage—St John's. Weeks had passed since her encounter with the dark humanoid shape behind the little white door in the attic of Kenmore's Female Five. She'd wanted to come to the orphanage sooner, but life had invariably got in the way. Her ten days off following her night shift had been spent in Gundagai with family. Then she'd returned to day shift for a couple more weeks, and a single day off was hardly enough time to set aside for this venture. There was too much life admin to be done. But now, three days into her next ten-days off, following the previous run of night shifts, she was here.

I wasn't making excuses, Bonnie said to herself as she climbed the stone stairs. *I wasn't procrastinating… It really was the earliest I could come…*

She looked up now as she walked, choosing perhaps the worst moment to take in the façade of the building. The walls appeared even more imposing from this angle, looming over her. The building wasn't that much bigger than the largest wards of Kenmore. The pointed roof probably gave it its domineering veneer—the building's tallest point—with the cross reaching for the heavens and the Virgin Mary praying beneath it. The red bricks were familiar, even though

St John's seemed more severely put together than Kenmore. This place was less art and more function. The only artistic thing about it was the delicately carved, pearl-white Virgin Mother lauding over Bonnie as she passed beneath the arched entranceway.

It was just after 6:00 a.m.—the time she'd been told to arrive—and already the orphanage was a hive of activity. She passed older boys tending to the garden and grass. Inside, she saw younger boys darting around, carrying loads of linen or other bundles, polishing the floors, dusting. The place *sparkled* with so much domestic labour. None of the orphans made eye contact with her as she entered, though she caught some surreptitiously glancing at the stranger in their midst after they'd passed by her.

"Miss Thatcher."

The strict, clipped voice that called Bonnie's name did not ask a question, but merely stated a fact. Perhaps even gave her an order. Bonnie turned towards a short, thin nun standing off to her right. Her white coif and guimpe—the collar and large circle of cloth across her chest—looked stiffer than the nursing uniforms next door in Kenmore. Though Bonnie couldn't see the woman's hair, her eyebrows dark grey, and her face was as wrinkled as an apple picked too young and then left in the summer sun to whither. She thought back to what Gerald and Patsy had called them when Bonnie had first asked about the orphanage. Not the Sisters of Mercy, but the Sisters of Misery.

"Yes, ma'am," Bonnie replied, too much like a student to her own ears. The nun eyed her up and down. Bonnie had deliberately chosen demure clothing for the occasion. A shirt buttoned all the way up to its collar, a simple dark blue cardigan, a thick skirt that reached to her ankles, and stockings and heels. Perfectly respectable. Even still, she felt inadequate beneath that glare. The feeling punched deeper as the woman scoffed and grunted.

"I'm Sister Margaret. Come this way." The nun walked back through the door whence she'd come, and Bonnie followed. The two emerged into a small administrative office. Bonnie closed the door behind her, pleased to have the sound of scurrying feet cut off by the thick wood. Sister Margaret circled her large wooden desk and took her time sitting down, then motioned for Bonnie to take the wooden stool before her.

Now it really does feel like I'm back at school. Bonnie sighed internally. *I'm doing this for Alice. For Roy.*

"How can I help you, Miss Thatcher? I hear you wanted to speak to me about one of our boys after we'd first opened."

"Yes, that's right. I—"

"I should tell you," Sister Margaret continued as though she hadn't been interrupted. "I can only spare a little time this morning. Mass begins just after 7:00 a.m., and I need to prepare."

"Yes, of course, I—"

"So I can't have too much dallying."

Bonnie twisted her fists into her skirt, teeth grinding. She forced herself to take measured breaths, despite the frustration bubbling in her stomach. Perhaps her fear of Alice's spirit hadn't been the only reason she'd delayed coming to the Catholic-run orphanage. *I didn't delay…*

She paused a moment to ensure the nun had really finished speaking before trying again. "Thank you, Sister Margaret." She paused again, and the nun inclined her head, indicating she could continue. The bubbles of frustration popped in her sternum. "As you know, I'm Bonnie Thatcher. I'm a trainee nurse next door at Kenmore, working in Ward Five. One of the patients—well, she's passed away now—one of the *former* patients had a son who used to live here. His name was Roy. Unfortunately, I don't have much to go on, other than that he would have been one of the first boys at the

orphanage and he was always running away. As one of the olde—"
Bonnie cut herself short, took a sharp breath, and continued. "…
As one of the longest serving sisters here, your colleague thought
you might be able to help me."

"Yes." Sister Margaret didn't lean back in her chair like many
would have when they reflected on the past. She remained as still
as that statue of the Virgin Mary, who still prayed above them,
somewhere, on the roof. "I've been here since the beginning. Since
the first foundation stone was laid and blessed in 1912, since the
orphanage opened its gates in December 1913."

"My, that is—" Bonnie began conversationally.

"I don't remember every young man who comes through these
doors." The nun continued as though Bonnie hadn't spoken.

No more pleasantries for you…

"But I do remember Roy. Indeed, he was one of our first boys.
His father gave him to us just after Christmas 1913. A young scrap
of a thing, always crying and snivelling. And *always* running away.
Off to your place, that Kenmore, looking for his mother." Bonnie
now knew not to speak, so she nodded her head vigorously. "Yes,
I remember Roy. Took a lot of moulding to get that one straight."

There was a good pause; Bonnie couldn't help herself, leaning
into the conversation as though she and the nun were old family
friends sharing a pot of tea. "It must have been difficult looking
after so many parentless children. There must have been plenty of
tears."

"Hah!" Sister Margaret slowly placed her folded hands flat on
the desk. She didn't so much roll her eyes as her entire head. "*Most*
of the little cretins had parents. Oh yes, we even knew where their
parents were. Most of them either couldn't afford to feed them
or—like Roy's parents—gave them up when the father tired and
decided to move on."

Bonnie was speechless. She knew some of her own charges had been left at the asylum for those same reasons, but she had never thought of what might happen to the children. She'd assumed the fathers still kept them. In some cases, evidently not.

"So what is it you need from me?" The question snapped her out of her dismal reverie.

"Well, I know it's been a long time, but I don't suppose you know what happened to him? To Roy?"

Sister Margaret clenched her hands together again. "I do." She took a long breath, taking her time before answering. "I lost count of the number of times he ran off on us. We *always* knew where to find him, though. I ended up having quite the friendship with your old matron because of that one. Only when the boy received news that his mother had died did he quieten down. Took to his chores and his lessons."

"Did he ever get adopted?" Bonnie instantly regretted asking the question. The nun's eyes hardened and her chin crinkled as she pushed her lower lip into her teeth, swirling her tongue around like she attempted to swallow something bitter. "I—I'm sorry, I don't mean to interrupt."

"Yes, well, if you *keep* interrupting, then I'll not be able to answer your questions, now will I?!" The nun took another two slow breaths, and then continued. "He was never adopted. He stayed here eight years or so, until he was old enough to take up work at one of the nearby cattle stations. He worked at those stations off-and-on for almost forty years, but he *always* came back to Goulburn. Heaven knows why he sought me out every time to let me know how he was doing. But he did. The Lord tests us."

Bonnie steeled herself to bridge the silence once more. "So, he's still in Goulburn then? I don't suppose you know where he lives?" The Sister raised an eyebrow so high it nearly disappeared beneath her bandeau. "I have some news about his mother. I thought I'd share it with him, if I could find him." The half-lie easily rolled off her tongue.

Why am I trying to find him? She chastised herself. *What good will it even do?*

"Yes. I know where he lives. The lazy boy just retired and moved into a nice little place on Joshua Street. Barely age fifty. Idle hands are the devil's tools! Me, I'll work until the Lord calls me home."

Bonnie suffered through another ten minutes of forced conversation with the woman before she finally had Roy's full address. With relief, she stepped out into the brisk air, breathing in deeply and thanking her lucky stars she didn't have to suffer the likes of Sister Margaret any longer. How Roy had made it through eight years, and then kept coming back, belied belief. Perhaps he'd been taught self-flagellation and took the visitations upon himself as punishment for his sins!

She looked up at the sky and saw that clouds had descended, covering the sun. No sign of rain yet, so she decided to walk the hour into town, detouring by Buna House first to grab her walking shoes. The walk gave her too much time to think. Her mind strayed through everything, from her own Catholic schooling experience, to what Roy must have gone through, to the nightly occurrences in Ward Five, and finally to a more reassuring train of thought. Remembering how happy she'd been to see the inebriates return to Ward Five. She supposed she should wish them recovery, perhaps a good husband, a new life. Those thoughts felt silly to her, though. She was just pleased they'd returned where she could take care of them. And where Lillian could return the favour with her famous coffee and rolls breakfasts.

As Bonnie approached Roy's cottage—small, but well-kept—a light drizzle began sprinkling the top of her hair. She didn't have any more time to second-guess herself, but unlatched the small gate and ran up the broken concrete path to the covered veranda. She hesitated only a moment with her hand raised to knock, and the door pulled open. A huge figure filled the doorframe. So tall, the top of his head was only just visible. Shoulders so wide they filled the opening from frame-to-frame. Not fat, just huge. A man built from decades of hard labour.

"Oh!"

"Can I help you?" The voice was not unkind, but nor was it kind. Flat, almost empty.

"I'm so sorry to bother you. I'm looking for Roy…"

"I'm Roy." The man didn't move. The shade cast by the entryway kept his features and facial expressions hidden.

"Oh…" She hated being *that* woman. The one who sighed, and squealed, and giggled, and said "oh" on repeat. "My name is Bonnie Thatcher. I'm a nurse over at Kenmore Hospital."

Had he stiffened at that name?

"I completely understand if you don't want to talk to me, but—"

"No…" A little emotion filled his voice. Perhaps eagerness? Perhaps desperation? His hands flinched as though to reach out to her. "No, please, come in." He stepped back so that the corridor of his cottage became visible, leading away to what looked like a small living room.

Bonnie looked at Roy one more time before stepping inside. Yes, she was a young woman on her own in a strange man's house. But it was her job to know who was dangerous and who was not. Her nurse's sixth sense. And for whatever reason, she decided she could trust the gentle giant. As he led her to a small sitting room, plainly and simply furnished but well-maintained and expertly cleaned, she felt that sense of safety grow.

"Tea?"

"Oh, no, thank you." She didn't want to stay any longer than she had to. She felt like an intruder; the longer she stayed, the less certain she was of why she'd come. *I can't exactly tell him I think his Mum is haunting the asylum!*

He sat on a sofa and encouraged her to sit in a matching armchair opposite him. While the house was immaculately clean, it also lacked the homey touches she'd expected. The cushions had come with the sofa, matching the print exactly. No throw blankets draped over the furniture to protect them. No flowers or vases or photographs.

"You live alone?" Alice spoke the words before she could properly think them through. It just seemed so obvious.

"Hm." He hunched forward with his elbows on his knees, clapped his two huge hands together, and looked over his shoulder as if taking in his cottage for the first time. "It's that obvious, is it?"

"No, no!" Bonnie lied and snapped her mouth shut. "It's lovely. I just didn't see any photographs. It's a silly observation."

"Nope, you're right." He remained slumped forward. He still hadn't made eye contact with her, she realised. Just like the other boys at the orphanage, he watched the world from his peripheral vision. "I never married. Just worked, went to church, came home. And before you know it, I'm fifty and tired, and can't be bothered." An awkward pause followed, and Bonnie wished she'd accepted that tea, just for something to do with her hands. "So you're here to talk about my mum, then?"

Bonnie nodded. Even though he hadn't raised his head, he still caught the gesture.

"I've been wondering when the hospital would send someone. Tell me what actually happened to her. How a young, fit woman died so young."

"Oh, no. I'm not here officially." Roy did look at her then, curious. She had to bite her bottom lip to stifle a gasp when his eyes fell on her. So deep, so dark, so piercing. Just like the eyes that had stared at her from the attic. There was no doubting it. Alice still haunted the asylum. He grunted at her, and she floundered for words. "I—I work in Ward Five. Female Five, that is. Where your mother stayed when she was with us all those years ago. Even after all this time, they still talk about her."

"Hm, how so? Is it about how she died?"

"I—" Bonnie lowered her gaze. "I'm so sorry, I don't really know why I came here at all. I really don't know that much at all. I'm so very sorry." She made it as if to stand, but Roy stopped her with a raised hand and an unexpected plea.

"Wait…" He let his eyes drop back to the floor, and Bonnie immediately felt a little less restless being out of their glare. Perhaps that was the real reason he kept his eyes down, not because of his time at St John's. "I didn't really know her at all. I was five when Pa took her away. Six when he sent me away, too, to St John's. I must have been nearly ten when she died. I remember her singing to me, holding me. I think I do, anyway. I remember her eyes. But you know, I have more memories of trying to get back *to* her than I do of any time spent *with* her. I can't explain it well, but it's like she was a missing piece of me. One I never got back. So, please stay. I'll listen to anything you have to say about her."

Bonnie cleared her throat, debating over what parts of Alice's story she actually wanted to share with him, and what parts she wanted to keep to herself. Either way, she didn't know much. In the end, curiosity won out during her small internal battle. "They still talk about her because she had a hard time, actually. She spent a lot of time in solitary. I also know she was kept away from other people for a long, long time. And I think she was so upset because she was trying to get back to you. She must have loved you very much."

"And?" he probed her, knowing there was something else. His large, docile exterior camouflaged his intelligence. "What else?"

"She didn't die when they told you she did," Bonnie finally admitted.

"What?"

"That's what they say, anyway, at the hospital," she quickly chimed in. "The staff at the time lied to…to stop you from running away."

The man sat, stoic. He reminded Bonnie of Sister Margaret and her ability to mimic statues. Finally, he stood. Bonnie leapt to her feet as well. "I should have known…" he muttered, clenching and unclenching his fists. "It never *felt* right. She's still there, isn't she?"

"Yes…" Bonnie whispered, before realising her mistake. He didn't mean as a spirit. He meant in flesh and blood. "Oh, no!" His dark gaze held her once again, wrapping her tight in a cold, steel grip. "Oh my God…" She put a hand to her head to break free. "I'm *so* sorry. I really shouldn't have come here like this. I just— She's *not* still there. She did pass away. I'm not sure exactly when, I'm sorry. Just that it wasn't when they told you. And when I said she was still there, I meant… People talk, and…they talk about Alice all the time."

"They think she's a ghost?" Roy's tone held no emotion. She couldn't tell if he believed her or thought she was as unwell as the patients she served. She felt dizzy and panicky, wishing she'd never come.

"I really didn't mean to upset you." Bonnie took a step towards the door. "I'm a fool, really, I am. I figured if she *was* still there, and I could tell her how well her son turned out, well…" Roy didn't stop her as she retreated backwards into the hallway. "I'll see myself out. Again, really, I am *very* sorry."

She didn't wait for Roy to answer, but turned and fled as fast as she could without sprinting. She maintained that pace all the way out the door, through the little gate, and through the rain back to Kenmore. Not caring that her hair became absolutely ruined and her clothes drenched through in the process.

BONNIE NEVER TOLD anyone what she'd done. She was too mortified at her behaviour, at how badly she'd handled the whole situation. She stayed quiet through her only social interactions that week, during daily breakfasts in Buna House. In fact, Lillian had been uncharacteristically content to sit in companionable silence as well, leaving the others to carry the conversations. The last seven days of her time off had been torturous, without enough work or leisure to keep Bonnie distracted. If she tried to read, the words on the page inevitably morphed into her horrid, stuttered dialogue with Roy. If she tried to watch TV, her mind wandered and replayed her escape down Roy's cottage hallway. Walking only gave her brain more oxygen, more blood flow, to energise it for further mental torment.

She was relieved when her next night shift came around, and she had work to pour all her efforts and concentration into. Her notes would be the most meticulous she'd ever made. She sat alone in the office, scribbling on the paperwork like a woman possessed. The ward creaked around her. The footfalls continued. The groaning in the walls did, too, as did the soft tapping. Bonnie ignored it as best she could. After her 4:00 a.m. rounds finished, she decided to dust the office.

A bang sounded from the attic. Was Alice angry that Bonnie was ignoring her? Could she ignore the tormented soul forever?

With a sigh, she stepped out into the dark hallway, the trusty Big Beam clutched in her hands. She passed through the hallways and locked doors to the base of the stairs almost automatically. She really needed to think this through, just like she should have done before seeking out Roy. But rational thought remained denied to her. She climbed the steps slowly, taking her time with each one, drawing out the chance of another terrifying encounter.

"Alice?" she whispered, finally on the landing, her ear pressed against the attic door. "Alice?"

Silence. She fit her key into the lock and stepped into the room, her palms both clammy and freezing. Everything appeared to be the same, though slightly mustier, perhaps. The tinge of an unpleasant odour in the air.

"I found Roy," she blurted, eyes fixed on the small white room, bracing herself for Alice's crazed spirit to rush her. It felt as though she stood in a metal box in the middle of a lightning storm. "I wanted you to know that he grew up. He's big and healthy. *So* tall. Like a gentle giant." No response, but she couldn't help herself. The words tumbled free. "He worked on cattle stations, made good money. He has a lovely cottage in town. And he loves you, Alice. He never stopped loving you. And he never gave up on you. I wanted you to know that. He only stopped coming because…because…"

Was that a noise now? She felt the hairs on her arms rise. Even the small soft hairs on her cheeks tugged on her flesh, as though pulled by a static charge. The energy in the room almost felt painful. She had to say it, or surely that force would crush her.

"Because they told him you'd died. They told him you weren't at Kenmore anymore, so he'd stop running away from St John's." She took a breath in and held it. This was it. The weight of the energy practically groaned as it pulled at the walls, beams, and roof.

And then…it stopped.

The attic fell quiet. Silent. Cold. Bonnie spun around, but all was still. *Is she gone?* She took a tentative step towards the small white room. She swiftly unlocked the deadbolt, then yanked open the door. The smell of fresh paint assailed her, but nothing more than that. *Did I do it?*

In a haze, Bonnie walked back down the stairs, down the hall, and to the office. It felt all too easy. Was that really all it took? To simply share the truth? The woman had haunted the ward for decades.

A few minutes later, still standing in her office, still staring at nothing as thoughts ran through her head, she heard another sound. This one was all too human. Shouting. Running? She hurried to the hall and took a right turn, unlocking the side door and stepping into the brisk night air. There *were* people. Most in night clothes. What were they doing? Why were they out there?

"Hey!" Bonnie yelled as she saw a familiar face. Bubbles looked at her and she could tell he wanted to continue running. At the last moment, he tore himself away from his task and sped over to her. She couldn't leave the ward. It was her charge, so she was grateful he'd come to her. "What is it? What's happening?"

"It's Male Seven," he breathed heavily. A few drops of sweat beaded the edge of his forehead, despite the chilly Autumn night. "It's on fire. It's burning down."

CHAPTER TWENTY-THREE

1917
31 DAYS AFTER ALICE'S DEATH

Harriet shook. She prided herself on keeping a stiff upper lip. On her composure in the face of any situation. But this was too much, even for her. Alice's death had been traumatic enough, for her, for everyone. Malaise had spread through Female Five like an infection. Some patients refused to eat. Some refused to get out of bed. Those who had known Alice best were the worst affected. No longer speaking. Even the staff were impacted. How could they not be?

Harriet tried to clear her throat as she felt withheld tears balling up, and groaned instead. The groan built like it had its own will, so she clamped her hands over her mouth. Two nurses had resigned after it had happened. Only one of the two had even been there when it happened. With Harriet. Had seen Alice die.

She breathed raggedly. This recent tragedy was so reminiscent of the first. She couldn't help but feel Alice was responsible for it. It was an insane thought. Utter lunacy. Alice was *dead*. And yet, there was no rational explanation this time.

"Nurse, are you alright?"

Harriet looked up. She hadn't seen the Superintendent arrive at the morgue. In fact, she hadn't seen much of anything, barely taken in her surroundings at all. She floated in that horrid memory of watching Alice die. Reignited by the similar death she'd found that morning.

"Sorry, sir." Harriet managed to inject a modicum of surety into her voice. She didn't even feel like she spoke at all. Surely someone else answered for her.

"We need you to answer a few more questions. We're, ah—That is, we're struggling to understand what happened." He motioned a doctor forward, who stood behind him. Yet another thing she'd failed to notice. "Can you tell us again what happened? From the top, if you please?"

"It was our first round of the evening," Harriet began in the same absent tone. She did not so much speak as listen to the words flowing out of her. "We came to Helen's—to Ms. Bellamy's—room. We opened the door and went inside. Found her on the floor. Naked, covered head to toe in burns. She was deceased, already turning cold. No sign of her clothes. No sign of any fire. The floor was not burnt. The bed, the walls, the curtains—there were no scorch marks on any of them."

"And when was the last time you saw Ms. Bellamy?"

"Well, I saw her at the handover. She was asleep, in her bed, in her nightgown."

"And the nightgown—?"

"We didn't find it." Harriet knew she was in shock. She struggled to comprehend her surroundings. She felt cold. Colder than she should, even in Autumn. The chill had seeped inside her, into her blood. "We looked everywhere. Under the mattress, in the pillowcase, behind the curtains. It was just gone."

"Could someone have accessed the room between handover and the first rounds?" the doctor asked next.

Could someone have gone to her room, unlocked the door, taken her somewhere else, taken her clothes, burnt her to death, and then returned her to her room? That's what he means.

"No. The other nurse on duty and I had the only keys. Plus, the building carries sound. We would have heard someone taking her, but we heard nothing." The doctor thoughtfully looked at the Superintendent and shook his head, clicking his tongue, obviously at a loss for words.

"Do you have *any* theories about how this could have happened?" The Superintendent tried one more time. Harriet was tired, now. So very tired.

Alice killed her, she thought. *She was always whispering in the woman's ear. And she came back from the grave to finish what she started. She burnt her to death without burning anything else in the room, reducing her clothes to ash, and then vanished back to Hell.*

"There's only one thing I can think of…" Harriet whispered. "Ever since Alice died, we've often found Helen by the fire. Especially *after* the fire has been put out, playing with the still-warm coals. You'll see she has old burns on her fingers. All I can think is that somehow, maybe she smuggled a hot coal back with her to her room…"

"And did you find the coal? Or any sign of it?"

Harriet sighed. It was all so confusing. "No, we didn't. No sign of soot in the bed. No sign of any coal in the room. But… Sir, *what* else? *Who* else? I—" Her voice caught as she breathed in deeply.

They let her out, Harriet thought forlornly to herself. She finally lost her ability to speak, and the two men turned to talk to themselves. At odd intervals, they gestured to the covered body, as if to instruct the other to find the answers no-one else could. *They let Alice out of the chair. It's their fault. All of them. The doctors. The nurses. The wardsmen. All their fault. They let this happen.*

And then Alice tormented Helen. Made her pace those hallways. Made her descend deeper and deeper into lunacy. Even after she died, she didn't leave. It's Alice. It must be Alice. Alice is still here. And it's all their fault!

1954
WINTER

BONNIE WIPED AWAY a tear that fell from her eyes as the car pulled into the Base Hospital car park. Gerald drove, but had been silent the entire trip. They both had been. The hospital had been *bedlam* that past month. If Bonnie had thought things had been strange before, they were nothing compared to what happened now. Thankfully, no-one had been hurt in the fire that consumed Male Seven. The old building had gone up quickly, decades of floor polish and kerosine giving the flames plenty of fuel. No-one knew how the fire had started. It could have been a cigarette. Faulty wiring. They'd probably never know.

The fire had been disruptive enough for everyone. At first, that's what Bonnie attributed to the patients' odd behaviour. The sadness and malaise. Refusing to eat. Refusing to speak. Refusing to lift their arms themselves so they could be bathed properly. It happened, sometimes. But usually only to one patient at a time. Not to every single one of them. A hive-mind depression.

And now this…

"Are you ready?" Gerald asked, flicking her cigarette butt out the car door after she opened it. The butt fell into a puddle of melting frost and sizzled itself out. The weather, too, was unseasonable. Goulburn always got cold, but *this* was almost unheard of. *Snow* had fallen in town, and even stayed on the ground for hours before the sun could melt it away.

"Fuck knows…" Bonnie sighed. Perhaps the malaise really was catching. "Sorry…"

"I never should have sworn in front of you," Gerald teased as she followed her cigarette butt, stepping into the puddle when she exited the vehicle. "All that innocence and naivety, and now look at you. Worse than a drunken station hand."

That made her think of Roy. The retired station hand. And how Bonnie felt she'd been the one to start all this. With her stupid questions, and her stupid talking. If she hadn't found Roy, hadn't stirred up Alice… *But surely, even if ghosts exist, they couldn't do all this?*

Gerald and Bonnie made their way through the car park and into the hospital. Bonnie let Gerald do all the talking, following behind her meekly as they navigated the hallways, finally coming to a room with four beds separated by thin curtains. Two of the beds were empty. A third had its curtains drawn. In the fourth was the person they'd come to see.

"Well, hello there," Gerald said fondly as she walked to the bedside.

"Me nurses from Kenmore!" Lillian tried to beam, but her voice came out more hoarse than normal, the words barely able to scratch their way out before she descended into coughing fits. Going into nursing mode, Gerald reached for the plastic cup of water while Bonnie rearranged the pillows behind Lillian's head.

"Oh, Lillian," Bonnie started, running a hand through the woman's wiry hair, then over her forehead. She had a fever; her skin boiled, and she looked clammy and pale. "*Why* did you do it?"

Lillian had run away from Kenmore two days prior. It had taken the staff a while to realise. No one had suspected that Lillian, who ensured she'd be sent to Kenmore for winter every year, would think to leave during the middle of a horrible storm that had seen Goulburn properly blanketed in white for the first time in years.

They still hadn't figured out *how* she'd escaped. Her bedroom door was locked, the bars on the windows tightly secured. It had then taken another full day for the cops to find her huddling under a bridge, blue all over and practically dead.

Gerald squeezed Lillian's hand as if to reassure her it was okay. She'd known the woman far longer. "It's okay Lillian, it's just us. We're your friends first, your nurses second, and snitches never."

"Good," Lillian barked. "Cos snitches get stitches." She half coughed and half hacked her lungs out. "I had to do it…" A tear fell from one eye then, and she sobbed as she breathed in. It felt wrong watching the woman cry. Like watching a pig fly, or a donkey dance. Lillian was tough.

"If anyone was hurting you," Gerald said firmly. "Or threatening you, you just tell me, and—"

"There's nothin' yous can do," Lillian whispered. The soft words were easier on her vocals but harder for the two nurses to hear. "S'not anyone livin' who's giving poor Lillian a hard time. It's the *voices*."

Bonnie exchanged glances with Gerald, who shook her head and shrugged. Outside of her alcohol addiction, Lillian had never displayed any symptoms of mental illness. Adult-onset schizophrenia was possible, but unlikely. She was too young for dementia, though that could happen early, in rare cases, she supposed. The logical diagnosis was more likely to be psychosis brought on by alcohol abuse. But Lillian had been in the hospital for weeks since her escape, all without a drop of alcohol. Bonnie had seen the withdrawal.

"I've been countin' 'em. There's two men, and five women, I think. At least! But one of the women, she's worse than the rest. That one voice. Always talkin' bout my children. The ones who were took. And *her* child too. All tooken. And then she whispered about fire and then…" Lillian cut off as coughs wracked her body again.

"And then Male Seven burnt down," Bonnie whispered, finishing Lillian's thought aloud. The woman nodded enthusiastically, even as Gerald tried to raise the cup of water to her lips again.

"And then the whispers got worse. Got louder. Tellin' me to goes after me kids." Lillian cried openly. "I ain't never gonna find 'em. What's worse, they ain't never gonna know I was even lookin' for 'em." Bonnie felt a tear run down her own face. "I didn't run 'cos that damn voice told me to find me kids. I done tried and tried that enough before. I ran 'cos I was scared. Too scared to stay. That voice wants me. She wants me soul. And she'll start lookin' for someone else's soul now, I knows it. 'Cos she ain't gonna get Lillian."

"Do you still hear the whispers now?" Gerald asked softly. Bonnie understood her intent. Pushing for a diagnosis. Still thinking schizophrenia, or dementia, or psychosis.

"They done stopped the moment I left that place. But they ain't the only thing I lost." Bonnie hugged Lillian as she coughed and sobbed, her whole body violently shaking. "They took me toes!" she cried, wriggling her foot beneath the blankets. Bonnie noticed the shape of the feet below the sheets looked wrong. Slightly too fat, slightly too short. "I done got frostbite and they done took me toes!"

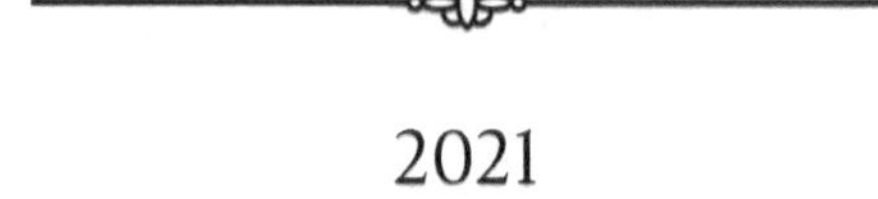

2021
16 OCTOBER, 14:09

DEVIN HAD FINALLY stopped screaming, but the noises in the walls of Kenmore refused to stop. The groaning, the pacing, the knocking.

Even whispering.. It only got louder the longer they waited. Hoping, praying, begging for it to stop. Just long enough for them to flee.

"There's voices," Devin panted. "You can hear it, too, right?" He sounded desperate. "Turn the camera on. Record it! It's not just me. There's fucking voices." Aiden hadn't stopped recording since they stood up. He *did* hear the voices. Or at least, he thought he did. No words he could truly discern. More like wind tickling leaves, but louder, closer. "Why didn't that cunt come back when she heard us screaming?"

Heard you *screaming*, Aiden thought, but again didn't speak. He couldn't bring himself to talk. The terror slowly leached away, replaced by something else. Depression. Acceptance of the end? He was giving up. If they got out of here, they'd probably be just as looney as the patients they'd kept locked up in here decades ago. No-one would ever believe them, could ever believe them. Even with the footage. They'd claim they'd faked it. Done CGI or something. No-one would want to believe it.

The whispers picked up, like they sprayed their murmured breaths directly into his ear. It felt cold, tickling him. Aiden yelled as he batted a hand at it, trying to rub away the sensation.

"Let's head for that side door on the other side of the rec room. Or one of the office windows. It's our best bet." Devin's voice still shook, but as he tried to take control, it became less high-pitched. Aiden just nodded. Both of them had their head torches on, the red illumination casting dark shadows in the hallway, warping the shapes of everything. Even the peeling strips of paint on the wall. Aiden found his eyes flicking from one dark spot to the next, wondering when any of them might stretch out and deepen to form the ghouls they'd previously seen.

The hallway appeared longer this time. Stretching infinitesimally into the night. Had the bedroom doors moved? Hadn't some of them been shut before? They all stood open now. The change was so minor that he couldn't tell if they *had* moved or not. He couldn't remember. But also so major, so confronting, that he almost couldn't move.

"Those things will be down there…" Aiden thought of the large monster polishing the floors and the creature stuck in the walls. Despite Devin's previous conviction, he also hadn't taken a step in that direction. "There's another way. Back the way we came. Through the attic and across the catwalk…"

The hallway groaned at them then. Sparks flashed at the corner of Aiden's vision, like he'd hit his head. The room seemed to sway and stretch. The sensation reminded him of being so drunk that the world refused to stand still. The walls and doors distorted, twisting his stomach into even more agonisingly nauseous knots.

"Y-yeah…okay…" Devin breathed, turning towards his left. That hallway looked far less confronting. Its corners refused to let their perceptions distort. Every single one of those doors was closed. "Let's go…"

The groaning of the building subsided as they took their chosen path. The stairs were closer than they'd thought, and they paused at the base, looking up at the first landing where it curved around to the left, hiding the rest of the steps from view.

"*Poor lost boys.*"

Aiden and Devin reached the first landing. They craned their necks to cast their lights on the next flight of stairs. Empty. They continued up. The echoes of their footfalls came back distorted, loud enough that they didn't hear the whispering.

"*Come to be found again.*"

On the second landing, they saw the white door above them. It was closed. *Had we closed it?* It didn't matter now. They were so close to getting out.

Aiden reached the door first. It opened easily when he pushed it, groaning as it swung inwards to reveal the attic. Quiet, empty. Only their footprints had disturbed the dust on the floor. *Who did we hear up here…?* Aiden thought to himself. A fist felt like it tightened around the middle of his spine, tugging backwards, urging him back down the stairs. *There can't be something worse than those things…*

Devin shoved past him, running to the opposite side of the attic. Still, the fist wouldn't release Aiden. Devin didn't wait, didn't slow, didn't even glance over his shoulder. Aiden took one more step forward, wrenching himself into the room. All his senses burst to life. It felt *wrong*. He felt like prey, the eyes of a hundred predators trained on him. He didn't know where to look, where the greatest danger might come from first.

He jumped and stumbled forward as Devin banged against the door on the furthest side. "It's locked! It's locked! It's fucking locked! It's— *Argh!*"

A deafening slam. Aiden spun around in time to see dust shake loose from the closed attic door.

Of course…of course it closed… This is where it wanted us all along.

Aiden froze as the sound of footsteps paced invisibly across the floor, coming closer. His breaths became colder and colder, difficult to draw inside his lungs. He swore he felt the wind rustle his clothes as they moved past. Still, no-one left footprints in the dust.

"Aiden!" Devin screamed as he raced back across the attic in a panic. "What the fuck?! Why'd you close it? Open it, open it!" His face had turned ghastly pale, and sweat ran off him like a river. Devin shoved him in the shoulder on his way towards the door they'd just come through. Aiden knew it was locked. Devin sobbed as he tried, hopelessly, to open it.

The pacing spirit passed by Aiden again; this time, the cold didn't abate after it passed. He felt close to losing consciousness. *I need to move. I need to try something. Why can't I move…?* Another part of his brain had taken over. Primal, basic, but inherently strong.

"D-D-Devin," Aiden finally gasped. All he could manage was to raise a single finger, barely to the level of his own navel, and point behind his friend. A third door came into focus. A small, white door. *"Devin…"* His friend heard the grating whisper finally, turning to look just as the door finished breezing open. Something waited inside. Not black like a shadow. Not invisible, like the pacer. A milky blue form. It looked like any sad soul you might see in a hospital, except for those eyes. Those black, deep, entrancing eyes.

As it stepped closer, whispers echoed around them again, coming from nowhere and everywhere, and painfully clear.

I doos the polishin'.

Let me out!

You're so beautiful.

Step-step-step…

Failed.

Lost.

Taken.

Abandoned.

More and more voices. Some they'd not yet heard, swirling around them, growing, whipping.

"Aiden…" Devin ran back and grabbed his friend. His hands pinched painfully. His fingers ripped and caught. "It's not real… It's n-n-n-"

Devin pulled on Aiden's bag in his haste to lead his friend towards the catwalk door. Never mind that it was still locked. It was a way *out*. The rip in the bookbag that had formed in the bathroom split wider. Aiden heard it tear, and then he heard the contents of his bag clatter to the wooden floor. Packets of food. Spare batteries.

A tripod. An old microphone. And a cylinder of butane from the burner.

It rolled towards the spectre, almost as though drawn. It smiled. Its mouth as gaping and dark as its eyes. It stepped forward, and the canister erupted into flames.

CHAPTER TWENTY-FOUR

1954
WINTER

LILLIAN CAME BACK to Kenmore, but not by choice. She'd stayed in the hospital ward for one month, but was due to return to Buna House the next day. The poor woman was terrified.

"I need to try to find answers for Lillian. If she runs away again, she might not survive this time." Bonnie paced the small Buna House living space. She wore both her cardigan and her coat. The lack of heating made the air feel biting, even inside. "Scrap that," Bonnie added as she blew on her hands, rubbing them together. "If she runs again, she *will* die. This winter is brutal!"

Pasty sat with Bonnie that evening. Gerald was on night shift, no doubt blaming the creaking floorboards and tapping fingers in the walls on rats and possums.

"I told you, I sit on the fence." Patsy pursed her lips and wriggled herself back further into the armchair. "If what you say is true, and *you* started all this by going after Roy, then why not just *let it be*? Surely it'll calm down on its own."

Truth be told, things had already calmed down. At least, the patients were back to their "normal" selves. There hadn't been any more unexplained fires or accidents. Just the usual weirdness.

"It won't be enough for Lillian, Patsy. It's *her* I'm worried about, not Alice."

"Well…you know who's been here longer than anyone else, don't you?"

Bonnie silently stared at Patsy, trying to catch her meaning.

"Hatchet…" Bonnie breathed. The woman lived in staff housing at the edge of the hospital, by the front fence. "You think she might know something?"

"She's worked at Kenmore all her life, and now she's pushing retirement. So, yeah… I'd say she does. She's sixty or so I'd say. So, if my math is correct, that means…"

"She's worked at Kenmore for at least forty years. She would have worked here when Alice was a patient!"

"Bingo." Patsy cocked a finger at her and then let her head fall back, closing her eyes. "But you're on your own with this one. I am *not* going to be in the same room when you ask Hatchet about ghosts. I sit—"

"—On the fence," Bonnie finished for her. "I know! Okay, wish me luck…"

"You're not going now, are you?" It was pushing 8:00 p.m., the light long faded. Hatchet might even be in bed already.

"What choice do I have? They think they'll release Lillian tomorrow. I don't think she'd stay here another night!"

BONNIE KNOCKED ON Hatchet's door, stamping her feet, and pushing her hands as far into her armpits as they would go. She could almost feel frost forming on her eyelashes. It was like stepping into a walk-in freezer. *I can't let Lillian go back into this.* She readied herself to knock again when a light came on inside, and she heard movement. *Thank God…*

"Who is it?" Nurse Hatchet called out, firmly. A no-nonsense tone that made Bonnie wonder who else might have knocked on the Charge Nurse's door at night.

"Ma'am, it's Nurse T-Trainee Bonnie!" She leant forward as she yelled through the door. Her teeth chattered bitterly. "I'm so sorry for d-disturbing you, but I'm worried for one of the p-patients. Well, one of the inebriates. I was hoping t-to t-talk to you—"

The door swung open. Bonnie looked down at the small woman, wrapped in a thick dressing gown, with curlers already in her hair and secured beneath a sleeping cap. The sight might have been comical in different circumstances.

"And why bother me, hm? I'm not on duty tonight."

"Sh-she's t-talking about a p-patient who used t-to live here. A l-long t-time ago." She struggled to get the words out through her chattering teeth.

"Of for Heaven's sake, come in out of the cold so I can understand you." Hatchet grabbed Bonnie's arm firmly and yanked her inside, closing the door behind her roughly, bolting it. The room glowed with warmth. There were no rules against fires here, and one burned brightly in the living room to their left. Hatchet strode straight to it, sitting in a red-upholstered armchair, and motioning for Bonnie to take the second.

She couldn't help her curiosity, and peered around her, stealing a glimpse of the woman's life. Embroidery was everywhere, finished and unfinished. On the cushions, in the frames on the wall, and in a basket by her chair. An old photo of a man and woman sat on the fireplace mantle, taken in the late 1800s, Bonnie guessed. Probably the woman's parents. Next to it was a photo of a group of nurses, standing out the front of Kenmore, but not quite as Bonnie knew it. No photos of children, though, and no husband.

"Well?" Hatchet impatiently tapped her fingers on the arm of her armchair.

"Ma'am," Bonnie said, her voice regaining its warmth. "This is going to sound a little weird, I'm sorry."

"I'm bloody well used to the weird!"

"Yes, sorry."

"And stop saying sorry. God damnit girl, spit it out."

Bonnie took another breath, preparing to lay it all out in one fell swoop. "One of the inebriates ran away a couple of months ago, in the middle of that horrid storm. Lillian. She got frostbite and lost most of her toes as a result. This is a woman who has been coming to Kenmore on-and-off for years, never missing a winter. She loves it here. Lillian left after the fire in Male Seven. She said she's been hearing voices, but she can *only* hear them here, at Kenmore. As soon as she leaves, the voices stop.

"Lillian says the source of the voices is a patient called Alice, from Female Five. A patient who died here. She is threatening to run away again, and I'm worried if she does, then she'll lose more than her toes out there. I was hoping you would have worked here when Alice was a patient, and might be able to give me some information on her. Information that I can share with Lillian, so she'll be less afraid and will stay. Or maybe you could even talk with Lillian, help reassure her."

Hatchet watched Bonnie for a long time, finally uncrossing her legs and leaning forward slightly. "Is that all?" Bonnie coughed and shuffled uncomfortably in her chair under the woman's gaze.

"I don't understand what you—"

"I know what they all say. I'm old, but I'm not deaf. They say that Alice is still in Ward Five. That she haunts it. That strange things happen. Things that no-one can explain." Bonnie just nodded her head; that admission, coupled with her pale face, was all the confirmation Hatchet seemed to need. "I also know what you all call me. Hell, you call it to my face often enough. I kind of got used to it."

"I'm sorry, ma'am…"

"Do you even *know* what my name is, hm? Has anyone been able to remember to tell you?" Bonnie shook her head. "My name is Harriet Davies. I've been at Kenmore for forty years, and I was a nurse at the area hospital for almost five years before that. I've known Alice all that time. You see, I spent a couple of weeks at the Reception House, before they transferred me to Female Five. We both arrived at the Reception House on the same day and then moved to Ward Five the same day as well."

Bonnie leant forward in her chair now, wanting to ask questions, wanting to pry, but unable to. She was utterly captured as the woman's story unfolded. Someone who *knew* the ghost.

"I watched that woman for four years. "Poor Alice", they sometimes called her. There was nothing "poor" about that woman. She was the most intense, strong, devilish woman I ever met. You know, they kept her tied to a chair for the first two years, or longer, after she arrived? She was so violent that not even a camisole could keep her fully restrained." Bonnie gasped before she caught herself, but Hatchet—Harriet—merely chuckled. "Yes, you might think it cruel. I did too, but still, I participated. We had no other way of subduing the demon of a woman at the time. We still washed her, after a fashion. We tended her sores when we could get close enough. Fed her when she'd let us.

"The screaming was bad, but the *tapping* was worse. The *tap-tap-tap-tap* of the blasted wonky chair leg. Eventually, the Superintendent let her out. He and the others thought they'd cured her. She stopped screaming, stopped scratching and biting and hitting. But those eyes of hers never changed. She just channelled all that vigour, all that intensity, another way. If anyone could force their essence to stick around after death, then it's Alice who'd find a way to do it. Those 'doctors' and all the rest made her what she was; they ultimately failed her. She should never have been allowed to roam the wards."

"There are rumours…" Bonnie spoke up into the silence. "About how she died. That she killed herself?"

Harriet sighed and closed her eyes then. Bonnie had seen enough people reliving trauma to know that the Charge Nurse struggled with the weight of her memories. "The rumours don't get to the half of it," she whispered. "Alice had been out, sleeping in the attic, over a year when it happened. She'd been whispering to the patients, some of the patients anyway, putting all sorts of horrid ideas in their heads. She must have decided it was enough at one point, because one winter, she just walked herself into the fireplace and burnt herself to death. We didn't even realise the cover had been pulled back. She didn't scream, not at first. The other patients didn't either. Just watched for a time. By the time I turned and saw it was much too late. Only when I locked eyes with hers—those dark, piercing eyes—did she start screaming again."

Harriet shuddered, forcefully blowing out a breath, her cheeks puffing up. "She's haunted *me* ever since, that's for sure." For just a moment, Bonnie caught a glimpse of a softer woman under the hard, cold Hatchet exterior. A woman who had been moulded and shaped by Kenmore just as much as Alice had been. "And I'm sure she's haunted others, too. Those strange things just kept happening after she passed."

"Like what?" Bonnie whispered, caught in the tight grasp of morbid curiosity.

"Deaths we couldn't explain or account for. The same *hauntings* that you all go on about now. The tapping. The footsteps started about a month later, after another patient, Helen, was found burnt to death in her room. The odd thing was, we never figured out *how* she burned. There were no scorch marks, no source of fire…"

"So the pacing isn't Alice? It's Helen?" The story-telling was morphing into a conversation, but Harriet let it, nodding along with Bonnie.

"Yes, I'd say so. Helen was always pacing after Alice got into her ear. And then, anytime someone got it into their head to go *digging* into Alice and her past, other things would start to happen. There have been fires on-and-off at Kenmore through my entire forty years. The laundry. The boiler. There could always be a rational explanation, yes, but it would be just like Alice to keep her fire burning. And the unexplainable deaths, too. A woman was found with her head so tightly shoved into her own rubber chamber pot that she suffocated to death. Another woman broke a window and slit her own throat. And there was a man who used to work in the gardens, who was as peaceful and calm as could be. Until the day he found the biggest rock he could carry and caved-in another patient's head with it."

Bonnie's mouth hung open, but she couldn't help it.

"Each time, the Ward Five patients would get melancholy. And yes, I *know*, that happens when someone you know dies. I'm not an idiot!" Hatchet's voice rose loudly, like she was used to defending herself. "But *not* like this. Every single one of the women, eating less, talking less, not following their routine. Like the whole damn haunting was contagious. And what's more, all those people who died had something in common. The women were all either abandoned by their husbands, or lost their children in some way or another, *before* coming to the asylum. And the man who died was a lost child himself. Never knew his mother, or his father."

"It's like she collected them," Bonnie breathed in shock, realising for the first time the severity of Lillian's plight. Perhaps she never should have come back to Kenmore. After all, Lillian's children had been taken from her, too. Another thought struck her. "Did you know Alfred? The patient who tended the gardens? The one who went missing?"

Harriet nodded.

"Would he be connected too, do you think?"

Harriet shrugged, massaging one temple with a bony finger. "I never knew his story. Perhaps. Why do you ask?" Her eyes narrowed as she watched Bonnie, and then some of the sharp Hatchet came back. "What did *you* do? I *told* you not to go meddling, didn't I?"

Bonnie took a deep breath and then let it spill out. "I found Roy." This was perhaps the first time Bonnie had seen the woman shocked. She gulped and averted her eyes. "I thought it might help…"

"Oh, you foolhardy girl!" Hatchet stood up and paced to the fire, its glow casting the wrinkles on her face in even deeper lines. "That's what started that blasted fire, isn't it?"

Bonnie bit her lip, but didn't acknowledge. "What do I do? What *can* I do?"

Hatchet scoffed and threw her hands in the air, pacing back to the armchair. "Don't give it attention!" she barked. "*Don't* feed the flames. Whatever it is! If it's Alice, or some horrible copy of her, whatever it is. *Leave it alone.* Ignore it."

"But Lillian…the inebriate. How can I help her?"

Harriet shook her head sadly. "If you figure that out, you let me know."

2021
16 OCTOBER, 03:14

THE FLAMES EXPLODED up and outwards. The boys collapsed onto the ground; Aiden fell on top of Devin and bore the brunt of the

247

heat. On instinct, he covered his face with his hand, yelping as his arm was scorched. Adrenaline numbed some of the pain, but the deep ache that seemed to pulsate from his bones told him he'd been badly hurt.

Devin shoved him off, then saw the state of his friend and roughly grabbed him by the shoulders and heaved him backwards. The flames licked up the white door, the chipped paint curling in on itself as it shrivelled under the intense heat. The roof seemed to welcome the flames greedily, lapping them up, sucking them to its very top. The acrid smoked stung and burned Aiden's throat. He coughed and gasped, the acidic air filling his lungs, the pain in his arm temporarily forgotten.

Devin paused his epic scramble long enough to grab Aiden's shirt and pull it over his nose. Aiden flicked his eyes up and saw Devin's skull bandana fully shielding his friend's mouth as well. Then his eyes fell back to the flames. To the woman who still stood in their midst, smiling, arms outstretched, welcoming. If the smoke hadn't been so hot and thick, Aiden would have screamed. The terror he felt at that *thing* embracing him forever rivalled even his fear of burning to death.

Devin finally fell, succumbing to the heat. Aiden turned, trying to put weight on his arms to stand, but collapsed as well. His arm could hold no weight. Devin suddenly yelled; he pawed at the bandana now *melting* to his face. It came away in sticky strings, like hot taffy.

I'm going to die…

Not as profound a thought as Aiden expected for such a momentous fate. He waited for his life to flash before his eyes, but only the flames licked around him. He thought he'd at least cry. *Shouldn't I feel sad?* Instead, he felt numb. Even the terror leached away as the realisation this would be the end slid home.

The deafening sound of splintering wood crashed behind him, and he wondered how long they had before the building fell in on itself. Bringing him, his friend, and their wondrous footage—their proof—down with it.

"Come on!" An unfamiliar voice screamed. Aiden twisted his head towards a shape rising up from the far end of the room.

Another spirit?

"Move it!" A woman, her short, blonde hair flecked with white. She was tanned, lean, and strong. He felt her fingers squeeze his upper arm and realised she was no ghoul. She was the caretaker.

Aiden half-scrambled, half-fell as he ran, pulling and pushing at his friend as much as Devin did to him. The catwalk door had been forced open. The crash he'd heard was the caretaker pushing her way inside. The catwalk stretched before them. Outside was *so* close. They were going to make it.

And then Alice screamed. The spectre's voice rattled the walls, the glass in the windows bursting outwards in flames.

"You don't want these two," the caretaker said firmly. "They're not lost. They're only naughty. I'm taking them home to their mothers."

In the chaos of getting down from the burning building, Aiden was again not quite sure what he'd seen and heard in the attic. Just like he couldn't be sure if he'd actually closed the doors behind him in the asylum. His memories blurred in a fog of shock and trauma. Lying on the grass, a safe distance from the flames but still feeling their heat, his arm resumed its throbbing. Eventually, the pain overwrought every other thought in his head. He was vaguely aware of Devin raving about ghosts, but the last words he fully caught before letting himself succumb came from the groundskeeper.

"I didn't realise insanity was catching."

1954
WINTER

"Why are you here again?" Gerald asked, walking a couple of paces behind Bonnie as she climbed the dark stairs towards the attic.

"It's for Lillian," Bonnie said over her shoulder. "I know you don't believe in ghosts and all that nonsense, but Lillian does. And I have an idea to help her get over her fear enough to *stay*. Not to run out into the winter and get herself killed."

Gerald shook her head, not understanding, but when she got to the top landing, she still pulled her keys free and twisted them into the lock of the white wooden door. She motioned for Bonnie to go ahead, following slowly after, a look of wry disbelief still etched on her face.

"Alice!" Bonnie called, turning immediately to the smaller, white wooden door to her left. Gerald scoffed, crossing her arms over her chest, but Bonnie ignored her. "I know you think that Lillian needs you…" She paused, waiting to see if anything would happen, if the tapping would recommence, or the door would start banging. Maybe a slight buzz filled the air. She leant into it. "But she doesn't need you," Bonnie said, almost desperately. "*I* need her. She's been like a mother to me here. Feeding me breakfast. Giving me advice. Looking out for me. Making me laugh."

Gerald let her arms relax as she watched. Perhaps she registered the slowly rising energy in the room after all, at least on some subconscious level.

"Please, Alice. Don't take Lillian away from me. Please leave her in peace. I *need* her. She's my mother now."

As quickly as the energy had built up, it dissipated. She heard only her own breaths heaving in and out of her chest.

"Well?" Gerald muttered. "Did it work?"

"We'll see," Bonnie murmured. "We'll see."

Either way, whether it worked or not, this was the end. Bonnie would never try to talk to Alice again. Would never respond to the knocking, or the tapping. She'd do as Nurse Hatchet—as Harriet—had told her.

Ignore it. Don't feed the flames.

CHAPTER TWENTY-FIVE

2021
16 OCTOBER, 04:30

BONNIE STUMBLED SLIGHTLY on the uneven ground, her hip twinging in pain, and every joint in her legs popped in response. Her eyes stayed transfixed on Female Five—or Ward Fifteen, as it was now known. The entire building was ablaze. Deep red glowed within its doors and windows. Water sprayed onto it from fire hoses made the air sizzle with brilliant purple sparkles. The sirens had awoken her, pulled her from her slumber so completely. Her old bones had known this was coming. The importance of it all was undeniable.

Her husband's hands felt for hers. The soft, dented palm and fingers clasping around her own. "Oh, James," Bonnie moaned. Mrs. Bonnie *Mason* now. Her voice broke just like her heart did at the sight of her Kenmore—her second home—engulfed in flames. The place where she'd made so many memories, both good and bad. The home to so many hundreds, thousands, of women. Where she'd heard Ethel talk about bees. Where she'd first met one of her best friends, Janet. Where Patsy and Gerald—long deceased now— had indoctrinated her into the ways of becoming a psych nurse, honing her sixth sense. Where her future husband had pranked her, and they'd shared their first dinners together.

Part of the building exploded, just like a log in a fireplace, but even more spectacularly. Shards flew into the air. The firemen shouted at one another; they couldn't save the building—that was a fool's errand now—but they needed to prevent the damage from spreading any further.

Another set of sirens wailed, and Bonnie turned to see an ambulance speeding off, gravel flying around its tyres. *So someone had been in there*, she thought. *Perhaps it wasn't you then, Alice? Or was it?*

As smoke, sparks, moroseness and memories swirled around her in the early hours of morning, apparitions appeared to her through her cataract-fogged eyes. She leant into it. There went Alfred, rushing by the building, trying to put the burning leaves back on their burning branches. There was Cora, staring at her reflection in the shattering glass, telling herself how beautiful she was. There was Bertha, too, mopping and polishing those blackening floors until they gleamed. Tears finished the job of fogging her vision, and she sobbed as she turned her head into James's chest, letting his arms enfold her.

The memories of her time as a caretaker of Ward Five and all its patients continued to flood her mind. She remembered Alice and Roy, and all the ghost stories the staff had shared about the two. She remembered how she'd managed to save Lillian over sixty years ago. At least, that's what she told herself. After she'd confronted Alice a final time, Lillian's voices had stopped and the woman had stayed at Kenmore until her six-month sentence was up. Then Bonnie never saw her again. She never knew where Lillian went, nor what happened to her. Only that her future hadn't included Kenmore. Bertha had returned, over-and-over, every winter. The woman had, in fact, died there peacefully in her sleep.

Harriet had retired as planned mere months after the final confrontation with Alice, dropping off the face of the earth as far as the young nurses were concerned. Bonnie often thought about the woman, wondering what her final years were like, and if she ever shook Alice's haunting off her shoulders. The longer Bonnie lived and thought of the woman, the more she came to realise: Harriet had been looking out for the patients in her own way. All that anger and firmness had only ever been directed at the nurses and the staff, never at the patients. Threatening to dump cold water on the *nurses'* heads if they let the patients stand in the cold too long. Getting so cross at Bonnie when she thought Bonnie had stolen Ethel's food. Becoming a hero in her and Gerald's eyes when defending the patients against Howard's whistling.

Bonnie wondered about Lucy, too, and what she'd done after she'd run off; she wondered if she was even still alive, or still clinging on to life just like Bonnie. Patsy had stayed at Kenmore until she'd retired as well, while Gerald had moved on to Sydney. Bonnie had stayed in touch with both of them until each had passed away. Gerald, unsurprisingly, of lung cancer a mere couple of years after she'd moved. Patsy had been the age Bonnie was now, she supposed, when she'd peacefully left to meet their maker. As fit in mind and body in her final moments as she had been all her years in Kenmore. Sitting on the fence until the very end.

No-one had been surprised to see James—or Bubbles, as he had been known back then—settle down with Bonnie. And Lillian had been right. Bonnie had never been bored with the prankster. She'd lived such a good, full life. Janet, who'd been cured by the chemical revolution and discharged, had children around the same time as Bonnie. They'd bonded again over the shared joy and tribulation of raising a family, and remained best friends until Janet had died. Cancer again, the bastard. Janet's middle son had died of cancer not long after, too, come to think of it.

So many lives, intertwining at such immeasurable and unexpected moments, before separating again.

"I hope you're free now, Alice," Bonnie whispered into James's chest, too low for him to hear over the chaos. "I hope you've finally found your Roy. That you're finally at peace."

I WATCH THEM come and go. The men. The women. Even the occasional children. The only constant is their passing. Forever moving through, never staying. One by one, they always leave. One way or another.

When this one left, though, she took a piece of me with her. Burning my walls and windows away in a cleansing, raging, passion-fuelled fire. The blaze seared my flesh away. Whittled down my bones. Sent parts of me scattering across the wind.

She took the others with her, too. The pacing woman. The beautiful woman. The suffocated woman. The slashed-throat woman. The bashed man. The polishing woman. The man in the walls—Alfred—who'd climbed inside me when they renovated me in the 1950s. What's left of his bones burnt and scattered in the inferno as well. All the others, too, the ones time forgot. All gone, one way or another, as I knew they would be.

And finally, her: Alice. The one they tied to the chair. The fire let them all go.

They are gone, but I remain. I may be falling apart, still. Slowly rotting. Parts of me continue to fade. But I remember. I remember them all, when no-one else will. When no-one else can.

I observe their loneliness. I see their imperfections. I feel their insanity. Once they come here, the world forgets them. They are abandoned. But not by me. Never by me.

I keep them all. I haunt them all. They are mine.

ACKNOWLEDGEMENTS

I acknowledge the traditional custodians of the land where this book is set, Australia's First Nations peoples, including the Mulwaree People. I pay my respects to their Elders past, present, and emerging, for they hold the memories, traditions, stories, and hopes of the First Nations people of Australia. We must always remember that under the roads, houses, towns, cities, ruins, and in the history of modern Australia, is a much deeper and much longer history.

I pay my respects to all the former staff and patients of Kenmore Asylum, Goulburn. While this is a work of fiction, I have been inspired by true events and personal accounts from family and staff at Kenmore and similar institutions across Australia. The term "asylum", a former nurse informed me, means "a safe place". While I do not deny that places like Kenmore were not a safe place for many, especially in the early days of mental health "treatment", Kenmore was certainly a haven for thousands of others. Walking the line between different people's experiences is as challenging as walking the line between the diverse, and often confronting, sides of our own human nature. I appreciate every account that was shared with me, most of which I will only hold in my heart. The world, perhaps, isn't ready yet for some of those stories.

There were so many people who shared their experiences and knowledge of Kenmore with me, helping to shape the story you have (or are about to) read. Thank you to Fran O'Flynn at the Goulburn Library for your own passion, and for putting me in touch with the fabulous Leoné Morgan: historian, Secretary of the now-closed Kenmore Museum, and former nurse of Kenmore. Leoné, I learnt so much from you, and was inspired not only by your stories and your research but also by your strength and grit of character. To all the former nurses of Kenmore who Leoné introduced me to, and who subsequently took the time to share your stories: my words cannot express my gratitude. You welcomed me into your circle of camaraderie without a second thought—I felt like a part of the Kenmore family.

To Canberra historian Doris Kordes, I share my whole-hearted appreciation for your enthusiasm and your research. Your thesis opened the world of Kenmore to my imagination. But more than that, you shared your precious time and passion with me. Thank you. I feel we are of a kindred spirit!

To my family: as always, your unwavering support helped me to make it through this book. This story was more challenging to tell than any other I have so far. I would often be exhausted or fighting headaches after writing some of the harder chapters—you were always there to comfort me. I love you.

Finally, to the *AMAZING* team at Graveside Press, words cannot express how grateful I am to work with you. Hannah, as soon as you said you'd fight off anyone with a fish to acquire this story, I knew in my heart you guys were the one. I was not mistaken!

My editor, Lauren, taught me so much, not just about the craft, but about myself. She lifted the manuscript to a whole new level. Kell polished *everything,* from the text to the cover to the process itself. The whole team made this book the absolute best it could be.

KENMORE ASYLUM

The original Buna House, Kenmore Asylum
photo credit: Goulburn Mulwaree Library

JJ Carpenter is the author of *The Corner of Her Eye*, a series of Australian ghost stories exploring the concept of purgatory.

JJ has been writing books since she was six years old—a collection of kooky tales she would staple together and hide in a shoebox under her bed. Penning her first novel at the age of 12, her love of all things creepy, supernatural and wild has never left her. Join JJ as she journeys through haunted places and chilling mysteries across the beautiful country, and rich history, of Australia.

She was born in Canberra, Australia. She spent her childhood in various locations, including the Barossa Valley, South Australia, and Hampshire, England. As an adult, she's spent much of her career living and working in the South Pacific: Solomon Islands (twice), Vanuatu, Fiji and beyond.

jjcarpenterauthor.com

CONTENT WARNINGS

THANK YOU!

Thank you for supporting Graveside Press and our authors. One of the biggest ways you can help is to leave a star rating or a review wherever you purchased your copy!

Stay spooky.

graveside-press.com